A TEXT BOOK OF

Structural Botany & Taxonomy of Angiosperms

(PAPER - III)

And Plant Ecology

(PAPER - IV)

FOR

B.Sc. Part - II (BOTANY) : Semester - III

As Per New Revised Syllabus of Solapur University, June 2015

Dr. D. N. KUTWAL
M.Sc., M.Phil, Ph.D.
H.O.D. of Botany Deptt.,
Shankarrao Mohite Mahavidyalaya, Akluj

Dr. V. S. SHIRASHYAD
M.Sc., M.Phil, Ph.D.
Ex. H.O.D. of Botany Deptt.,
Walchand College, Solapur

Dr. M. N. JAGTAP
M.Sc., M.Phil, Ph.D
H.O.D. of Botany, Deptt.,
D.B.F. Dayanand College, Solapur

R. S. SURYAVANSHI
M.Sc.
H.O.D. of Botany, Deptt.,
Vidnyan Mahavidyalaya, Sangola

R. L. SAVALAJKAR
M.Sc., M.Phil
Associate Professor
Department of Botany
Shankarrao Mohite Mahavidyalaya, Akluj

Dr. K. U. GARAD
M.Sc., Ph.D.
Assistant Professor
Department of Botany
Shankarrao Mohite Mahavidyalaya, Akluj

N3654

B.Sc. Part-II : Botany (P-III & IV) (Sem. III) **ISBN 978-93-5164-798-0**

First Edition : June 2016

Published By:

NIRALI PRAKASHAN

Abhyudaya Pragati, 1312, Shivaji Nagar
Off J.M. Road, Pune – 411005
Tel - (020) 25512336/37/39, Fax - (020) 25511379
Email : niralipune@pragationline.com

☞ DISTRIBUTION CENTRES

PUNE

Nirali Prakashan : 119, Budhwar Peth, Jogeshwari Mandir Lane, Pune 411002, Maharashtra. Tel : (020) 2445 2044, 66022708, Fax : (020) 2445 1538, Email: bookorder@pragationline.com, niralilocal@pragationline.com

Nirali Prakashan : S. No. 28/27, Dhyari, Near Pari Company, Pune 411041 Tel : (020) 24690204 Fax : (020) 24690316 Email : dhyari@pragationline.com, bookorder@pragationline.com

MUMBAI

Nirali Prakashan : 385, S.V.P. Road, Rasdhara Co-op. Hsg. Society Ltd., Girgaum, Mumbai 400004, Maharashtra Tel : (022) 2385 6339 / 2386 9976, Fax : (022) 2386 9976 Email : niralimumbai@pragationline.com

☞ DISTRIBUTION BRANCHES

JALGAON

Nirali Prakashan : 34, V. V. Golani Market, Navi Peth, Jalgaon 425001, Maharashtra, Tel : (0257) 222 0395, Mob : 94234 91860

KOLHAPUR

Nirali Prakashan : New Mahadvar Road, Kedar Plaza, 1st Floor Opp. IDBI Bank Kolhapur 416 012, Maharashtra. Mob : 9850046155

NAGPUR

Pratibha Book Distributors : Above Maratha Mandir, Shop No. 3, First Floor, Rani Jhanshi Square, Sitabuldi, Nagpur 440012, Maharashtra Tel : (0712) 254 7129

DELHI

Nirali Prakashan : 4593/21, Basement, Aggarwal Lane 15, Ansari Road, Daryaganj, Near Times of India Building, New Delhi 110002 Mob : 08505972553

BENGALURU

Pragati Book House : House No. 1, Sanjeevappa Lane, Avenue Road Cross, Opp. Rice Church, Bengaluru – 560002. Tel : (080) 64513344, 64513355,Mob : 9880582331, 9845021552, Email:bharatsavla@yahoo.com

CHENNAI

Pragati Books : 9/1, Montieth Road, Behind Taas Mahal, Egmore, Chennai 600008 Tamil Nadu, Tel : (044) 6518 3535, Mob : 94440 01782 / 98450 21552 / 98805 82331, Email : bharatsavla@yahoo.com

niralipune@pragationline.com | www.pragationline.com
Also find us on f www.facebook.com/niralibooks

PREFACE

We are very much delighted to present this book **'Structural Botany and Taxonomy of Angiosperms (Paper III) and Plant Ecology (Paper IV)'** for B.Sc. Part-II students as per new revised syllabus of Solapur University, June 2015.

The book covers all aspect of syllabus of Botany, B.Sc. part-II, Semester-III. We have tried to present the topics in simple words. The illustrative diagrams are given wherever necessary. At the end of each unit Questions are given for practice purpose.

The information of Botany Paper-III and Paper IV is compiled in such a way that it meets all the demands of students. We have referred standard books and articles to prepare this book. We are grateful to authors and publishers of these reference books.

Authors are grateful to Management and Principals of Shankarrao Mohite Mahavidyalaya, Akluj, Walchand College, Solapur, Dayanand College, Solapur and Vidnyan Mahavidyalaya, Sangola for their continuous encouragement and guidance.

We are thankful to the faculty members of all the colleges of Solapur University for their constant support.

We are thankful to Shri. Dineshbhai Furia, Shri. Jignesh Furia and the entire staff of **Nirali Prakashan** for taking keen interest in publishing this book and bringing out in attractive form and well in time.

The authors welcome suggestions for improvement from the readers.

– **Authors**

SYLLABUS

(PAPER – III) : STRUCTURAL BOTANY & TAXONOMY OF ANGIOSPERMS

UNIT – I

1. Meristems **(07)**

1.1 Introduction and Classification of meristems

1.2 Functions of meristems

1.3 Theories of structural development :

(a) The Apical cell theory

(b) Histogen theory

(c) Tunica corpus theory

UNIT – II

2 Permanent Tissues

2.1 Structure and functions of simple tissues

2.2 Structure and functions of complex tissues

2.3 Types of vascular bundles

UNIT – III

3. Tissue System and their Functions **(07)**

3.1 Epidermal tissue system

3.2 Secretory tissue system

3.3 Mechanical tissue system

UNIT – IV

4. Primary Structure of Plant Organs **(06)**

4.1 Primary structure of monocot root and stem - (maize)

4.2 Primary structure of dicot root and stem - (sunflower)

UNIT – V

5. Secondary Body of the Plant **(10)**

5.1 Normal secondary growth in dicot root and stem.

5.2 Periderm, lenticles and annual rings

5.3 Basic structure of wood and its types

5.4 Anomalous secondary growth in *Bignonia* and *Dracaena* stem.

UNIT – VI

6. Taxonomy of Angiosperms (11)

Study of Angiosperm families with respect to classification, morphology of vegetative and reproductive parts, floral formula, floral diagram, diagnostic features and economic importance. (any five examples.

(a) Combretaceae (b) Asclepiadaceae

(c) Amaranthaceae (d) Liliaceae.

(PAPER – IV) : PLANT ECOLOGY

UNIT – I

1. Introduction (06)

1.1 Climatic factors

1.2 Edaphic factors

UNIT – II

2. Community Ecology (08)

2.1 Form and structure of communities

2.2 Classification and physiognomy

2.3 Community characteristics

UNIT – III

3. Ecosystem (11)

3.1 Concept and types

3.2 Components and organisation of ecosystem

3.3 Ecological pyramids, food chains and food webs

3.4 Energy flow in ecosystem

3.5 Biogeochemical cycles – Nitrogen, oxygen, carbon

UNIT - IV

4. Ecological Succession **(06)**

4.1 Concept and process

4.2 Primary and secondary succession

4.3 Hydrosere and xerosere

UNIT - V

5. Ecological Adaptations **(08)**

5.1 Concept

5.2 Xeric, hydric and mesic adaptaions

UNIT - VI

6. Pollution **(06)**

5.1 Introduction

5.2 Air pollution – Definition, Sources of air pollutants, their effects and control measures.

5.3 Water pollution – Definition, Sources of water pollutants, their effects and control measures.

CONTENTS

PAPER - III

PAPER - IV

PAPER - III

1

CHAPTER

MERISTEMS

1.1 INTRODUCTION

Meristem or meristematic cells are immature, thin walled cells that have the capacity of division and redivision. These cells bear abundant protoplast, prominent nucleus and the vacuoles are almost absent. The intercellular spaces are absent in the meristematic tissue.

When a seed germinates the radicle emerges out first. The apex of the radicle bears meristematic cells. The root system develops due to the activity of these cells. Later, plumule develops into shoot system bearing leaves and branches. The shoot develops due to the activity of dividing cells situated at the apex of the shoot. This growth is known as **primary growth**. The vascular cambium and phellogen undergo division and form secondary tissues. The secondary tissues increase the girth of the plant. These meristems undergo division and form daughter cells which differentiate into permanent cells and construct the complex plant body.

1.1.1 Characteristics of Meristematic Tissue

- They are living, undifferentiated tissues composed of immature cells
- They are thin walled.
- They may be rounded, polygonal, oval or rectangular in shape
- They have the capacity to divide indefinitely and hence these cells are in a continuous state of division
- They have dense granular cytoplasm
- The cells are compactly arranged without intercellular spaces

- Vacuole is absent, if present, it is of very small size
- The nucleus is large, prominent and conspicuous
- These cells are metabolically highly active and therefore lack food reserve
- Plastids are usually absent. If present they are found only in the proplastid stage
- They usually are found in the apices of root and shoot

1.1.2 Classification of Meristems

Meristems can be classified on the basis of their position, origin, function and plane of cell division.

1. **Classification of Meristem based on Position:** On the basis of position in the plant body the meristems are classified as

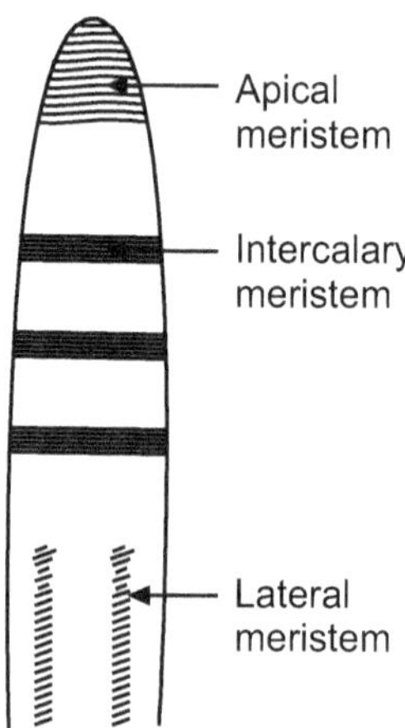

Fig. 1.1: Different meristem based on position

(a) Apical Meristem: This meristem lies at the apex of root and stem of vascular plants. Due to the activity of the apical meristem the length of the plant/organ increases. There may be one or many dividing cells. In lower plants e.g. Bryophytes only one apical cell is present whereas in higher plants many dividing cells occur. They may be terminal as in stems and sub-terminal as in roots. The apical meristem is responsible for primary growth of the plant. During the formation of leaves and elongation of stem some meristematic cells are left behind from shoot apex and they form axillary buds.

These are capable of producing a branch or flower.

(b) Intercalary Meristem: These are the portions of apical meristems that have remained in the permanent tissues at the nodal region. Such meristems are found in stems of grasses. They are responsible for the increase in the length of stem. Rapid growth of grasses is due to the activity of both apical and intercalary meristems.

(c) Lateral Meristem: Lateral meristem consists of cells which divide periclinally (parallel to the axis). They add cells laterally and increase the girth of the axis. The tissues formed by the activity of lateral meristem are known as secondary tissues. The cork cambium (phellogen) and vascular cambium are the examples of lateral meristem. **(Fig. 1.2)**

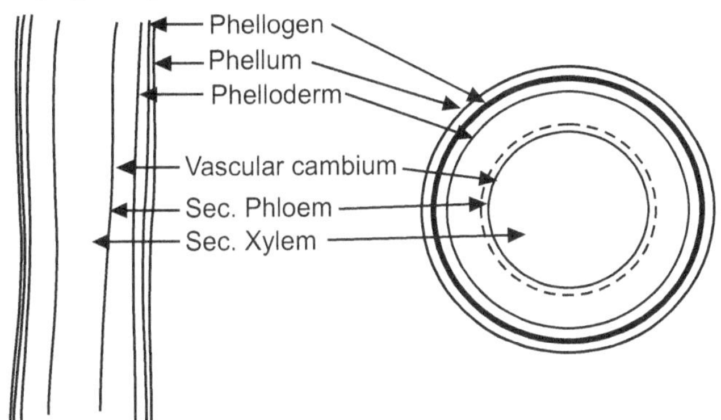

(a) L. S. of stem showing lateral meristems (secondary meristems) and their derivatives

(b) T. S. of stem showing lateral meristems and their derivatives

Fig. 1.2: Lateral meristems

2. **Classification of Meristems based on Origin:** On the basis of origin, the meristems are classified as:

(a) Primary Meristem: Both apical and intercalary meristems are primary in origin. They are responsible for the formation of primary plant body. Primary meristem is embryonic in origin. The main primary meristems are apices of root, stem and leaves. Intercalary meristem of grasses is also an example of primary meristem.

(b) Secondary Meristem: These originate from the permanent tissues and occur laterally in stems and roots. Some of the primary permanent tissues gain the power of division and become meristematic. Phellogen (cork combium) is an example of secondary meristem. Phellogen undergoes division and forms Phellum (cork) on the outerside and phelloderm (Secondary cortex) on the inner side. **(Fig. 1.2)**

The secondary meristem, phellogen is formed from mature cells of epidermis or cortex.

3. **Classification Based on Function:** Based on function, Haberlandt classified the meristem as (i) Protoderm (ii) Pro-cambium and (iii) Ground or fundamental meristem. He proposed that the apical meristem of root and stem is distinguished into three tissues. **(Fig. 1.3)**

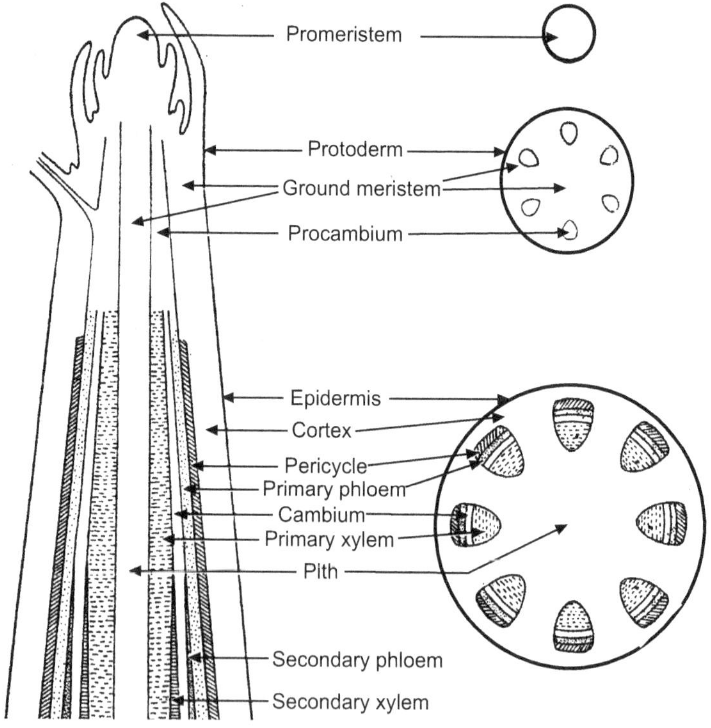

Fig. 1.3: Classification of meristems based on function (a) L.S. of dicot stem (b) T.S. of dicot stem

(i) Protoderm: It is the outermost layer of meristem which develops into epidermis. Protoderm is single layered meristem found at the apex of root and stem.

(ii) Pro cambium: The isolated strands of slightly elongated cells situated in the central regions of stem apex are known as "Pro cambium cells". These cells divide and redivide. The daughter cells differentiate into vascular tissues- xylem and phloem i.e. vascular bundle.

(iii) The Ground or Fundamental Meristem: It develops into ground tissue and pith. The ground tissue consists of large, thin walled, isodiametric, parenchymatous cells. Later it differentiates into hypodermis, cortex, endodermis, pericycle and pith.

4. **Classification of Meristem Based on Plane of Cell Division:** On the basis of plane of cell division the meristems are classified as

(i) Mass Meristem: In mass meristem growth takes place by division of cells in three planes or all planes, as a result there is mass increase e.g. embryo development, sporangia development, endosperm formation.

(ii) Plate Meristem: In plate meristem cells divide mainly in two planes – so that there is plate like increase in the area. One layered plate meristem forms epidermis. Two or many layered plate meristem is prominent in leaf development.

(iii) Rib Meristem (File meristem): It undergoes division in only one plane, anticlinally producing rows or columns of cells. This leads to the increase in length of organs. Rib meristem plays an important role in the development of young roots, pith and cortex of young stems.

1.2 FUNCTIONS OF MERISTEMS

- The seed germinates and the embryo develops into an independent plant by the addition of new cells at the apex of radicle and plumule. Thus the apical meristems produce root and shoot system of primary plant body.
- The addition of new cells is restricted to certain parts of the plant body. The derivatives differentiate into different tissues to perform different functions.

- Lateral meristems form secondary tissues.
- The addition of secondary xylem, phloem, cork, secondary cortex leads to the increase in the girth of the axis.
- Apical and intercalary meristems are responsible for the rapid growth in length of some monocots.
- The primary growth initiated in the apical meristem sometimes produce flowers.
- The cambia (meristems) help in healing of wounds in plants.
- In perennials, the meristems keep the plant in growing state.

1.3 THEORIES OF STRUCTURAL DEVELOPMENT

Several theories dealing with the methods of origin of the patterns formed and their histological and morphological significance have been proposed. These theories are explained below.

(i) Apical Cell Theory

This theory was put forth by Hofmeister in 1857 and supported by Nageli. Nageli first coined the term 'meristem' and proposed that the apical meristem consists of a single apical cell. The apical cell is considered as the structural and functional unit of apical meristem. It is responsible for the construction of the plant by growth. This apical cell divides and forms different tissues and plant body. This theory is true with many cryptogams (Algae, Bryophytes and Pteridophytes) and is not applicable to higher plants like phanerogams.

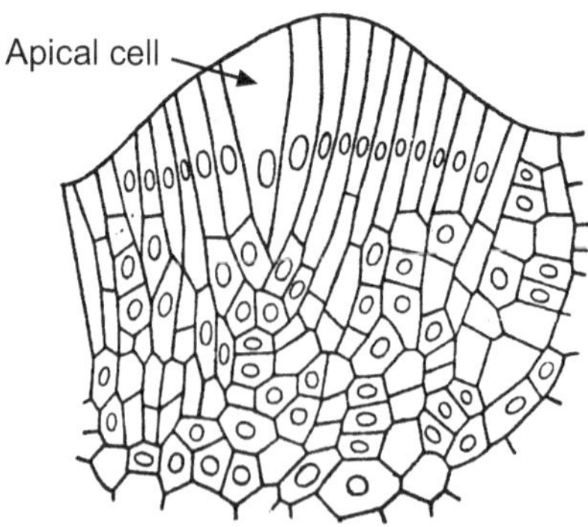

Fig. 1.4: Apical cell

(ii) Histogen Theory (Histogen – tissue builder)

This theory was proposed by Hanstein (1870). According to this theory apical meristem is divisible into three zones/histons viz : Dermatogen, Periblem and Plerome. **(Fig. 1.5)**

(a) Dermatogen: (Derma = Skin, gen = produce) This is the single outermost layer of cells which gives rise to epidermis in stem and epiblema in roots. The epidermis shows cuticle while the epiblema has no cuticle. In root apex, just outside the periblem, the dermatogen cuts off many new cells forming the calyptrogen. This calyptrogen gives rise to root cap.

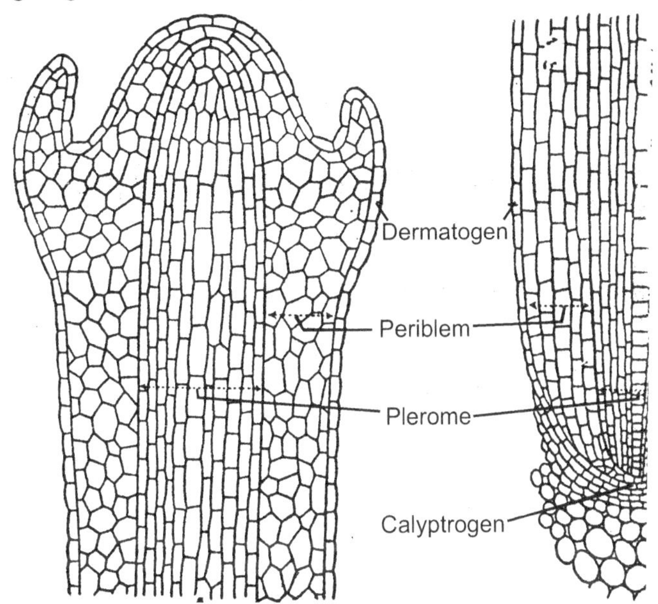

Fig. 1.5: Three histons according to the Histogen Theory

(b) Periblem: (Peri = around, blema = covering) The periblem lies internal to the dermatogen. It lies between dermatogen and plerome. At the apex it is single layered but in the lower side it is multi-layered. The daughter cells of periblem form the cortex, hypodermis and endodermis.

(c) Plerome: (pleres = full) It occupies the central portion of the axis. It lies internal to the periblem. The strands of elongated cells of plerome form procambium. The procambial strands differentiate into vascular bundles. Some cells remain undifferentiated and form cambium. The plerome forms the central cylinder of the stem known as 'Stele'. Pericycle, medullary rays, pith, and vascular bundles are differentiated by plerome.

(iii) Tunica – corpus Theory

This theory was proposed by Schmidt (1924). According to this theory, the apical meristem consists of two zones. The outer zone is Tunica. It consists of one or more peripheral layers of cells. The tunica cells are small and undergo anticlinal division to form epidermis. Corpus is the undifferentiated mass of larger cells enclosed by Tunica. The corpus cells divide in many planes and form cortex, vascular tissues and pith. This theory is widely accepted. **(Fig. 1.6)**

In Pteridophytes there is no distinction of Tunica and Corpus (*Selaginella*), weakly differentiated in *Lycopodium* (Pteridophytes). In Gymnosperms (*Sequoia*) tunica and corpus are differentiated whereas in Angiosperms, Tunica and Corpus layers are distinct.

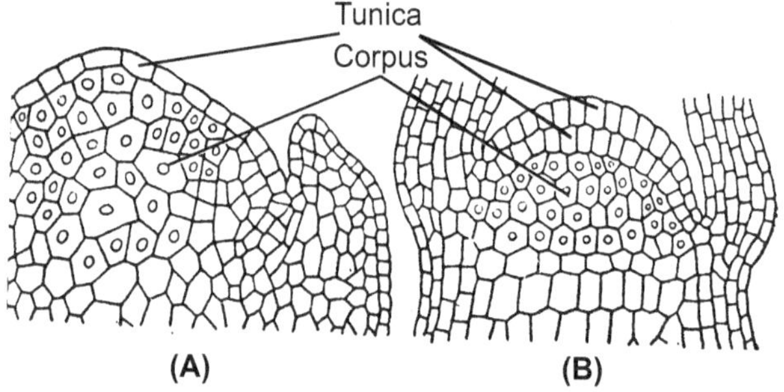

Fig. 1.6: L.S. of Shoot apex showing Tunica and Corpus

EXERCISE

I. Multiple Choice Questions

1. The meristematic tissue consists of --------- cells.

   (a) mature (b) immature

   (c) differentiated (d) permanent

2. The cells having the power of division and situated at the tip of axis are known as --------.

   (a) apical meristem (b) lateral meristem

(c) intercalary meristem (d) secondary meristem

3. Apical, Intercalary and Lateral meristems are classified on the basis of their --------.

(a) origin (b) function

(c) position (d) plane of cell division

4. Primary and secondary meristems are categorised on the basis of their ---------.

(a) plane of cell division (b) function

(c) position (d) origin

5. Protoderm, pro-cambium and fundamental meristems are classified on the basis of their ----.

(a) origin (b) function

(c) position (d) plane of cell division

6. Mass, plate and rib meristems are categorised on the basis of their --------.

(a) position (b) origin

(c) function (d) plane of cell division

7. Primary plant body develops due to the activity of --------.

(a) lateral meristem (b) cambium

(c) phellogen (d) apical meristem

8. Phellogen is -------- meristem.

(a) apical (b) intercalary

(c) primary (d) lateral

9. --------- meristem is responsible for increase in the girth of stem.

(a) apical (b) intercalary

(c) lateral (d) primary

10. Apical meristem is responsible for --------.

(a) increase in height (b) increase in thickness

(c) decrease in height (d) increase in girth

11. The cork cambium is also known as --------.
    (a) phellum (b) phellogen
    (c) phelloderm (d) dermatogen
12. The derivatives of -------- meristem develop into secondary tissues.
    (a) apical (b) primary
    (c) intercalary (d) lateral
13. The primary tissues develop from -------- meristem.
    (a) apical (b) apical and lateral
    (c) intercalary and lateral (d) lateral
14. The permanent tissue that regains the power of cell division is known as -------- meristems.
    (a) apical (b) intercalary
    (c) primary (d) lateral
15. The derivatives of protoderm develop into -------- tissue.
    (a) epidermal (b) conducting
    (c) vascular (d) pith
16. Procambium derivatives develop into ---------tissue.
    (a) epidermal (b) mechanical
    (c) conducting (d) secretory
17. The derivatives of --------- develop cortex and pith.
    (a) pro-cambium (b) ground meristem
    (c) protoderm (d) vascular cambium
18. Mass, rib and plate meristems are classified on the basis of ----------.
    (a) position (b) function
    (c) plane of cell division (d) origin
19. Apical cell theory was proposed by --------.
    (a) Hofmeister (b) Nageli
    (c) Hanstein (d) Schmidt

20. Tunica corpus theory was proposed by --------.
    - (a) Hofmeister
    - (b) Hanstein
    - (c) Schmidt
    - (d) Starsburger
21. Hanstein proposed --------- theory.
    - (a) Apical cell
    - (b) Histogen
    - (c) Tunica corpus
    - (d) Dermatogen
22. --------- forms root cap.
    - (a) Calyptrogen
    - (b) Dermatogen
    - (c) Periblem
    - (d) Pleurome

ANSWERS

1-a;	2-a;	3-c;	4-d;	5-b;	6-d;	7-d;	8-d;
9-c;	10-a;	11-b;	12-d;	13-a;	14-d;	15-a;	16-c;
17-b;	18-c;	19-a;	20-c;	21-b;	22-a.		

II. Two Marks Questions

1. What is meristem?
2. Write any two important characteristics of meristems.
3. Classify meristems based on position and function.
4. Classify meristems based on function and plane of cell division.
5. Which are the three zones of meristems according to histogen theory?
6. Write any two functions of meristems.

III. Four Marks Questions

1. Classify meristems on the basis of their origin.
2. Comment on the Apical cell theory.
3. Discuss Histogen theory.
4. Give the functions of meristems?

IV. Five Marks Questions

1. Classify and comment on the meristems with respect to their origin and functions.
2. Discuss any two theories of structural development of plant organs.
3. Comment on the characteristics of meristematic tissues.

V. Seven Marks Questions

1. What are meristems? Discuss in brief the characteristics and functions of meristems.
2. Discuss the theories of structural development of plant organs.
3. Classify and comment on the meristems with respect to their origin, functions and plane of cell division.

2
CHAPTER

PERMANENT TISSUES

A tissue is a group of cells which are alike in structure and function and have a common origin. Plant tissue may be classified into meristematic and permanent. Meristematic tissue consists of cells that have the power of division (meristos = division) while permanent tissue is composed of cells that have lost the power of division and attained definite size and shape.

Permanent tissues are formed by the differentiation of the daughter cells of meristematic cells. Permanent tissues may consist of living or dead cells, their walls may be thin or thick and they may be of primary or secondary type. The primary permanent tissues are formed from apical and intercalary meristems. The secondary permanent tissues are formed from lateral meristems.

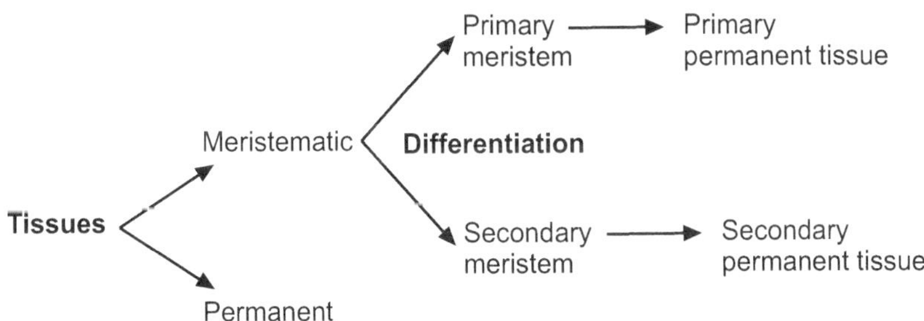

Permanent tissues are classified as simple and complex tissues. Simple tissue is made up of only one type of cells (homogeneous). Complex tissue is made up of more than one type of cells (heterogeneous) that perform the same function.

The common simple tissues are parenchyma, collenchyma and sclerenchyma. Complex tissues are xylem and phloem.

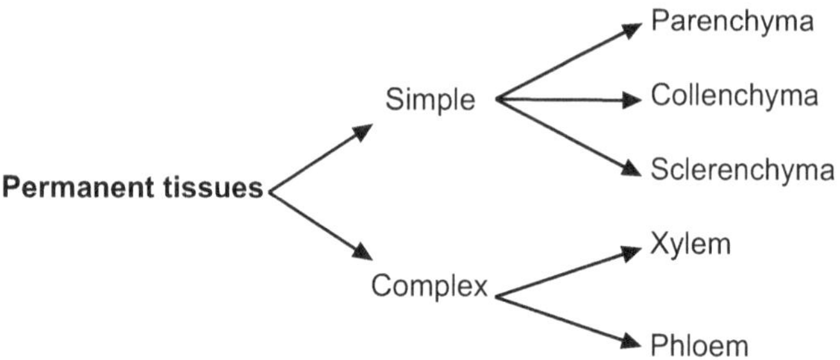

2.1 STRUCTURE AND FUNCTIONS OF SIMPLE TISSUES

2.1.1 Parenchyma: *(Para = beside, enchein = Pour) Semiliquid substance poured beside other tissues which are formed earlier.*

Parenchyma is the most common plant tissue. Parenchyma consists of isodiametric, thin walled living cells. The cell wall is made up of cellulose. The cells contain cytoplasm, nucleus, vacuole, etc. The cells may be oval, rounded, or polygonal in shape. They are not elongated. Parenchyma tissue makes up the major portion of many organs in plants e.g. pith, cortex, pulp of fruits, endosperm of seeds. They also occur with xylem and phloem. Ontogenetically parenchyma is a primitive tissue.

The main function of parenchyma is storage of food material and to provide rigidity to the plant body. In some hydrophytes, the intercellular spaces between the cells become wide and filled with air. Such a parenchymatous tissue having large intercellular space is known as **Aerenchyma**. It helps in the exchange of gases and provides buoyancy to plants. **(Fig. 2.1 b)**

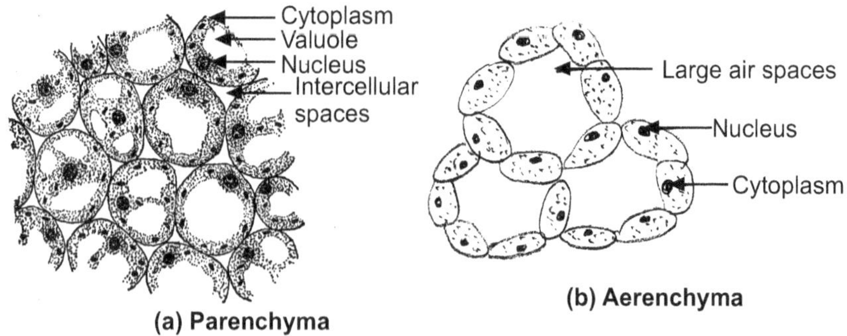

(a) Parenchyma

(b) Aerenchyma

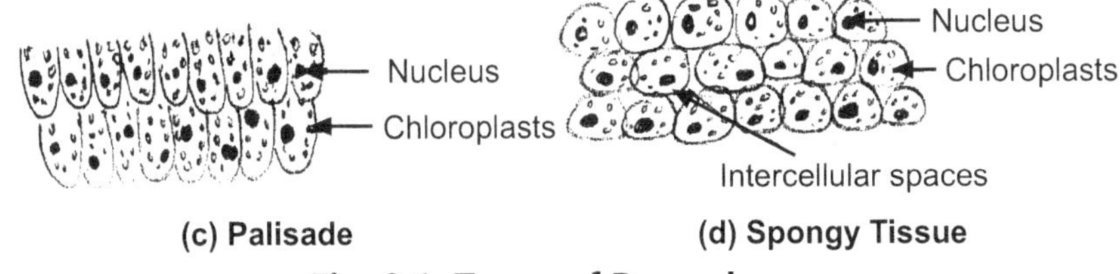

(c) Palisade (d) Spongy Tissue

Fig. 2.1: Types of Parenchyma

In mesophyll of leaves and other green parts of plants parenchyma tissue contains chloroplasts. Such a tissue is known as **Chlorenchyma (Fig. 2.1 c, d).** When the chlorenchyma cells are elongated, barrel shaped and without intercellular spaces it is known as Palisade tissue. (**2.1 c**) If the cells are rounded with intercellular spaces it is called as spongy tissue (**2.1 d**). In most monocots, the leaves are isobilateral with spongy mesophyll tissue whereas in dicot leaves the tissue is differentiated into dorsal **Palisade** and ventral **Spongy** tissue. The function of chlorenchyma is photosynthesis.

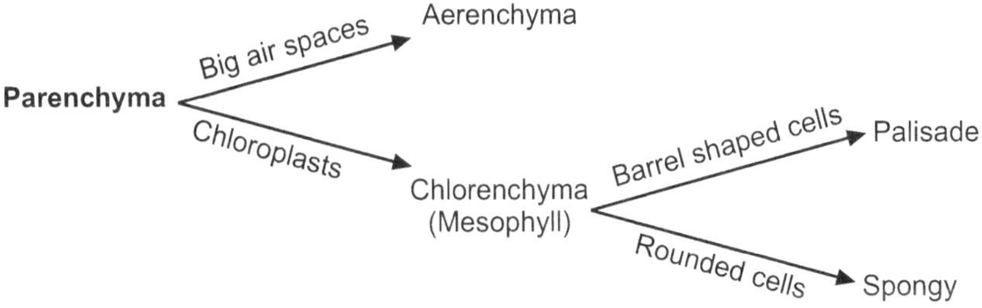

2.1.2 Collenchyma: *(kolla= glue, enchein – pour)*

It is made up of elongated living cells. The cells may be oval, spherical, or polygonal. The corners or intercellular spaces are thick due to the deposition of cellulose, hemicellulose, and pectin. The cell wall is unevenly thickened.

The collenchyma is found under the epidermis e.g. hypodermis of herbaceous stems, leaves and floral parts of dicots. Collenchyma tissue gives mechanical support, elasticity and tensile strength to the young stem and petiole of leaf. As the cells are living and provide mechanical strength, the tissue is rightly called as **"Living Mechanical Tissue"**. Sometimes chloroplasts are present in the collenchyma cells. These cells are responsible for photosynthesis.

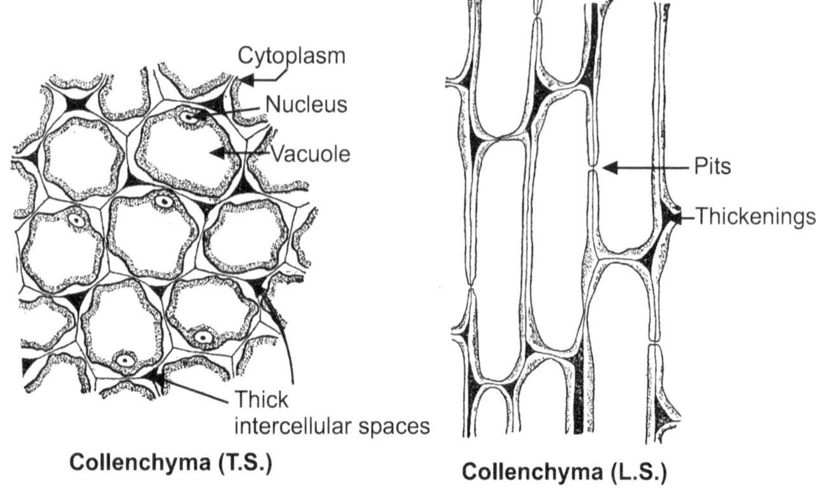

Collenchyma (T.S.)

Collenchyma (L.S.)

Fig. 2.2: Types of Collenchyma

2.1.3. Sclerenchyma: *(Scleros = hard)*

It consists of long, narrow cells with thick, hard secondary walls due to the deposition of lignin. Sclerenchyma is a **dead mechanical tissue**. The sclerenchyma cells are compactly arranged without intercellular spaces between them. The cells are joined together with the help of middle lamella. It occurs in hypodermis, pericycle, secondary xylem and phloem. They are also found in the endocarp of almond and coconut. Sclerenchyma tissue helps to withstand various strains which leads to stretching, bending of plant organs without any damage to the soft cells. Sclerenchyma cells can be classified as fibres and sclereids. **(Fig. 2.3)**

(a) Fibres: These are long, elongated cells with pointed ends with a small lumen. The thick lignified walls have many pits. The length of fibres varies. In Jute hemp the length ranges from 20 mm to 550 mm. These long fibres are commercially used. **(Fig. 2.3 b)**

The fibres associated with xylem are known as "Xylem fibre". The fibres associated with cortex cells are known as "Cortical fibres". The fibres originating from phloem are classified as 'bast fibres'. Some fibres are lignified. Some are non-lignified. In *Linum* the wall is made up of cellulose.

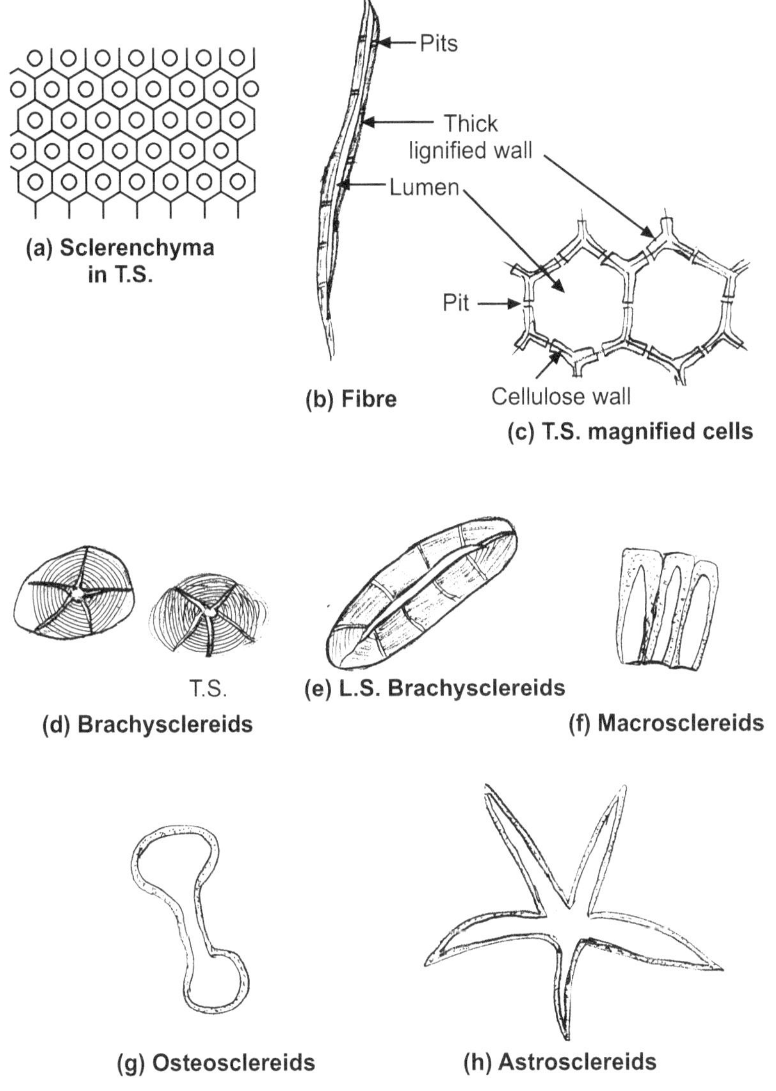

(a) Sclerenchyma in T.S.

(b) Fibre

(c) T.S. magnified cells

(d) Brachysclereids

(e) L.S. Brachysclereids

(f) Macrosclereids

(g) Osteosclereids

(h) Astrosclereids

Fig. 2.3: Types of Sclerenchyma

(b) Sclereids: *(Stone cells or sclerotic cells):* These are spherical, oval or cylindrical, highly thickened dead and single celled structures. These have a narrow lumen. The walls have pits. Sclereids occur singly or in groups in different parts of the plants like leaves, fruits, seeds etc. They provide mechanical support. The sclereids are classified into four categories.

(i) Brachysclereids: These are short and more or less isodiametric, commonly found in cortex, phloem, pith of stems and in the pulp of fruits. **(Fig. 2.3 d, e)**

(ii) Macrosclereids: These are rod shaped and form palisade like epidermal layer in seeds and fruits, cortex of xerophytic leaves and stems. **(Fig. 2.3 f)**

(iii) Osteosclereids: These are single celled elongated bone shaped, and are broad at both ends and narrow in the middle. These commonly occur in the seeds, fruits, and xerophytic leaves. **(Fig. 2.3 g)**

(iv) Astrosclereids: These are star shaped sclereids, commonly found in intercellular spaces of leaves, petioles of hydrophytes (Lotus). **(Fig. 2.3 h)**

The hardness of seed coat and the gritty pulp of pear fruits is due to sclereids.

2.2 STRUCTURE AND FUNCTIONS OF COMPLEX TISSUES

The complex tissue consists of more than one type of cells which work together as a unit. Complex tissues help in the transportation of water, minerals and food (organic material). These are also known as conducting or vascular tissues. The complex permanent tissues are of two types:

1. Xylem or wood
2. Phloem or bast

1. Xylem or wood

Xylem conducts water and minerals from roots to all parts of the plant. It also provides mechanical strength to the plant. Xylem consists of

(a) Tracheids

(b) Tracheae (Vessels) (*Sing: trachea*)

(c) Xylem fibres (wood fibres)

(d) Xylem parenchyma or wood parenchyma

(a) Tracheids: These are fundamental cells of the xylem. Tracheids have long tube like cells with pointed ends. They have thick and lignified walls. These are dead cells without protoplast. The tracheids have various kinds of thickenings like annular, spiral, reticulate, scalariform, pitted, etc. Water can pass through the empty lumen as well as from tracheid to tracheid through the pits in their walls.

Ferns and gymnosperms have only tracheids whereas angiosperms have tracheids and vessels. The main function of tracheids is conduction and they also provide mechanical support. **(Fig. 2.4 a)**

(b) Vessels (Tracheae): These are long cylindrical tube-like structures. Each vessel has lignified walls and a large central cavity called lumen. The vessel cells are also devoid of protoplasm. Vessels are present in angiosperms and absent in pteridophytes and gymnosperms.

Vessels are made up of a row of cells placed end to end in which the transverse partition walls are dissolved. The diameter of vessel is much greater than that of tracheids. **(Fig. 2.4 b)**

(c) Xylem fibres or wood fibres: These are elongated thick walled dead cells associated with tracheids. The lumen of the fibres is much narrow or completely absent. These cannot conduct water; their main function is to provide mechanical strength. **(Fig. 2.4 c)**

(d) Xylem parenchyma or wood parenchyma: These parenchyma cells are associated with xylem. In secondary xylem they occur vertically. The radial transverse series of the cells forms the wood ray or xylem ray parenchyma. **(Fig. 2.4 d, e)**

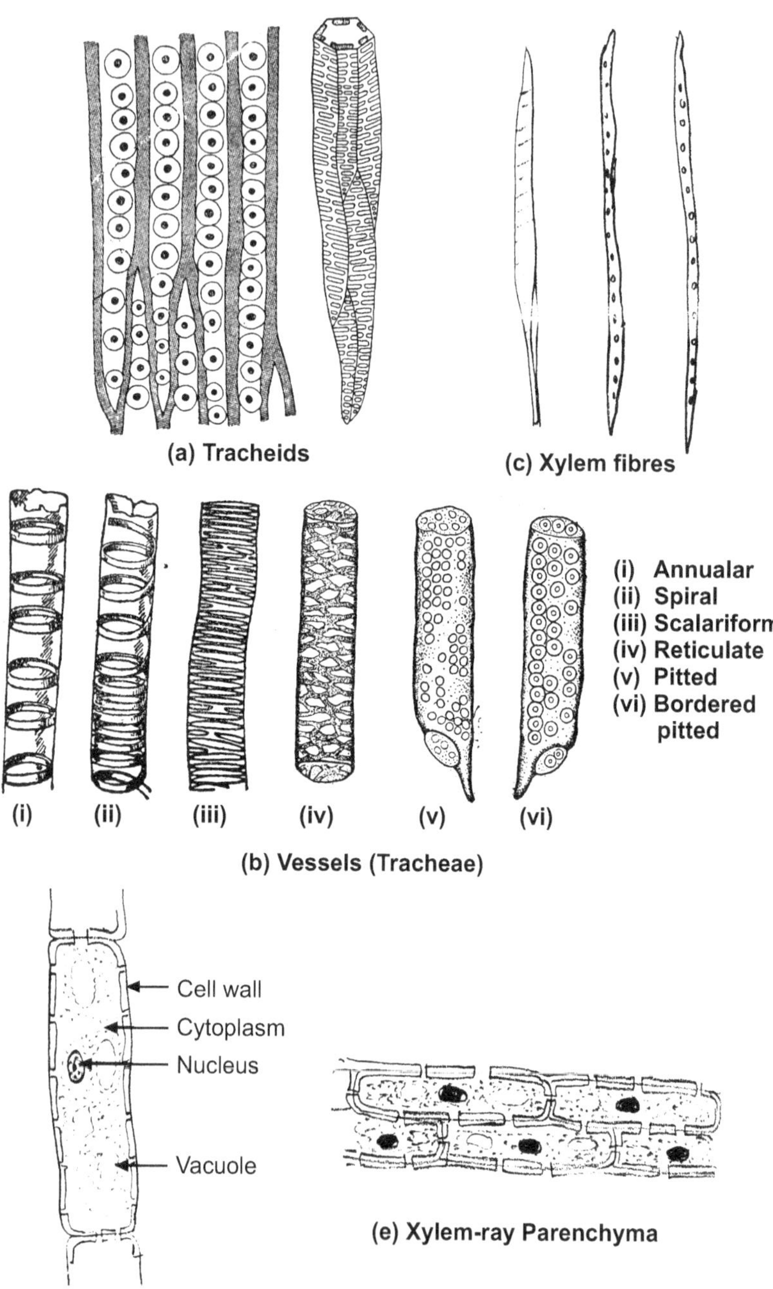

Fig. 2.4: Xylem elements

These parenchyma cells are small, thin walled living cells. Their walls are made up of cellulose. They store food materials in the form of starch, fat and may store other substances like tannin. Xylem parenchyma cells are involved in lateral and radial conduction of water in the form of medullary rays. They also help in the conduction of water upward through the vessels and tracheids.

2. Phloem

Phloem is a thin walled, living, complex conducting tissue. It conducts food materials from leaves to other parts of the plant. Phloem consists of (i) Sieve tube (ii) Companion cells (iii) Phloem fibre and (iv) Phloem parenchyma.

In pteridophytes only sieve cells and phloem parenchyma are present. In some gymnosperms, sieve cells, phloem parenchyma and phloem fibres are present but sieve tubes and companion cells are absent. In angiosperms sieve tubes, companion cells, phloem parenchyma, phloem fibres, sclereids and secretory cells are generally present. **(Fig. 2.5)**

(i) Sieve tube: This is the most important cell element of the phloem. Sieve tube consists of longitudinal rows of cells. The cell wall is thin. It contains protoplast. The cross walls of the sieve tubes are highly perforated and are called **sieve plates**. The cytoplasm of the neighbouring sieve tubes is usually connected by the cytoplasmic strands through the sieve plates. Nucleus is absent in sieve tube. The functions of sieve tubes are controlled by the nucleus of the companion cells. **(Fig. 2.5 a)**

(ii) Companion cells: These are specialised parenchyma cells associated with sieve tubes. The sieve tube elements and companion cells are connected by pit fields. These pits are present between their common longitudinal walls. The companion cells help in maintaining the pressure gradient in the sieve tubes. The companion cells are present only in angiosperms. **(Fig. 2.5 a)**

(iii) Phloem parenchyma: These are elongated, cylindrical cells with dense cytoplasm and nucleus. The cell wall is composed of cellulose and has pits. The phloem parenchyma stores food material and other substances like resins, latex and mucilage. Phloem parenchyma is absent in most of the monocotyledons.

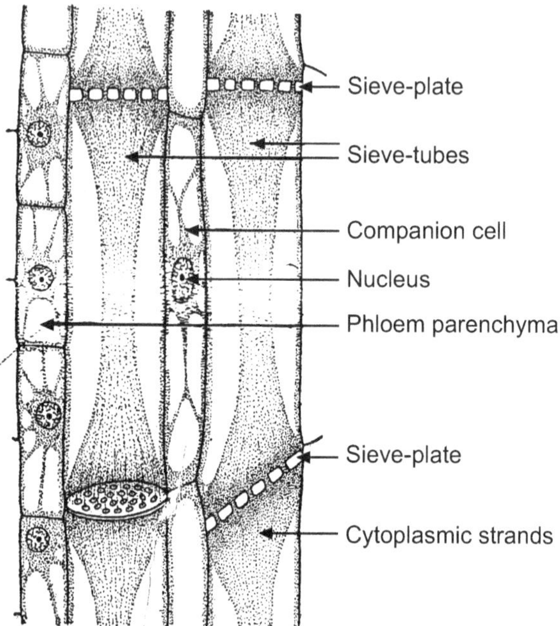

Fig. 2.5 (a): L.S of Phloem

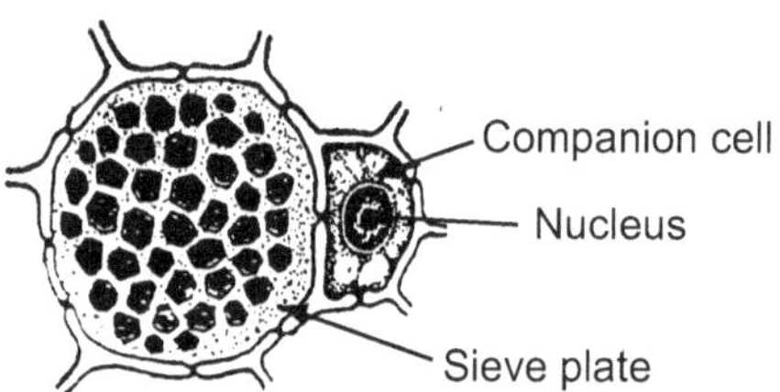

Fig. 2.5 (b): T.S of Sieve tube

(iv) Phloem fibres (Bast fibres): These are sclerenchymatous cells associated with phloem. Generally absent in primary phloem but are found in the secondary phloem. These are much elongated, unbranched and have pointed ends. The wall is very thick. They provide strength to the sieve tubes. Phloem fibres of jute, flax and hemp are used commercially.

2.3 TYPES OF VASCULAR BUNDLES

The vascular bundle consists of xylem and phloem and sometimes cambium. On the basis of the arrangement of xylem and phloem, vascular bundles are classified into three types **(Fig. 2.6)**.

1. Radial Vascular Bundle

When xylem and phloem are arranged in different radii, the vascular bundles are known as Radial vascular bundles. In this type the xylem and phloem lie radially side by side. These are primitive type of vascular bundles and are commonly found in the roots. **(Fig. 2.6 a)**

2. Conjoint Vascular Bundles

In conjoint type of vascular bundle the xylem and phloem occur in the same radius. Phloem is situated on the outer side and xylem towards the centre. This type of vascular bundles occurs in stems and leaves.

Conjoint vascular bundles are of two types

(a) Collateral (b) Bicollateral

(a) Conjoint Collateral Vascular Bundles

In this type phloem occurs only on the outer side of xylem and forms a bundle. Conjoint, collateral vascular bundle may be open or closed.

(i) **Conjoint collateral open vascular bundle:** In dicotyledonous stems, cambium is present in between phloem and xylem. It is called open type. The cambium produces secondary xylem and phloem. **(Fig. 2.6 b)**

(ii) **Conjoint collateral closed vascular bundle:** In the monocotyledonous stem the cambium is absent, hence, it does not form secondary tissues. Such a vascular bundle without cambium is called conjoint collateral and closed. **(Fig. 2.6 c)**

(b) Conjoint Bicollateral Vascular Bundle

In this type of vascular bundle phloem is present on both sides of the xylem. Cambium is also found in two patches, on both the sides of xylem. Bicollateral vascular bundles are found in the members of family Cucurbitaceae. **(Fig. 2.6 d)**

3. Concentric Vascular Bundles

When one of the vascular tissue (xylem or phloem) surrounds the other, the vascular bundle is called concentric. These vascular bundles are always closed. Concentric vascular bundles are of two types.

(i) Amphicribral (Hydrocentric): In this type phloem surrounds the xylem. It is found in ferns, *Lycopodium*, *Selaginella*. **(Fig. 2.6 e)**

(ii) Amphivasal (Leptocentric): When xylem surrounds the phloem, the vascular bundle is called amphivasal (Leptocentric) concentric vascular bundle. Ex.: *Dracaena*, *Yucca* stem. **(Fig. 2.6 f)**

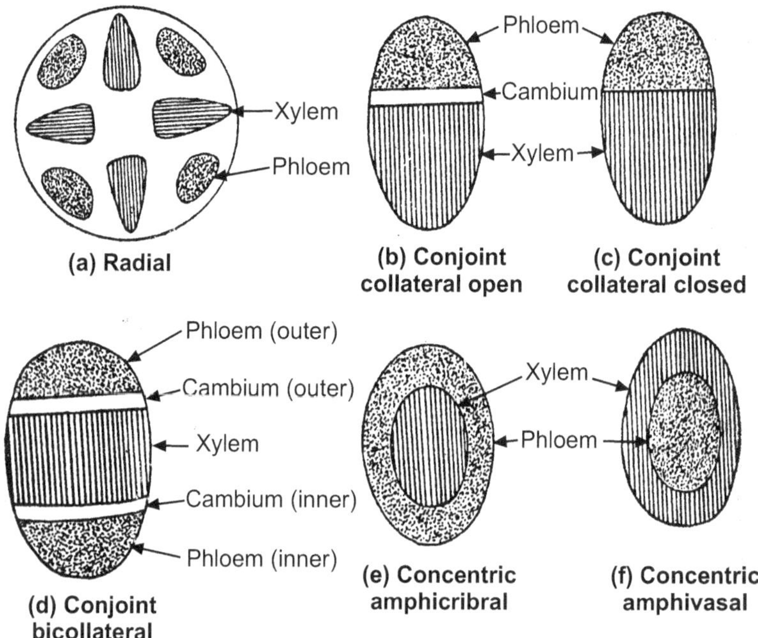

Fig. 2.6 : Types of Vascular Bundles

EXERCISE

I. Multiple Choice Questions

1. Group of cells having same size, shape, origin and function is known as ---------.

   (a) tissue (b) tissue system

   (c) living tissue (d) dead tissue

2. Collenchyma is a --------- tissue.

   (a) meristematic (b) simple living

   (c) simple dead (d) complex

3. Parenchyma cells having big airspaces are known as -------.

   (a) chlorenchyma (b) sclerenchyma

   (c) aerenchyma (d) collenchyma

4. -------- is a living mechanical tissue.

   (a) sclerenchyma (b) xylem

   (c) collenchyma (d) parenchyma

5. --------- cells have lignified walls.

   (a) sclerenchyma (b) parenchyma

   (c) collenchyma (d) chlorenchyma

6. -------- are lignified complex cells

   (a) sclerenchyma (b) collenchyma

   (c) sclereids (d) tracheids

7. --------- are lignified simple cells.

   (a) tracheids (b) collenchyma

   (c) sclereids (d) vessels

8. Sclereids are -------- celled structures.

   (a) simple, lignified and single

   (b) simple, non-lignified single

   (c) complex, lignified and single

   (d) complex, non-lignified and single

9. Living elements of xylem are ---------.
   (a) vessels (b) tracheids
   (c) fibres (d) xylem parenchyma
10. --------- are main water conducting elements in angiosperms.
   (a) vessels (b) tracheids
   (c) xylem fibres (d) xylem parenchyma
11. -------- elements have cytoplasm but nucleus is absent.
   (a) sieve tube (b) companion cell
   (c) phloem parenchyma (d) phloem fibres
12. --------- are the only thick walled elements in phloem.
   (a) sieve tubes (b) companion cells
   (c) phloem parenchyma (d) phloem fibres
13. Companion cells are present only in -------.
   (a) gymnosperms (b) angiosperms
   (c) pteridophytes (d) bryophytes
14. Tissue having only one type of cells is known as -------- tissue
   (a) glandular (b) complex
   (c) simple (d) special
15. Complex tissue consists of -------- cells.
   (a) different types of (b) same type of
   (c) all living (d) all dead

ANSWERS

1-b;	2-b;	3-c;	4-c;	5-a;	6-d;	7-c;	8-a;
9-d;	10-a;	11-a;	12-d;	13-b;	14-c;	15-a.	

II. Two Marks Questions

1. What is permanent tissue?
2. Enlist simple and complex tissues.
3. Give functions of parenchyma.

4. What is the function of collenchyma and sclerenchyma?
5. What are the components of xylem tissue?
6. Enlist the elements of phloem tissue.
7. What is simple tissue?
8. What are complex tissues?
9. What is the function of xylem and phloem?
10. What types of vascular bundles are present in dicot and monocot stem and root?
11. What are radial types of vascular bundle?
12. What is diarch, exarch xylem?
13. What do you mean by endarch xylem?
14. Give the functions of vascular cambium.
15. Give the characteristic feature of palisade tissue
16. Give the characteristic features of spongy tissue.
17. Draw the diagram of amphivasal concentric type of vascular bundle.
18. What is amphicribral type of vascular bundle?
19. What is conjoint bicollateral vascular bundle? Where do they occur?
20. Give the characteristic features of angiosperm root vascular bundles.

III. Four Marks Questions

1. What is vascular bundle? Comment on concentric vascular bundles
2. What is vascular bundle? Comment on conjoint collateral vascular bundles
3. Discuss different types of sclereids you have studied.
4. Comment on collenchymas.

IV. Five Marks Questions

1. Comment on the types of vascular bundles.

2. Discuss the functions of permanent tissues.
3. Describe the structure of xylem
4. What is conducting tissue? Describe the structure of phloem
5. Discuss the structure and function of parenchyma and collenchyma.
6. Structure and function of sclerenchyma.

V. Seven Marks Questions

1. Give an account of simple tissue.
2. Explain the structure of complex tissue with neat labelled diagrams.
3. What is conducting tissue? Describe the types of vascular bundles.

3
CHAPTER

TISSUE SYSTEMS AND THEIR FUNCTIONS

Introduction

Cell is the basic unit of life. A group of similar cells constitute tissue and many tissues come together giving rise to a tissue system.

A plant tissue system can be defined as a functional unit, which connects all organs of a plant. The tissue system is made up of various permanent tissues grouped together to perform a similar function, irrespective of its position in the plant body. In a plant organ different types of tissue systems are present. These tissue systems are categorised as epidermal, secretory and mechanical tissue according to their role in plant body.

3.1 EPIDERMAL TISSUE SYSTEM

The term 'epidermis' refers to the outermost layer of cells on the primary plant body. [Epidermis (Greek) epi-means – above; derma-means – skin] It is also known as dermal tissue system.

It constitutes the outer covering of the plant body. It is a protective tissue that protects the internal tissue of the plant body. This tissue also helps in storage of water, secretion and photosynthesis.

The epidermal tissue system is made up of epidermis, cuticle, stomata and various outgrowths of different epidermal cells. Thus the epidermal tissue system is structurally and functionally variable.

A) Epidermis

Epidermis covers the outer surface of plant body such as root, stem, leaf, flower, fruit and seed. The cells of epidermis are living parenchmatous and variable in shape, size and arrangement. These cells are always closed and attached without intercellular spaces. The cells are elongated or tubular in shape. Mostly the epidermis occurs in single layer but in many plants it is multilayered. **(Fig. 3.1)**

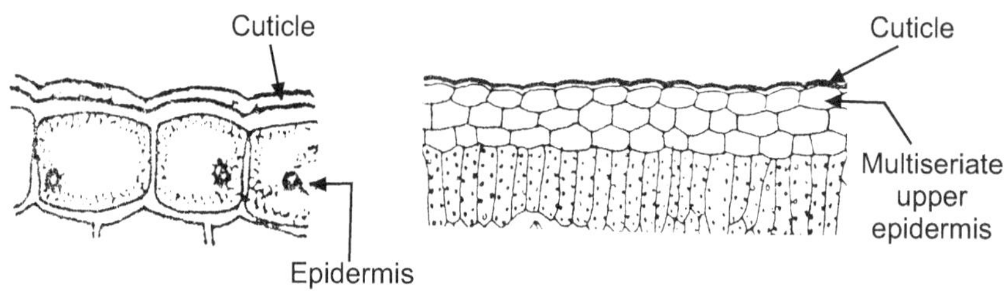

(a) Single layered epidermis (b) Multiple or Multilayered epidermis

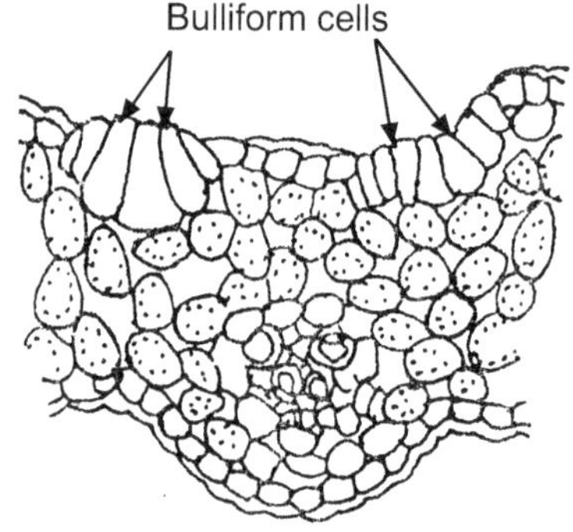

(c) Epidermis with Motor or Bulliform cells

Fig. 3.1: Types of Epidermis

i) Single layered epidermis

It is a continuous layer which is one celled in thickness. The cells are elongated, parenchymatous and closely arranged. The walls of epidermal cells are unevenly thickened. Some cells are thin walled while others are thick walled.

ii) Multiple or multilayered epidermis

It is made up of 3-5 layers of cells. The cells are compactly arranged without intercellular spaces and are thin walled. It reduces the rate of transpiration. Such type of epidermis is found in leaves of many plants like *Nerium* and *Ficus*.

iii) Epidermis with Motor/Bulliform cells

In the leaves of monocots, a peculiar type of large sized and thin wall cells occur in the epidermis. These cells are called motor cells or bulliform cells. These cells are uninucleate and without chloroplast. E.g. Maize leaf

Functions of Epidermis

- Epidermis serves as the outer covering that protects the internal tissues against mechanical injuries, harmful chemicals and invading bacteria.
- Thick walled epidermis and multilayered epidermis reduces the rate of transpiration i.e. they prevent excessive evaporation of the water.
- Epidermal cell acts as store house of water.
- It also helps in photosynthesis and secretion.
- Motor cells of epidermis stores the water and avoid rolling or folding of leaf.

B) Cuticle

It is the layer of waxy, fatty substance known as cutin. It is present on the outer wall of the epidermal cells of the aerial parts of plant body. The thickness of cuticle depends on the environmental condition of the plants. The cuticle is very thin in shady plants while it is thick in the plants which grow in dry condition or dry climate. The surface of cuticle may be smooth or waxy or possess waxy rods. In *Ficus* a waxy bloom is present on the upper epidermis.

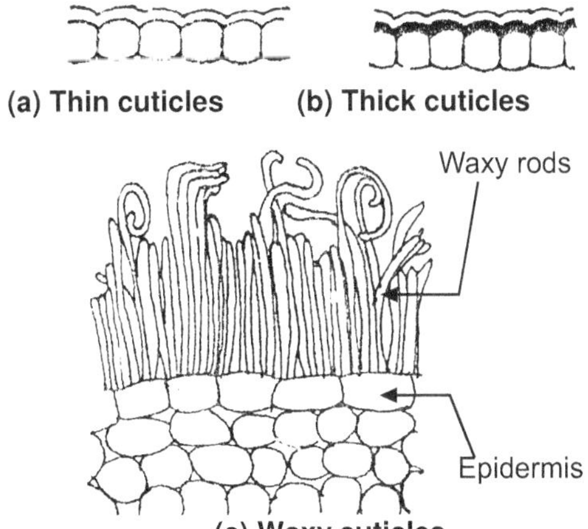

(a) Thin cuticles (b) Thick cuticles

(c) Waxy cuticles

Fig. 3.2: Types of cuticles

The waxy rods are present in the cuticle of sugarcane leaf. In *Musa* (Banana Leaf) cuticle project into the radial walls as peg like bodies. Cuticle is absent in epidermis of root and submerged aquatic plant.

Functions of cuticle

- Thick cuticle prevents the loss of water from the underlying parts.
- The waxy cuticle prevents wetting of leaf.
- The waxy bloom on the epidermis reflects sunlight and thus prevents excessive heating of internal tissues.

C) Stomata

The stomata are minute openings or pores present in the epidermis of the plants. Each stoma remains surrounded by two cells called guard cells. An opening present between the guard cells is known as the aperture. The guard cells are surrounded by subsidiary cells. A cavity present just below the stomata is called the stomatal chamber. The guard cells are living and contain chloroplast. Due to the uneven thickening of wall, the guard cells help in the opening and closing of stomata. It also helps in the exchange of gases that takes place between the internal tissues and the atmosphere.

Stomata are usually found on the aerial parts of the plants but they are most commonly found in the leaves. They are present on both upper and lower surface of leaf but are more abundant in number on the lower surface of the leaf.

In floating leaves stomata are present on the upper surface only.

Types of stomata

Structurally stomata can be divided into five different types.

- **Anomocytic or Ranunculaceous – (Anomocytic = irregular celled):** In this type the stomata remains surrounded by five subsidiary cells which are quite alike the remaining epidermal cells. This type of stomata is found in dicotyledons. Example: Ranunculaceae, Malvaceae, Papaveraceae
- **Anisocytic or Cruciferous – (Anisocytic = unequal celled):** In this type the stomata remains surrounded by three subsidiary cells. Of these three one is distinctly smaller than the rest. This

type of stomata is found in dicotyledons. Example: Cruciferacea, *Solanum*, *Nicotiana*

- **Paracytic or Rubiaceous – (Paracytic =parallel):** In this type the stomata is surrounded by two subsidiary cells which lie parallel to the guard cells. This type of stomata is found in dicotyledons. Example: *Vigna*
- **Diacytic or Caryophyllaceous – (Diacytic = cross celled):** In this type the stomata remains surrounded by a pair of subsidiary cells. The wall of the subsidiary cells lies at right angle to each other. This type of stomata is found in dicotyledons. Example: Acanthacea, Caryophyllaceae
- **Gramineous:** In this type the central portion of guard cells is narrower than the ends. The guard cells are dumb bell shaped. They are surrounded by subsidiary cells. Stomata remain arranged in parallel rows. This type of stomata is found in monocotyledons. Example: Cyperaceae and Gramineae.

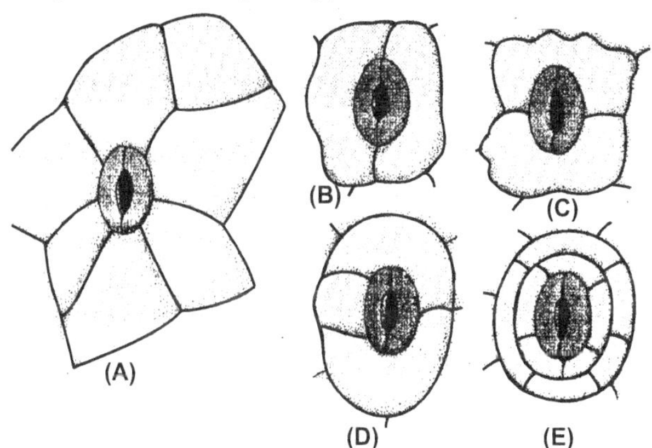

(A) Anomocytic, (B) Paracytic, (C) Diacytic, (D) Anisocytic, (E) Graminaceous

Fig. 3.3: Types of Stomata

Functions of Stomata

- The function of stomata is to regulate transpiration and exchange of gases.
- Stoma plays an important role in the vital phenomenon of photosynthesis and respiration.
- Sunken stomata reduce the rate of transpiration.

D) Epidermal Outgrowth/Appendages

The outgrowths which are present on the epidermis are called epidermal appendages. These are of three types Trichome, Emergence and Root hairs.

I) Trichomes

These are unicellular and multicellular appendages. These are variable in structure and function in different parts of plant body. The trichome cells may be thin walled and living or thick walled and dead cells.

Foster (1949) classified the trichomes in to four groups: i) Hair ii) Scale iii) Colleters and iv) Water vesicles. On the basis of morphology, trichomes are of two types

1) Non glandular 2) Glandular

1) Non glandular trichomes

These are epidermal outgrowths without gland cells. They may be unicellular or multicellular hairs.

a) Unicellular trichomes

These are simple, tubular, elongated epidermal cells. The unicellular trichomes may be unbranched or branched and elongated, twisted or lobed hairs. **(Fig. 3.4)**

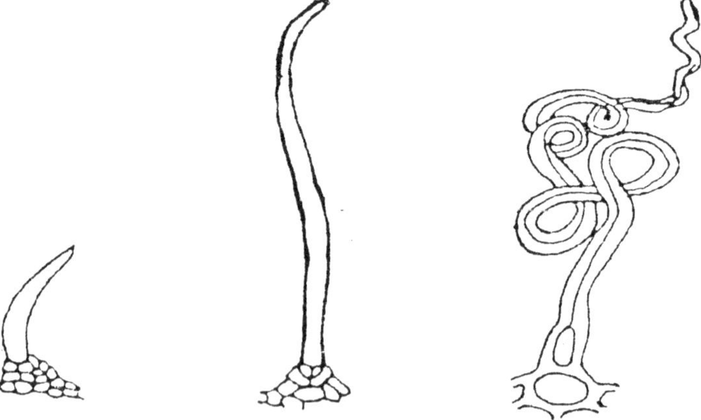

(a) Unbranched short hair *Cassia* (b) Unbranched long hair of *Gossypium* (c) Unbranched elongated twisted hair of *Banksia*

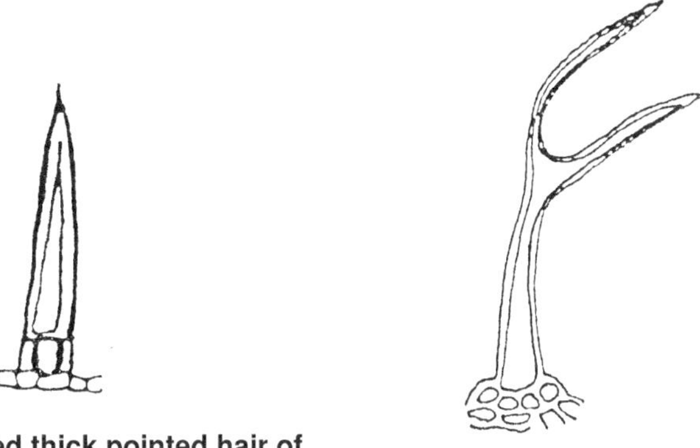

(d) Unbranched thick pointed hair of *Lantana*

(e) Lobed hair of *Amaranthus*

Fig. 3.4 : Unicellular Trichomes

b) Multicellular Trichomes (Colleters)

They are made up of many cells. The basal part of multicellular trichomes is broad and remains embedded in the epidermis called foot. The upper part is relatively narrow and is called body. Multicellular trichome may be uniseriate or biseriate or exhibit different cells. In some plants they are dendroid (tree like) or stellate, star shaped. **(Fig. 3.5)**

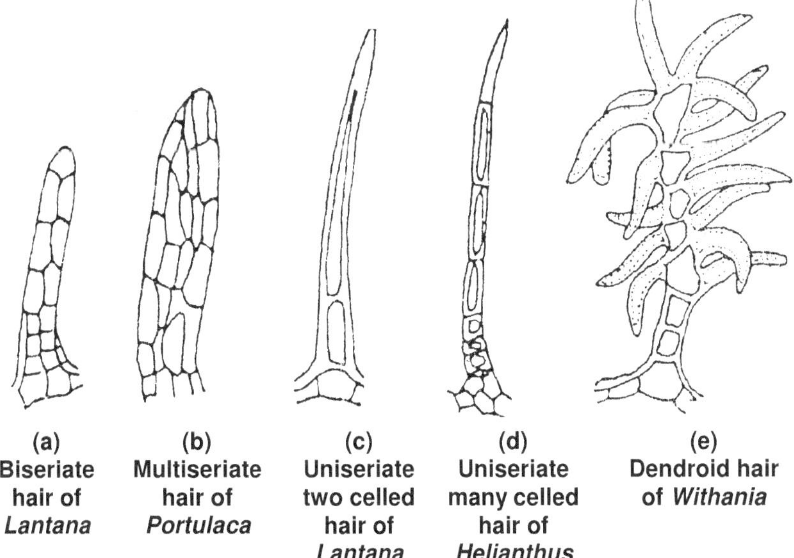

(a) Biseriate hair of *Lantana*

(b) Multiseriate hair of *Portulaca*

(c) Uniseriate two celled hair of *Lantana*

(d) Uniseriate many celled hair of *Helianthus*

(e) Dendroid hair of *Withania*

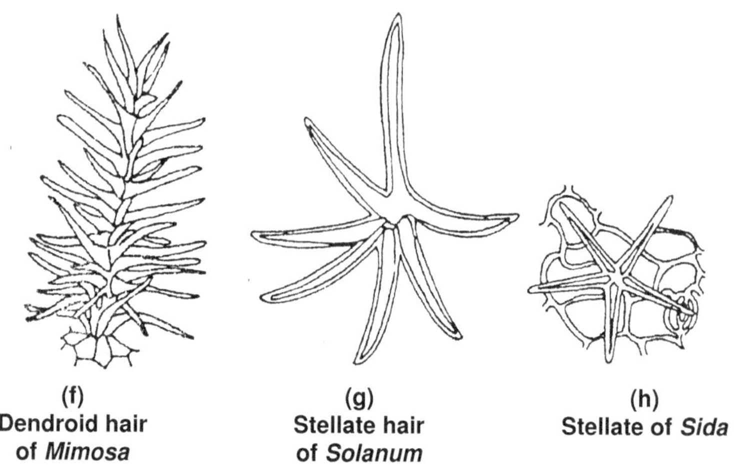

Fig. 3.5: Types of Multicellular Trichomes

2) Glandular trichome

These are unicellular and multicellular glandular trichomes. They are found on bud scale, stipules and foliage leaves. It consists of basal stalk and globular unicellular or multicellular head. It consists of sticky substance. In some plants like *Urtica* the trichome consists of basal swollen portion with poisonous liquid and upper pointed structure called stinging hair. In *Nicotiana*, glandular trichome consists of distinct foot embedded in epidermal cells. In some plant these trichome shows unicellular head and two celled head e.g. *Lantana* and *Leucas* stem consists colleters with two celled and many celled head. **(Fig. 3.6)**

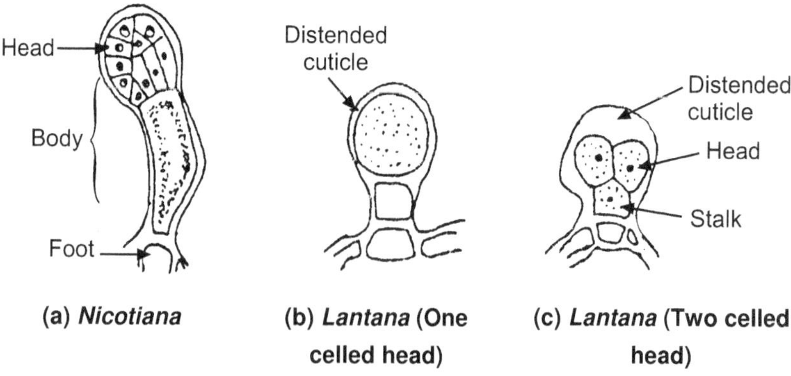

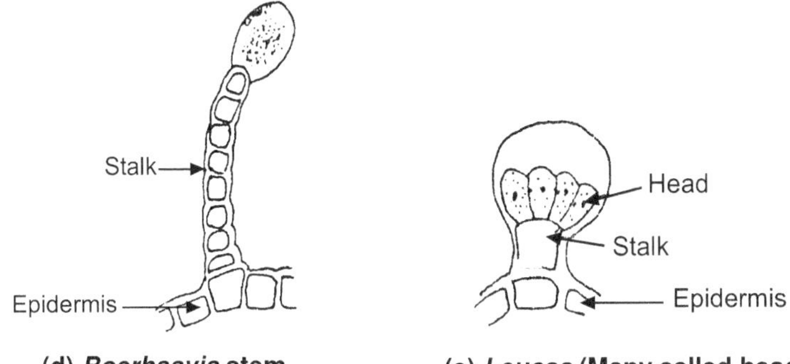

(d) *Boerhaavia* stem **(e) *Leucas* (Many celled head)**

Fig. 3.6: Type of Glandular Trichomes

Function of trichomes

- Trichomes are hairs or epidermal extensions on the stem or leaf which are helpful in reducing transpiration and heating effect of sunlight.
- Trichomes protect plant body from the outer environment
- Hairs on the seed help in the seed dispersal.
- Hairs on the stigma help in pollination.
- Root hairs help in the absorption of water.

II) Emergence

Emergence is different from trichome. It is formed by the epidermis and part of cortex. E.g. Prickles of Rose and *Smilax*. **(Fig. 3.7)**

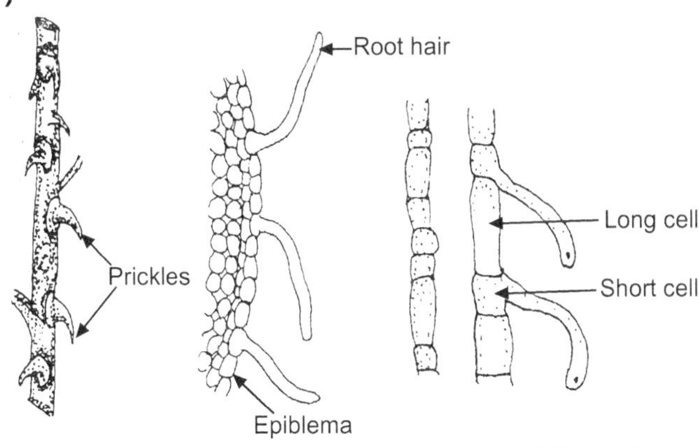

(a) Prickles on Rose stem **(b) Epiblema with root hairs** **(c) Trichoblast**

Fig. 3.7: Emergence

III) Root Hairs

Root epidermis fundamentally differs from shoot epidermis in origin and in absence of cuticle and stomata. Root hairs are not out growth like trichomes but they are prolongation of epidermal cells. The root hairs develop just behind the zone of cell division. The root hairs are unicellular, unbranched and are direct lateral extension of the epidermal cells of root.

The wall of root hairs is thin, composed of cellulose and pectic material. It has vacuolated protoplast and nucleus embedded near the tip. In some plant, root epidermis consists of two types of cells i.e. short cell and long cell. The short cell shows dense cytoplasmic contents. The hairs are formed from short cells which are called trichoblast. **(Fig. 3.7.c)**

Functions

- Absorption of water and mineral salts from the soil.

3.2 SECRETORY TISSUE SYSTEM

Secretory tissue system includes special group of cells or tissue which are directly concerned with secretion or excretion from the plant body. The secretory substances may be deposited but not utilised by plants e.g. (resins, rubber, tannin and crystals) while some other substances take part in function of the plant e.g. (enzymes and hormones). Some cell material produced by cytoplasm is stored in specialised structure called glands or ducts. Most of these secretory products are not useful to the plants but have great economic value to human beings e.g. latex, oils, resins, mucilage, honey. The secretory substances are secreted by special plant structure like hydathodes, glands, ducts, etc. The tissue concerned with secretion of gums, resins, volatile oils, essential oils, nectar, latex, etc are called secretory tissue system.

They may occur as isolated patches in any part of plant or may form well organised structure. They may be external or internal in position.

The secretory tissue system is classified into two groups.

1. Glandular tissue
2. Laticiferous tissue

1) Glandular tissues

These tissues consist of special structure called gland. The glands are well organised secretory structures composed of various types of cells. The glands may secrete oil, resin, nectar, digestive enzymes, water, etc. The gland may be external or internal in position. Glandular tissues are of two types A) Extra glands B) Internal glands.

A) Extra glands

They are generally superficial and occur on the stem and leaf epidermis as glandular outgrowth. There are three types of extra glands. a) Glandular hair b) Digestive gland c) Nectaries.

a) Glandular hairs

These are found in many plants and are of various types – i.e. unicellular and multicellular hairs. The wall of the hair may be thick or thin. In *Nymphaea* the leaves consists of a mucilage gland that develops from the epidermis. Each gland has a multicellular stalk and elongated slime secreting cell at apex which prevent wetting of leaves. In *Geranium* the leaves possess glandular hairs which have multicellular stalk with globular head at the top which secrete the oil. In *Urtica*, glandular hair is of stinging type. The tip of hair is made up of silica. **(Fig. 3.8)**

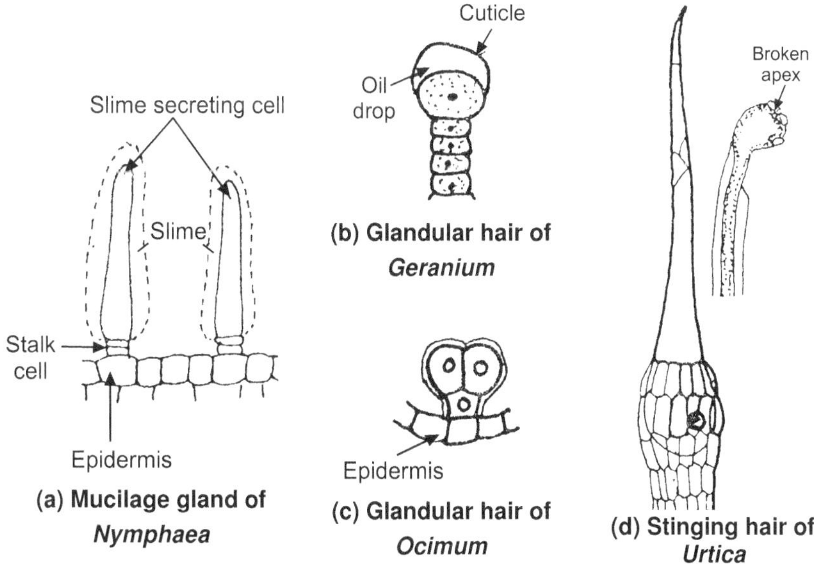

Fig. 3.8: Glandular hairs

b) Digestive gland

In certain insectivorous plants there are special glands which secrete a substance which acts upon the insect body. The protein from the insect body is digested by this secreted substance. The product of digestion can then be absorbed by the plant. E.g. *Drosera, Nepenthes.* **(Fig. 3.9)**

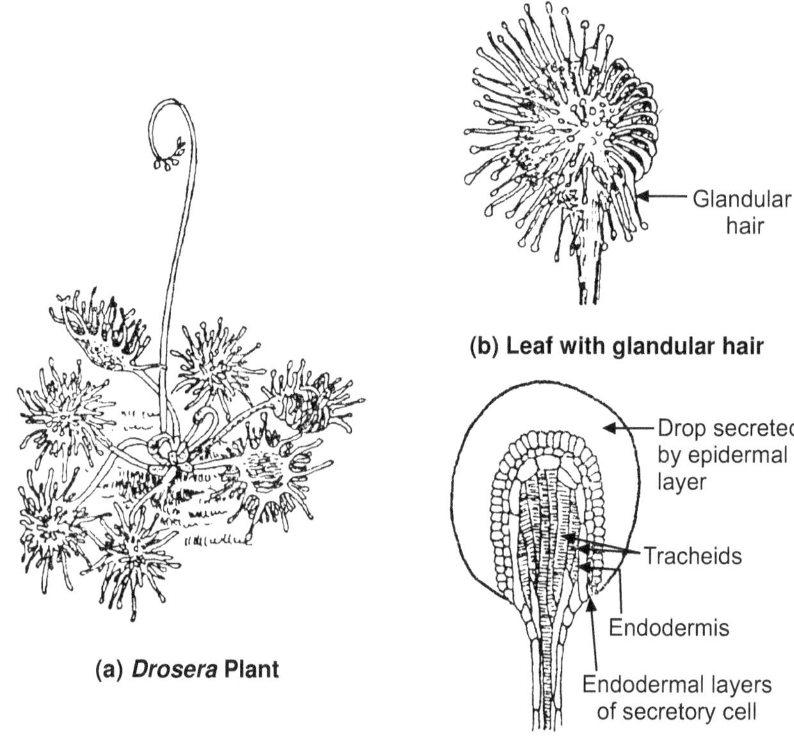

(a) *Drosera* Plant

(b) Leaf with glandular hair

(c) Digestive gland

Fig. 3.9: Digestive glands

In *Drosera* the secretory glands are present on the leaf surface and is differentiated into stalk and swollen gland. In addition to the mucilagenous or viscous substance; these glands also secrete protein digesting enzymes which hold and digest the protein component of the insect. The secretory gland has two layer of cells. These cells are thin walled. The tracheids are present at the center of gland. The stalk of gland is multicellular.

c) Nectaries

These are special glands usually located on floral parts. They secrete sugary substance - nectar or honey and thus they attract pollinating insects. These glands are superficial usually consisting of epidermal cells. In some cases gland cells are columnar where as in others these cells may be normal epidermal cells. The nectaries may occur on floral parts or extra floral parts. There are two types of nectaries i.e. i) Floral nectary and ii) Extra floral nectary.

i) Floral nectary

The floral nectary in *Euphorbia* is situated on the margin of involucral cup of cyathium inflorescence. The gland cells are vertically elongated, columnar peg like and contain granular cytoplasm with a large nucleus. These cells are present in the inner wall of the nectary. The nectar secreted through wall of gland cells is exposed upon the outer surface of nectary. Due to this the pollinating insects are attracted and help in the pollination. E.g. *Euphorbia*, *Citrus*, etc. **(Fig. 3.10)**

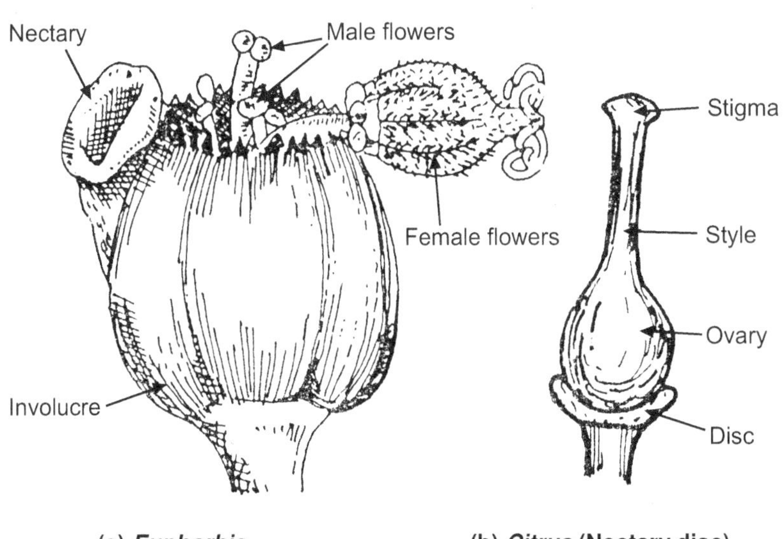

(a) *Euphorbia* (b) *Citrus* (Nectary disc)

Fig. 3.10: Floral nectary

ii) Extra floral nectaries

This nectary is present on the extra floral part of plant like leaf, stem, stipule or petiole. The extra floral nectary occurs on the stipules of *Vicia* of family Leguminosae and also at the junction of petiole and lamina of *Ricinus*, *Canna*, *Euphorbia*, *Vicia*, etc. **(Fig. 3.11)**

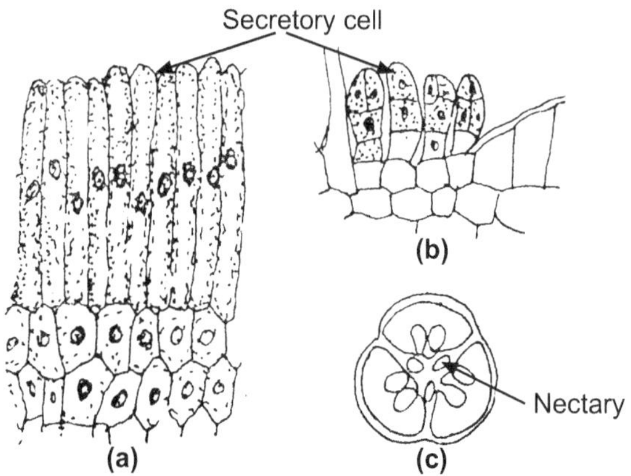

Fig. 3.11: Extra Floral nectary: In Sectional view (a) *Euphorbia* (b) *Vicia* (c) Septal nectary from ovary of *Canna*

B) Internal glands

There are three types of glands i.e. a) Oil gland or cavity b) Resin duct and c) Hydathodes **(Fig. 3.12)**

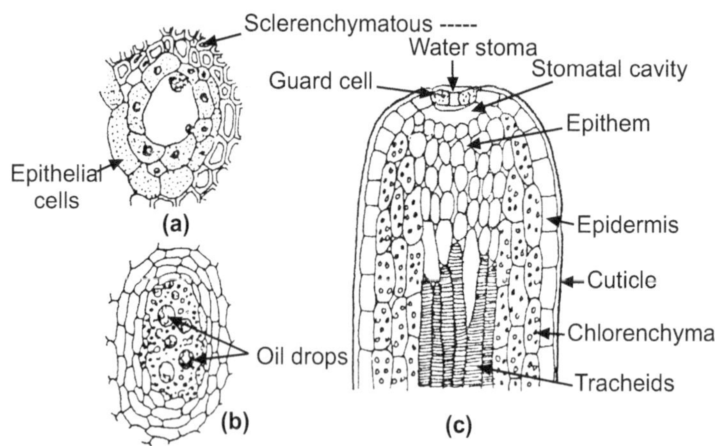

Fig. 3.12: Types of Internal glands: (a) Resin duct (b) Oil duct from peel of *Citrus* fruit (c) L.S. of Hydathode

a) Oil gland or cavity

These are internal gland without an opening. These glands are formed lysigenously (by breaking or disintegration of cells). After the disintegration of cells, a cavity is formed called the oil cavity. The oil secreted by these plants is stored in these cavities. Each gland or cavity has peripheral layer of thin walled secretory cells. These cells secrete the oil. The characteristic oil glands are present on the rinds of fruits like lemon or citrus and oranges. These oil cavities remain filled with essential oil and other substances. These oils are volatile and odoriferous. E.g. *Citrus* leaf

b) Resin duct

These are also internal structures without an opening. The resin ducts are commonly observed in gymnosperms like *Pinus* and angiosperms like Sunflower. In *Pinus* resin ducts are commonly present in the cortical and vascular regions. In longitudinal section these ducts form canal. In transverse section these ducts are circular in outline and consist of thin walled parenchymatous cells called epithelial cells. In the central part, cavity is present. It is formed schizogenously (by separation of cells in the middle lamellae). In sunflower stem resin ducts are present in cortex.

c) Hydathodes

These are specialised internal structure present in many plants through which exudation of water takes place. These are specialised water stomata through which water is released. This phenomenon of exudation of water is known as guttation.

Hydathodes are generally present at the tip or margin of leaf of those plants which grow in moist place. In these plants absorption of water takes place rapidly by roots but rate of transpiration is reduced. Generally water drops are seen in the morning on the leaves of many plants which indicates position of hydathodes. Each hydathode is a mass of epithelial cells and an opening in epidermis called water stomata. Guard cell of water stomata is small and without chloroplast. There is vein connection with epithelial cell which supplies water. The water secreted by hydathode may contain salt. Hydathodes are found in *Arum*, Fern, *Pistia*, Water hyacinth, etc.

2) Laticiferous tissue

The tissue which secretes latex is known as laticiferous tissue.

Latex is a watery fluid present in many flowering plants. Latex is usually milky, yellowish or pinkish in colour. Latex is viscous and colloidal in nature. It consists of sugars, proteins, gums, alkaloids, enzymes, rubber, starch, etc. The laticiferous tissue is found in large number of plants belonging to families like Apocynaceae, Asclepiadaceae, Asteraceae, Euphorbiaceae, Musaceae, Papaveraceae etc. There are two types of laticiferous tissue i.e. a) Latex cells b) Latex vessels **(Fig. 3.13).**

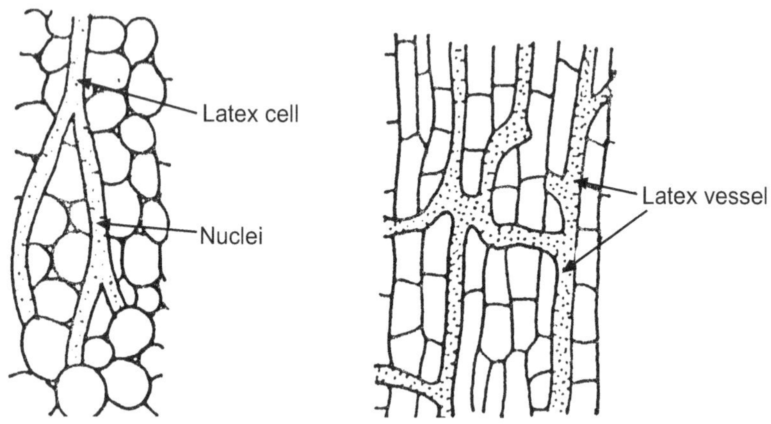

Fig. 3.13: (a) Latex cells from *Euphorbia tirucalli*
(b) Latex vessels from *Launaea* root

a) Latex cells

These cells are also known as non articulated laticifers. The latex cells are single cells, they may be branched or unbranched. They are uninucleate and much smaller in size during embryonic stage. Later they grow, elongate and show branching. The latex cells contain a large number of nuclei, hence they are known as coenocytes. The cell walls are made up of cellulose and are usually thin. A thin layer of cytoplasm is present next to the cell wall. The latex cells are common in the plants like *Calotropis, Catharanthus, Euphorbia, Nerium, Cryptostegia* , etc.

b) Latex vessels

These vessels are also known as articulated ducts. They are compound structures resembling xylem vessels in origin but latex vessels are living and multinucleate. The cells may be even irregular and they are formed by the fusion of many latex cells by dissolution of their septa. These ducts are branched and form complex network. These vessels are also coenocytes without septa. Such latex vessels are commonly found in plants like Papaya, Banana, *Achras*, *Launaea*, etc.

Function of secretory tissue system

- Glandular hair performs secretory and excretory functions and secretes various products.
- Stinging hair provides protection to the plants from animals.
- A mucilage gland of *Nymphea* secretes the slime which spread along the leaf surface and prevents the wetting and rotting of leaves.
- Nectaries secrete a sugary solution to attract insects for pollination.
- Digestive glands secrete protein digesting enzymes for the digestion of protein from bodies of insect.
- Hydathodes help in guttation.
- Laticiferous tissues store the food in the form of starch and also absorb substances from adjoining tissue.
- In the plants like *Argemone*, *Calotropis*, *Nerium*, the latex is poisonous and protect the plants against grazing animals.

3.3 MECHANICAL TISSUE SYSTEM

In many terrestrial plants, aerial shoot system grows vertically upward and the underground root system grows in the downward direction. The plant body stands erect with proper anchorage provided by the roots. The various organs of the plant body are subjected to various kinds of strain and stress. Large plants encounter different types of strains such as bending stress, longitudinal pulling and shearing stresses. These plants not only have to stand erect but have to support the weight of their branches and foliage. For the sufficient resistance against these various strains and stresses, the plant body requires some mechanical support. Therefore plants develop some specific tissues which give mechanical support to the plant body. Thus a group of cells in plants which gives mechanical support to the plant organs is called mechanical tissues.

Types of Mechanical tissues

There are various types of mechanical tissues i.e. i) Collenchyma ii) Sclerenchyma iii) Xylem iv) Phloem Fibre **(Fig. 3.14)**

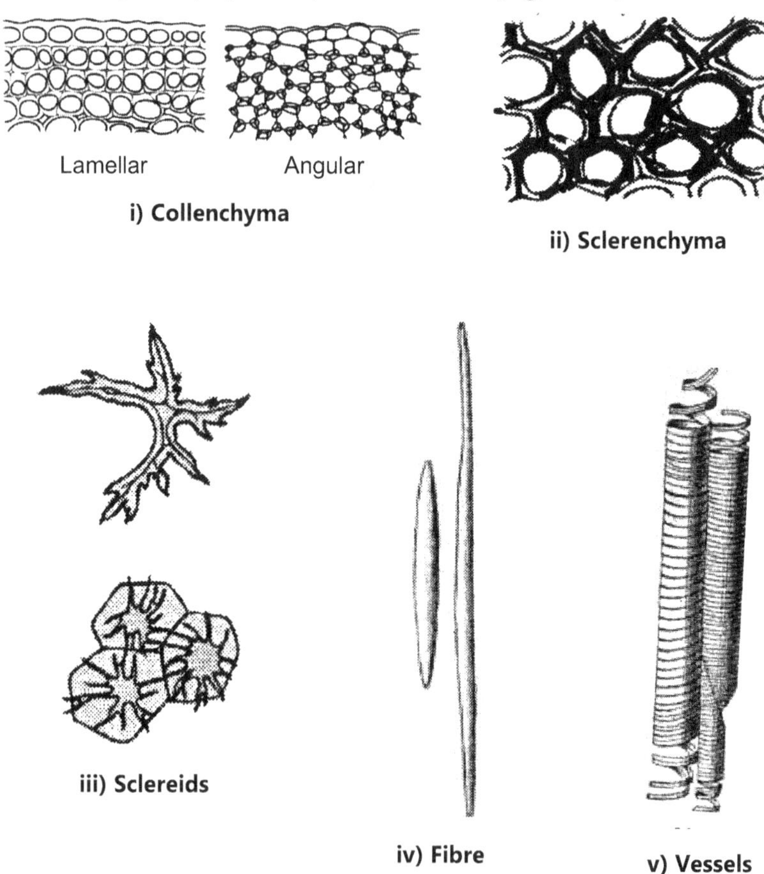

Fig. 3.14: Types of Mechanical Tissues

i) Collenchyma

It is the main supporting permanent tissue of growing organs of plants consisting of only one type of living cells. The most important characteristic is that the cell wall of collenchyma cells is unevenly thickened with cellulose and pectose. The cells have a tremendous capacity of elasticity. The collenchyma cells occur either in continuous long bands or as cylinders in the peripheral region of the aerial organs of plant. Collenchyma gives sufficient strength and elasticity to the growing organs of plant e.g. *Cucurbita*. In older organs, collenchyma may become rigid due to changes in cell wall composition. As the collenchyma cell walls are not lignified, they are flexible. This property makes the collenchyma cells ideal for support and protection against breakage in growing shoots.

ii) Sclerenchyma

It is a simple permanent tissue. Often, the cell dies after its cell wall is fully formed. The cells lack protoplasm i.e. dead cells. The walls of the cells are thick due to heavy deposition of lignin. In T.S. the sclerenchyma cells appear polygonal or hexagonal. Sclerenchyma cells are usually found associated with other cell types. It is found in stems, leaf veins, hard outer covering of seeds and nuts.

The sclerenchyma present in higher plants show two distinct types - sclerenchyma fibres and sclereids.

a) Sclerenchyma fibres: It is composed of elongated, pointed, thick walled and closely arranged dead cells. The sclerenchyma fibres usually occur in patches or bands. They may occur in cortex, pericycle, xylem and phloem regions. The sclerenchyma fibre gives mechanical strength to plants and help to withstand strain and stress.

b) Sclereids: These are short, isodiametric dead cells with thick walls. They are hard, stone like in nature and give rigidity to the organs. These cells occur in soft tissue like cortex, phloem, seed coat and mesocarp of fruit. The sclereids vary in types such as brachysclereids, osterosclereids, astrosclereids, macrosclereids, etc.

iii) Xylem

It is complex permanent tissue. It is composed of tracheids, vessels and xylem fibres. The tracheids and vessels are primarily meant for conduction of water and minerals. They possess thick lignified walls. As the walls are thick and lignified it also gives mechanical support to the plants. The sclerenchyma is associated with xylem fibres. They also possess thick walls and provide mechanical strength to the plant organ.

iv) Phloem Fibre

The sclerenchyma fibers in the phloem are called phloem fibres. These are thick walled, lignified cells found in phloem. These cells are elongated tapering cells, found particular in the stem. These phloem fibres also give mechanical strength to the plant organs.

EXERCISE

I. Multiple Choice Questions

1. In insectivorous plants digestive glands secrete digesting enzymes for the digestion of ------ from bodies of insect.
   a) Lipids b) Proteins
   c) Nucleic acids d) Carbohydrates
2. For mechanical support against strain and stress the distribution of --------- in the different organs of plant body is very important.
   a) Mechanical tissue b) Secretory tissue
   c) Epidermal tissue d) All of these
3. ------- secrete a sugary solution for attracting insects for pollination.
   a) Nectaries b) Mucilage glands
   c) Digestive glands d) None of these
4. Multilayered epidermis is found in ------
   a) *Nerium* b) Lotus
   c) Maize d) Sunflower
5. In monocot stomata guard cells are -----
   a) Bean shaped b) Crescent shaped
   c) Dumb bell shaped d) Rod shaped
6. The epidermal cell form a continuous layer on the surface of all organs in a plant body which form a protective system called -------
   a) Epidermal tissue system b) Secretory tissue system
   c) Mechanical tissue system d) Vascular tissue system

7. Multiple epidermis is found in ------ leaf
   a) Sunflower b) Maize
   c) Sugarcane d) *Nerium*
8. The stoma is bound by specialised epidermal cells called the -----
   a) Guard cells b) Subsidary cells
   c) Epidermal cells d) none of these
9. The glandular trichomes are found in -------
   a) *Euphorbia* b) *Drosera*
   d) Tomato d) Orchid
10. Pith and cortex of the stem are the parts of ---------
    a) Vascular tissue system b) Dermal tissue system
    d) Ground tissue system d) Epidermal tissue system
11. Water secreting glands are known as ---------
    a) Nectaries b) Digestive gland
    c) Hydathodes d) Epithelial cells
12. The tissues giving mechanical strength to the plant are called ------
    a) Excretory tissue system b) Secretory tissue system
    c) Mechanical tissue system d) Epidermal tissue system
13. The living mechanical tissue is ----------
    a) Parenchyma b) Sclerenchyma
    c) Collenchyma d) Aerenchyma
14. Laticiferous vessels are found in --------
    a) Phloem b) Xylem
    c) Cortex d) Pith
15. Latex vessels occurs in ---------
    a) *Hevea* b) Maize
    c) Water lily d) Sunflower
16. Epidermal outgrowths are known as ----------
    a) Spines b) Trichomes
    c) Periderm d) Prickles

17. Bulliform cells are present in the leaves of --------------
    a) Sunflower   b) Maize
    c) *Ficus*   d) *Euphorbia*
18. Sunken stomata are present in stomatal pits of ---------- leaves
    a) *Nerium*   b) Maize
    c) Sunflower   d) Sugarcane

ANSWERS

1-c;	2-b;	3-a;	4-a;	5-a;	6-c;	7-a;	8-d;
9-a;	10-d;	11-d;	12-c;	13-c;	14-c;	15-c;	16-a;
17-b;	18-b						

II. Two Marks Questions

1. Define epidermal tissue system.
2. Enlist the different types of epidermal trichomes
3. Define stomata.
4. State the functions of epidermal tissue system.
5. What is the significance of secretory tissue system?
6. What are the types of mechanical tissues?
7. State the functions of multiple epidermis.

III. Four/Five Marks Questions

1. Describe the structure of typical dicot stomata.
2. Explain structure of epidermis
3. Comment on Trichomes
4. Write in brief about internal secretory structure.
5. Discuss about the structure of collenchyma and sclerenchyma

IV. Seven marks questions

1. Describe in brief the epidermal tissue system
2. Describe in brief the secretory tissue system
3. Describe in brief the mechanical tissue system

4

CHAPTER

PRIMARY STRUCTURE OF PLANT ORGANS

4.1 PRIMARY STRUCTURE OF MONOCOT ROOT AND STEM

The primary growth of a plant body is brought about by the activity of primary meristems, i.e. by apical meristem. Primary growth is studied by observing a transverse structure of the plant structure. The transverse section of the plant organ is differentiated into outer epidermis, the inner ground tissue and vascular tissue.

4.1.1 Primary Structure of Monocot Root (Maize)

The primary root arises from root apical meristem which is situated at sub terminal position and remains protected by the root cap. The transverse section of a monocotyledonous root shows distinct regions: the epiblema, cortex, endodermis and the stele.

(i) Epiblema (Piliferous layer): Epiblema or piliferous layer is the outermost layer of root. It is single layered and made up of thin walled, barrel shaped, compactly arranged paranchymatous cells. They take part in the absorption of water. This layer is without cuticle and stomata. Some epiblema cells produce unicellular elongated structures called root hairs.

(ii) Cortex: Cortex is a major component of the ground tissue of root. The cortex can be distinguished into two regions. The outer region is made up of two or three layers of thick-walled cells placed immediately inside the epiblema. It is known as hypodermis. Inside the hypodermis there are many layers of parenchymatous cells. It forms the inner region of the cortex. It is represented by several layers of loosely arranged parenchyma cells. Intercellular spaces are prominent. The cortex is mainly meant for storage of water. The cells also allow free movement of water into the xylem vessels.

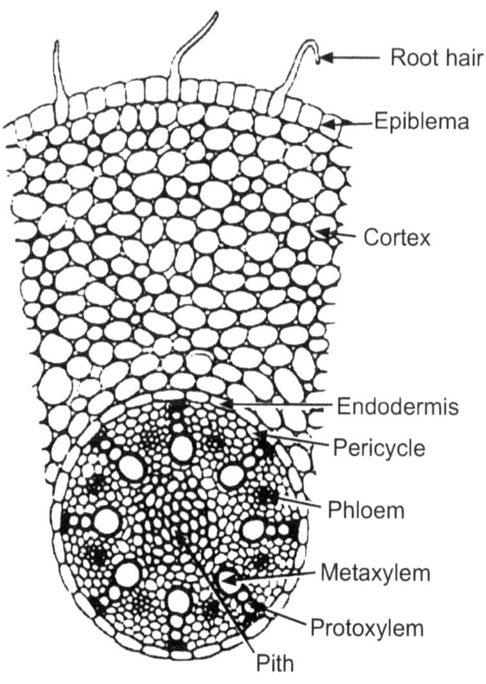

Fig. 4.1: T.S. of Maize root

(iii) Endodermis: It is the innermost layer of cortex formed by compactly arranged barrel-shaped cells. Some of the cells in the endodermis are thin-walled and are known as passage cells. The passage cells allow water to pass into the xylem vessels. The remaining cells in the endodermis are characterised by the presence of thickening on their radial walls. These thickenings are known as casparian thickenings. They are formed by the deposition of a waxy substance called suberin. The casparian thickenings play an important role in creating and maintaining a physical force called root pressure.

(iv) Stele: Stele is the central cylinder of the root consisting of pericycle, conjunctive tissue, pith and vascular bundles.

- **Pith:** It is large, well developed and occupies the centre of the root. It is parenchymatous.

- **Pericycle:** The pericycle is made up of a single layer of cells. In young roots it is thin-walled while in older roots it is thick walled. The ring of pericycle is broken opposite the protoxylem groups. It has abundant protoplasm.
- **Conjunctive tissue:** It is represented by a mass of loosely arranged parenchyma cells found in between the vascular bundles. The cells are specialised for storage of water.
- **Vascular bundles:** There are separate bundles of xylem and phloem arranged on different radii. Vascular bundles are radial in arrangement. Xylem and phloem form an equal number of separate bundles. There are nine to twenty bundles each of xylem and phloem. The vascular bundles are more numerous than in the dicot root. Hence, the condition is described as polyarch.
- **Xylem:** The protoxylem is placed towards the periphery. The xylem is, therefore, exarch. The xylem is made up of annular, spiral and pitted vessels.
- **Phloem:** The phloem is made up of sieve tubes and companion cells.

Characteristic Features of a Monocot Root

- Presence of thin walled cells in the epiblema.
- Absence of cuticle and stomata.
- Presence of unicellular root hairs.
- Presence of passage cells and casparian thickenings in the endodermis.
- Presence of parenchyma cells in the pericycle.
- Presence of conjuctive tissue.
- Presence of distinct pith.
- Presence of radial vascular bundles with polyarch condition and an exarch xylem

4.1.2 Primary Structure of Monocot Stem (Maize)

The transverse section of a typical monocot stem (Maize) shows the following characteristic features:

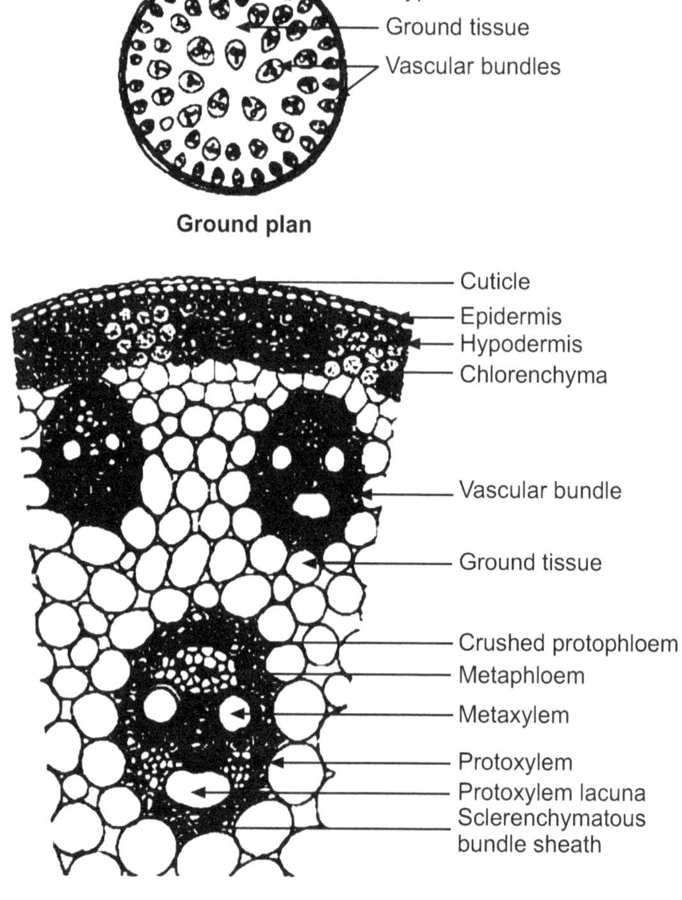

Fig. 4.2: T.S. of Maize stem

i) Epidermis: The outermost layer of cells is known as epidermis. It is formed of single layer of very tightly packed parenchymatous oblong cells. There is a thick layer of cuticle on the outer wall. The cuticle is yellow in colour. Stomatal openings are present in the epidermis. Each opening is guarded by a pair of guard cells. In surface view the guard cells appear dumb-bell shaped. There is a triangular subsidiary cell on the outside of each guard cell. There are no epidermal outgrowths.

ii) Ground tissue: Inside the epidermis there is a ground tissue. The ground tissue is not differentiated into cortex, endodermis, pericycle and pith. It can be distinguished into two regions. Immediately inside the epidermis there are a few sclerenchymatous layers. The major portion of the ground tissue is occupied by parenchyma. The parenchyma cells enclose prominent intercellular spaces. The thickness of the sclerenchymatous layers differs according to the age of the stem. In young stems there may be one layer of sclerenchyma while in fully developed stems there may be as many as six layers. The sclerenchymatous part of the ground tissue is known as hypodermis. It provides mechanical power to the plant.

iii) Vascular bundles: The vascular bundles are irregularly scattered in the parenchymatous part of the ground tissue. The vascular bundles at the periphery are smaller while bundles at the centre are larger and are well developed. Each vascular bundle consists of xylem and phloem. Cambium is absent. Xylem and phloem are laterally placed hence the vascular bundle is described as conjoint, collateral and open. Each vascular bundle is surrounded by a sclerenchymatous layer known as bundle sheath.

- **Xylem:** The xylem is V or Y shaped. Small vessels are placed towards the centre of the stem. Annular, spiral and pitted patterns are met with in xylem. The annular vessel is placed near a cavity known as lysigenous cavity. The cavity is formed by absorption of some cells. Xylem parenchyma is present around the protoxylem.
- **Phloem:** Phloem is placed outside the two pitted vessels. Phloem is made up of sieve tubes and companion cells. Phloem parenchyma and phloem fibres are absent in moncot stem.

Characteristic Features of a Monocot Stem

- Absence of trichomes.
- Presence of stomata.
- Presence of a hypodermis made up of sclerenchyma.

- Presence of undifferentiated ground tissue.
- Presence of numerous vascular bundles irregularly scattered with centrifugal arrangement.
- Vascular bundles are conjoint, collateral and closed with endarch xylem.
- Presence of only two protoxylem and two metaxylem vessels in each bundle.
- Presence of a lysigenous cavity.
- Absence of phloem parenchyma and phloem fibres.
- Presence of a bundle sheath made up of sclerenchyma.

4.2 PRIMARY STRUCTURE OF DICOT ROOT AND STEM

4.2.1 Primary Structure of Dicot Root (Sunflower)

The transverse section of a typical dicot root shows the following characteristic features

(i) Epiblema (Piliferous layer): The single outermost layer is the piliferous layer. It is made up of thin-walled living cells. Cuticle is not developed on its outer wall. Some cells of the piliferous layer produce outgrowths in the form of hairs. The hair is unicellular and they absorb food material from the soil.

(ii) Cortex: The cortex is made up of many layers of parenchyma. The cells contain leucoplasts and starch grains. The innermost layer of the cortex is known as endodermis. It is made up of egg-shaped cells. The radial walls of the endodermal cells are thickened. Small spots, dark in colour, are present on the thickened walls. These are known as casparian spots.

(iii) Pith: It occupies a small area inside the xylem bundles and is made up of parenchymatous cells.

(iv) Stele: Stele consists of pericycle, conjunctive tissue and vascular bundles.

- **Pericycle:** Pericycle is the outermost layer of the stele. It lies immediately inside the endodermis. It is made up of a layer of thin-walled living, parenchymatous cells. It is an important layer in dicotyledonous roots. It becomes meristematic when secondary growth takes place. It also gives rise to rootlets.

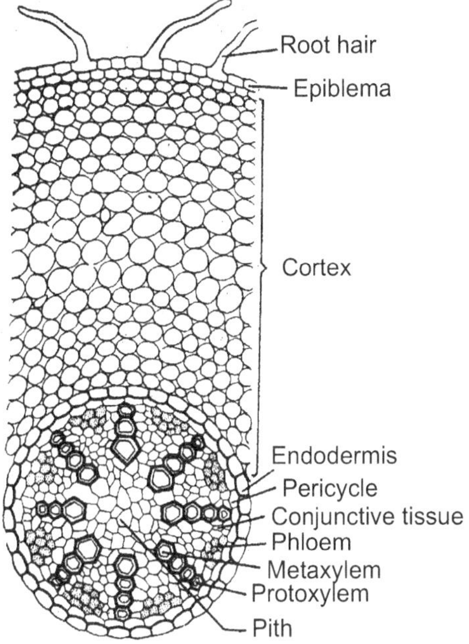

Fig. 4.3: T.S. of dicot root

- **Conjunctive Tissue:** Conjunctive tissue is represented by a group of radially arranged parenchyma cells found in between the vascular bundles. The cells are specialised for storage of water.
- **Vascular bundles:** There are separate vascular bundles of xylem and phloem. The bundles of xylem and phloem alternate with each other and they are placed on different radii. The arrangement of the vascular bundles is, therefore, radial. There are four xylem and four phloem bundles. The stele is, therefore, described as tetrarch.
- **Phloem bundles:** Each phloem bundle is made of sieve tubes, companion cells and phloem parenchyma.

Characteristic Features of a Dicot Root

- Presence of thin walled cells in the epiblema.
- Absence of cuticle and stomata.

- Presence of unicellular root hairs.
- Absence of hypodermis.
- Presence of passage cells and casparian thickenings in the endodermis.
- Presence of uniseriate pericycle made up of parenchyma.
- Presence of conjunctive tissue.
- Presence of radial vascular bundles exhibiting tetrarch condition with exarch xylem.

4.2.2 Primary Structure of Dicot Stem (Sunflower)

The transverse section of a typical dicot stem shows the following characteristic features

i) Epidermis: It is the single outermost layer of parenchymatous rectangular cells. The cells are closely arranged with no intercellular spaces. The cells appear flat in transverse section. Cuticle is formed on the outer walls of the epidermal cells. They are thus strengthened and are able to protect the tissues lying inside it. Choroplasts are present in the epidermal cells. Stomatal openings are present at regular intervals. The guard cells are crescentric or half-moon shaped. Some epidermal cells produce outgrowths in the form of multicellular hairs.

ii) Cortex: The cortex lies just below the epidermis. It is further distinguished into hypodermis, general cortex and endodermis.

- **Hypodermis:** The collenchymatous patch lying inside the epidermis is known as hypodermis. It is made up of 3 or 4 layers of cells. The cells contain chloroplasts. Collenchyma is a strengthening as well as photosynthetic tissue. Inside the stomatal openings, instead of collenchyma, there are thin walled loose cells.
- **General cortex:** The general cortex is made up of many layers of parenchymatous cells. Chloroplasts are also present in the parenchyma. Resin ducts are found in the general cortex. Each duct is surrounded by a layer of thin-walled living cells. This layer is known as epithelial layer. The epithelial cells secrete resin which is poured into the duct or cavity and excreted.

- **Endodermis:** The innermost layer of the cortex is known as endodermis. It is wavy and made up of egg-shaped cells. The cells of the endodermis contain starch grains. Because of the abundance of starch grains in these cells, this layer is also called as starch sheath. The endodermis and the casparian strip is not well developed in most dicot stems.

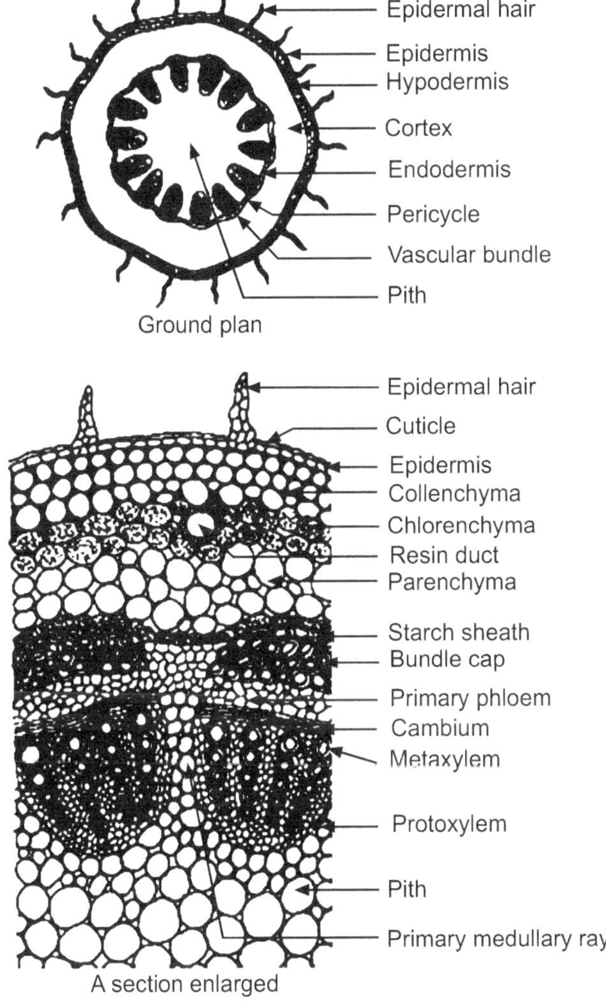

Fig. 4.4: T.S. of Sunflower stem

iii) Stele: The stele includes all tissues lying inside the endodermis. It includes tissues lying inside and around the vascular bundles, and pith.

- **Pith:** It occupies the centre of the stem and is made up of parenchymatous cells. Sometimes the thin walled cells break and a cavity is formed. Resin ducts also occur in the pith.
- **Pericycle:** Pericycle is placed inside the endodermis. It is made up of many layers. The part of the pericycle outside the vascular bundle becomes sclerenchymatous. This thick walled part of the pericycle is known as hard bast. The part of the pericycle in between the vascular bundles remains parenchymatous.
- **Medullary Rays:** They are found in between the vascular bundles. They are meant for the storage of food.
- **Vascular bundles:** Many vascular bundles are present in the stem. They are arranged in ring. Each vascular bundle consists of xylem, phloem and cambium. Xylem and phloem are laterally placed. The bundles are, therefore, described as conjoint, collateral and open.
- **Cambium:** It is a meristematic tissue. The cells of the cambium divide and give rise to xylem towards inside and phloem towards outside. This is a part of the bundle and, therefore, known as fascicular cambium (fascile – Bundle)
- **Xylem:** It lies towards the centre of the stem. The smallest element of xylem is placed towards the centre of the stem. The xylem is made up of annular, spiral and pitted vessels.
- **Phloem:** The phloem is placed immediately inside the hard bast. It is made up of thin- walled cells. It is also called as soft bast. The phloem consists of sieve tubes, companion cells and phloem parenchyma.

Characteristic Features of a Dicot Stem

- Presence of cuticle and trichomes.
- Presence of stomata.
- Presence of hypodermis made up of collenchyma.
- Presence of a wavy endodermis containing numerous starch grains.

- Presence of a bundle cap above each vascular bundle, formed by sclerenchyma.
- Presence of eight vascular bundles, arranged in the form of a broken ring.
- Presence of conjoint, collateral and open vascular bundles with an endarch xylem.

EXERCISE

I. Multiple Choice Questions

1. Casparian strips are present in ---------.
   (a) Cortex (b) Epidermis
   (c) Stele (d) Endodermis
2. The outermost part of the stele consists of one or more layers of parenchymatous cells. The outer layer of this parenchyma is called ---------.
   (a) Cortex (b) Epidermis
   (c) Stele (d) Pericycle
3. The type of arrangement in which protoxylem lies towards the outside and metaxylem lies towards the inside is called: ---------.
   (a) Mesarch (b) Endarch
   (c) exarch (d) None
4. When xylem is present towards the inner side and phloem is present towards the outer side of vascular bundle, it is known as
   (a) Collateral (b) Bicollateral
   (c) Concentric (d) Amphivasal
5. When one type of vascular tissue (xylem or phloem) completely surrounds the other type of tissue it is known as ---------.
   (a) Collateral (b) Bicollateral
   (c) Concentric (d) Diarch
6. Endodermis is present in ---------.
   (a) Monocot (b) Dicot
   (c) Gymnosperm (d) None
7. Cambium is absent in ---------.
   (a) Monocot (b) Dicot
   (c) Gymnosperm (d) None

ANSWERS

1-d; 2-d; 3-c; 4-a; 5-c; 6-b; 7-a;

II. Two Marks Questions

1. Describe in brief the epiblema layer of root.
2. Write any two characteristic features of dicot root as observed in transverse section.
3. Write in brief about phloem in dicot stem.
4. Comment on the vascular bundles in dicot stem.
5. Describe in brief the role of cambium.
6. Describe the vascular bundle in monocot stem.
7. What type of vascular bundles are present in root?
8. Write any two functions of epiblema of root.
9. Write any two characteristic features of monocot root.
10. Write any two characteristic features of dicot stem.

III. Four/Five Marks Questions

1. Draw neat labeled diagram of monocot root.
2. Draw neat labeled diagram of monocot stem.
3. Draw neat labeled diagram of dicot root.
4. Draw neat labeled diagram of dicot stem.
5. Describe the vascular tissue in monocot root.
6. Write a brief account of cortex observed in transverse section of typical dicot stem.
7. Write a brief account of ground tissue observed in transverse section of typical monocot stem.
8. Comment on the vascular tissue in typical dicot stem.
9. Write any five characteristic features of dicot stem.
10. Write any five characteristic features of monocot stem.
11. Write any five characteristic features of dicot root.
12. Write any five characteristic features of monocot stem.

IV. Seven Marks Questions

1. Describe in detail the structure of monocot root as observed in transverse section
2. Describe in detail the structure of dicot root as observed in transverse section
3. Describe in detail the structure of monocot stem as observed in transverse section
4. Describe in detail the structure of dicot stem as observed in transverse section.

5
CHAPTER

SECONDARY BODY OF THE PLANT

Introduction

The growth of the roots and stems in length with the help of apical meristem is called the primary growth. Apart from primary growth most dicotyledonous plants exhibit an increase in girth. This increase in girth is called the secondary growth. Two lateral meristems are involved in secondary growth; namely vascular cambium and cork cambium.

The secondary tissue is formed by the activity of vascular cambium and cork-cambium. The cambium forms secondary tissues in the stelar region and cork-cambium forms secondary tissues in the cortical regions. Secondary growth occurs only in dicot stem and root. It is usually absent in monocot root and stem.

5.1 NORMAL SECONDARY GROWTH IN DICOT ROOT AND STEM

5.1.1 Normal Secondary Growth in Dicot root

In dicot roots, the secondary growth is initiated by the activity of cambium and cork cambium.

a) Activity of cambium

Cells of the conjunctive tissues just below the phloem becomes meristematic and form strips of cambium. These strips grow laterally and join the pericycle cells outside the protoxylem. Thus a continuous wavy band of cambium is formed. The cambial cells below the phloem are more active on the inner side. Because of this the cambium and phloem are pushed outside. The cambium now becomes circular or a ring is formed. Now the entire ring produces secondary xylem on the inner side and secondary phloem on the outer side. The primary xylem and the pith may be crushed. In between the secondary vascular tissues there are primary and secondary medullary rays. The roots also show variable activity during different seasons and form annual rings. However, unlike in stem, the annual rings do not become distinct.

b) Activity of cork cambium

The cells of the pericycle become meristematic, and are called cork cambium or phellogen. Similar to stems it forms cork or phellem on the outer side and secondary cortex or phelloderm on the inner side. Bark also forms in roots. Sometimes lenticels may also develop.

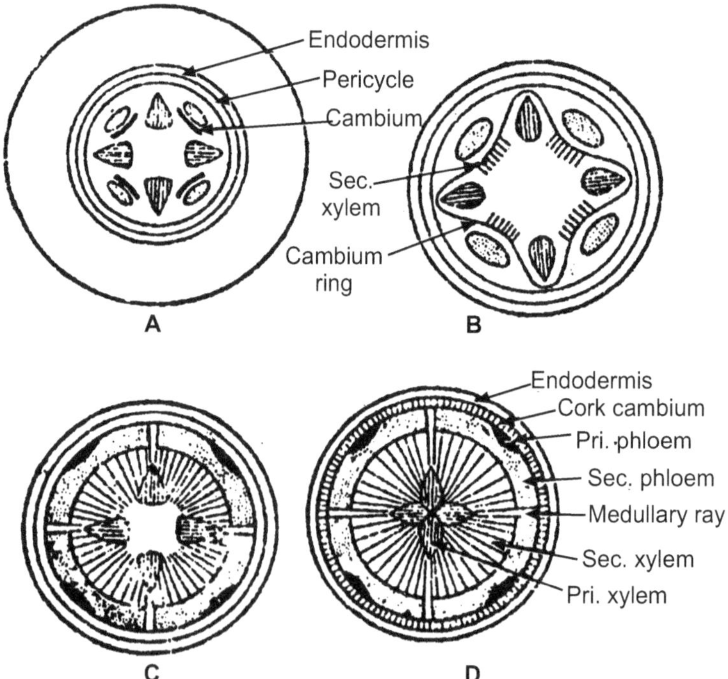

Fig. 5.1: Diagrammatic stages of secondary growth of root

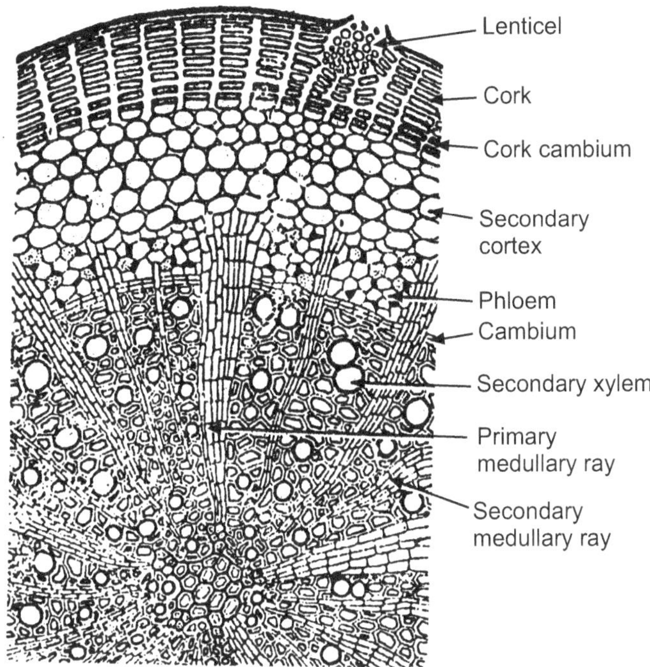

Fig. 5.2: T. S. of dicot root after secondary growth

5.1.2 Secondary Growth in Dicot Stem

In dicot stem, secondary growth takes place through the following steps:

a) Formation of Cambium Ring

Formation of the cambium ring is the first step of secondary growth. The cambium of vascular bundles becomes meristematic. At the same time some of the medullary ray cells lying at the level of cambium also become meristematic and form a strip of interfascicular cambium together with intrafascicular cambium and form a complete circular ring, which is called cambium ring. The cambium ring forms the secondary tissues in the stelar region.

The vascular cambium consists of two types of cells, the fusiform initials and the ray initials. The fusiform initials are vertically oriented and divide to form the elements of xylem and phloem. The cells of ray initials are smaller and isodiametric which give rise to vascular rays of parenchymatous cells.

b) Formation of Secondary Vascular Tissues

The cambium ring cuts off new cells, both on outer and inner sides. The new cells formed on the outer side gradually modify into the elements of secondary phloem. The cells formed on the inner side gradually modify into secondary xylem.

- **Secondary Phloem:** It consists of sieve tubes, companion cells, phloem parenchyma and phloem fibres. The primary phloem present on the outside gets crushed and is represented by small patches.
- **Secondary Xylem:** Secondary xylem consists of vessels, tracheids, wood fibres and wood parenchyma. The vessels or trachea are most abundant in secondary xylem and are usually shorter than that of the primary xylem. The cambium ring forms more tissue on the inner side than on the outer side. As a result, secondary xylem forms the main bulk of the plant body and is generally called the wood. Its width increases with age. The primary xylem persists as conical projections towards the pith.

c) Vascular rays:

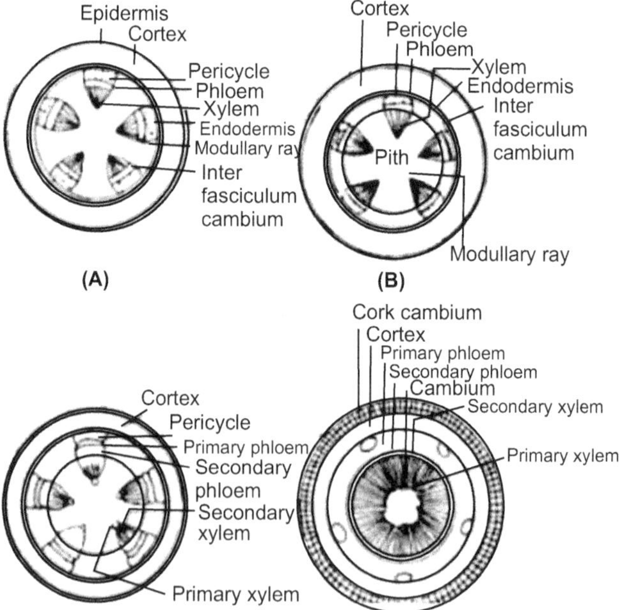

Fig 5.3 : Secondary Growth in Dicot Stem

Ray initials of the cambium ring form some narrow bands of parenchymatous cells. These cells extend radially from the pith to the phloem. These are called secondary medullary rays or vascular rays. The rays present in xylem are called xylem rays while the rays present in phloem are called phloem rays.

5.2 PERIDERM, LENTICELS AND ANNUAL RINGS

5.2.1 Periderm

As the stem continues to increase in girth due to the activity of vascular cambium, the outer cortical and epidermal layers are broken down. In place of these layers new protective layers must be developed. Hence, sooner or later, another meristematic tissue called cork cambium or phellogen develops, usually in the cortex region. Phellogen is a thick layered region made of narrow, thin-walled and nearly rectangular cells. Phellogen cuts off cells on both sides. The outer cells differentiate into cork or phellem while the inner cells differentiate into secondary cortex or phelloderm. The cork is impervious to water due to suberin deposition in the cell wall. The cells of secondary cortex are parenchymatous. Phellogen, phellem and phelloderm are collectively known as periderm. Due to activity of the cork cambium, pressure builds up on the remaining layers peripheral to phellogen and ultimately these layers die and slough off. Bark is a non-technical term that refers to all tissues exterior to the vascular cambium, therefore including secondary phloem. Bark refers to a number of tissue types, viz., periderm and secondary phloem. Bark that is formed early in the season is called early or soft bark. Towards the end of the season late or hard bark is formed.

Structure of periderm components

1) **Phellogen:** The phellogen is a secondary meristematic tissue by its origin and function. It is originated from permanent cells and produces secondary tissues which are involved in the formation of the secondary plant body. The phellogen is a lateral meristem present in the extra stellar region or surface region. The cells of phellogen add secondary tissue by tangential division which increases the diameter of the axis. The phellogen is simpler in its structure which is composed of only one type of initial cells. The

initial cells appear rectangular in transverse section and in longitudinal tangential section they seem to be polygonal. The protoplasm of the phellogen cells contains vacuoles of different size. The cells of phellogen are compactly arranged without intercellular spaces except in the lenticel regions. The phellogen exhibits seasonal variation in its activity like vascular cambium due to which the cork is formed in layers of different thickness.

2) Phellem: Phellem is also recognised as cork and shows rectangular flattened cells in transverse section while in tangential section the cells appear polygonal in shape. In transverse section of the stem the cork cells appear to be arranged in compact radial rows with no intercellular spaces.

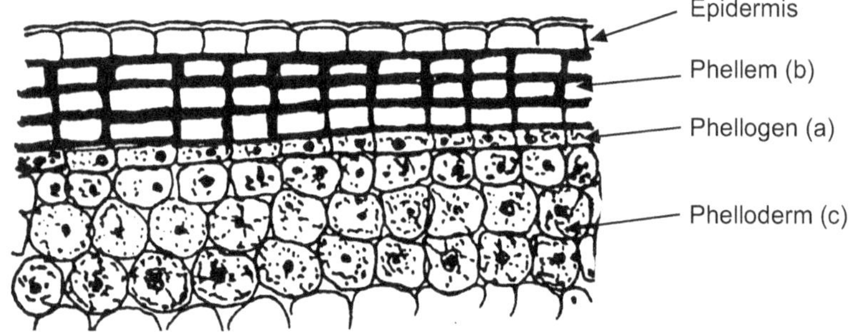

Fig. 5.4: Component of periderm

The cork cells are dead cells. There are two types of cork cells

- The hollow, thin walled and radially widened cells and
- Thick walled and radially flattened cells.

In plants like *Eucalyptus*, thick walled flattened cells are generally filled with dark resiniferous or tanniniferous substances. Some plants like *Butea* show presence of both types of cork cells.

The primary wall of phellem or cork cells generally consists of cellulose but sometimes it shows presence of suberin or lignin. Internally the primary wall is lined by a relatively thick layer of suberin. This suberin layer in many plants consists of fine alternating lamellae of suberin and wax. The suberin layer is impermeable to water and gases and it is not affected by acids. The protoplasts of phellem cells is lost after the various wall layers have been formed and then the lumen becomes filled with air or dark coloured substances.

3) Phelloderm: The cells of phelloderm are living cells with non-suberized walls. They are similar to normal parenchymatous cells. In multilayered phelloderm these cells are arranged in radial rows. In some plants the phelloderm cells contain chloroplasts which carry out photosynthesis e.g. *Tinospora* stem. Some plants do not show development of phelloderm.

5.2.2 Lenticel

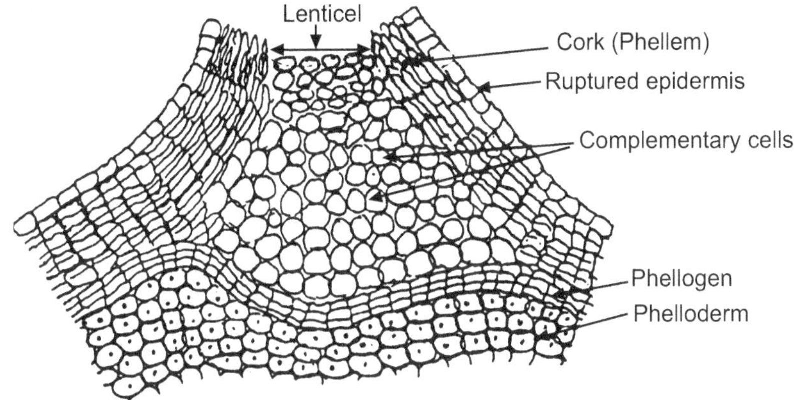

Fig. 5.5: Structure of lenticel region

At certain regions, the phellogen cuts off closely arranged parenchymatous cells on the outer side instead of cork cells. These parenchymatous cells soon rupture the epidermis, forming a lens shaped openings called lenticels. Lenticels permit the exchange of gases between the outer atmosphere and the internal tissue of the stem. These occur in most woody trees.

5.2.3 Annual Rings

The activity of vascular cambium is greatly affected by the variations in the climate. It is more pronounced in temperate regions. The cambium stops dividing in winter. In the spring season or early summer, the cambium becomes more active and produces a large number of vessels with wider lumen. These are called spring wood or early wood.

During the autumn or winter season, the cambium becomes less active and produces vessels with narrow lumens. Tracheids and wood fibres are formed in large numbers. These woods are called autumn wood or late wood. Hence, the annual rings are formed year after year. In the oldest part of the tree, annual rings can be used in determining the age of a tree. This determination of age of trees is called dendrochronology.

In tropical regions, the climate is more or less uniform. Therefore, the annual rings are not well developed and does not correlate with the age of tree.

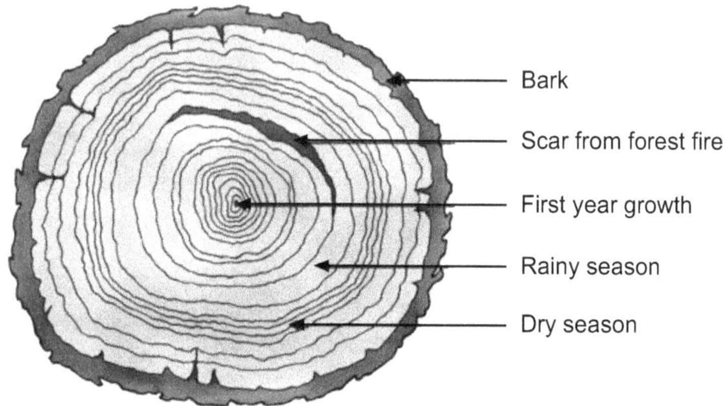

Fig. 5.6 : Annual Rings

5.3 BASIC STRUCTURE OF WOOD AND ITS TYPE

The solid mass of secondary xylem produced during successive years in many perennial trees together form the wood of commercial importance. The wood is the accumulation of secondary xylem for many years and therefore there is no difference in the basic structure of wood and secondary xylem. The secondary xylem consists of vessels, tracheids, wood fibres and wood parenchyma. The vessels or trachea are most abundant in secondary xylem and are usually shorter than that of the primary xylem. The cambium ring forms more tissue on the inner side than on the outer side. As a result, secondary xylem forms the main bulk of the plant body and is generally called the wood. Its width increases with age.

5.3.1 Types of wood

i) Sapwood and Heartwood

In older stems, the woody trunk is differentiated into two regions. The outer light coloured region is called sap wood or alburnum and central dark coloured region is called heart wood or duramen. The cells of sapwood are living and functional. They take part in conduction of water and storage of food. The heartwood consists of dead cells. During the growth process the rings of sap wood gradually convert into heartwood. The living cells of sap wood lose their protoplast and water content. The lumen of the xylem vessels get blocked by the ingrowth of the parenchyma cells. The adjacent parenchyma tissue enters through the pits of vessels and gradually enlarge to form a balloon like structure, which is called tyloses. The cells in this region are filled with tannin and other similar substances due to which heart wood becomes dark in colour. The heartwood is stronger and more durable than sapwood. The heartwood becomes resistant to the attacks of bacteria and fungi due to the presence of antiseptic oils.

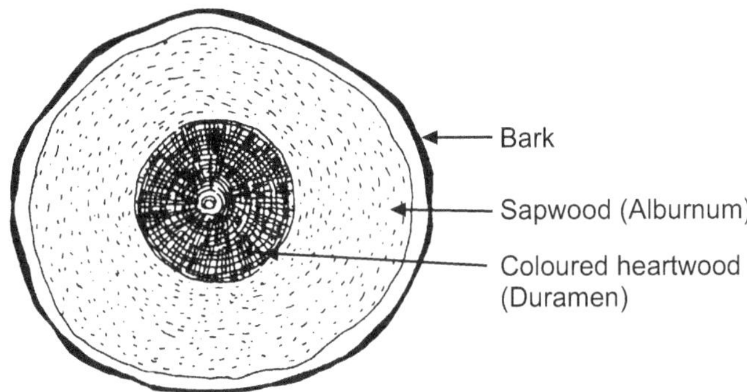

Fig. 5.7: T. S. of tree trunk showing heartwood and sapwood

ii) Porous and Non-Porous Wood

On the basis of presence or absence of vessels the woods are classified as non porous and porous woods. When vessels are absent in the wood it is considered as non-porous wood. i.e. Gymnospermous wood. When vessels are present in the wood it is considered as porous wood, i.e. Angiospermic wood.

The porous woods are further classified as

a) Diffuse porous wood

In angiospermic wood when the vessels in the wood are more or less uniform in diameter and distributed throughout the wood or when there is only a gradual change in size or distributed throughout the growth ring, the wood is termed diffuse porous wood (Eg. *Acasia, Eucalyptus*)

b) Ring porous wood

In this type of porous wood vessels are of different diameters. The vessels produced in the beginning of the season (early wood) are distinctly larger than those produced at the end of the season (late wood). This type of wood is present in plants like *Quercus, Fraxinus* and *Pistacia*. Ring porous wood is considered phylogenetically more advanced than diffuse porous wood.

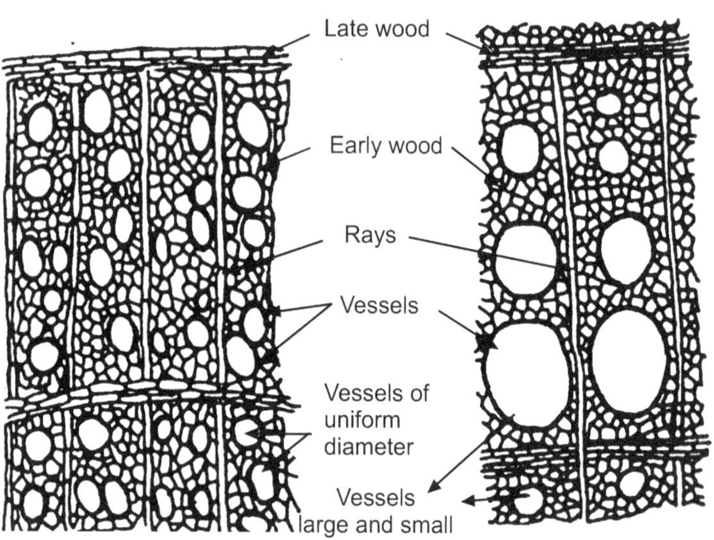

Fig. 5.8: A-Diffuse porous wood B-Ring porous wood

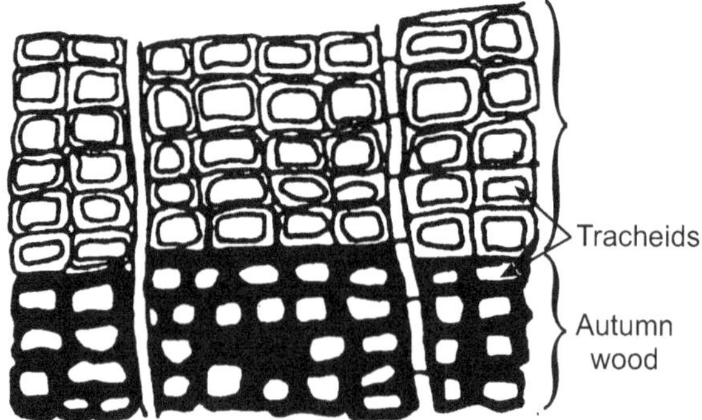

Fig. 5.9: Non-porous wood in gymnosperm

iii) Woods with apotracheal and paratracheal parenchyma

On the basis of distribution of wood parenchyma or axial parenchyma the woods are categorised as

a) Woods with apotracheal parenchyma

In this type of wood, generally parenchyma is present in the form of thin or broad bands or layers in the wood and is independent of distribution of vessels.

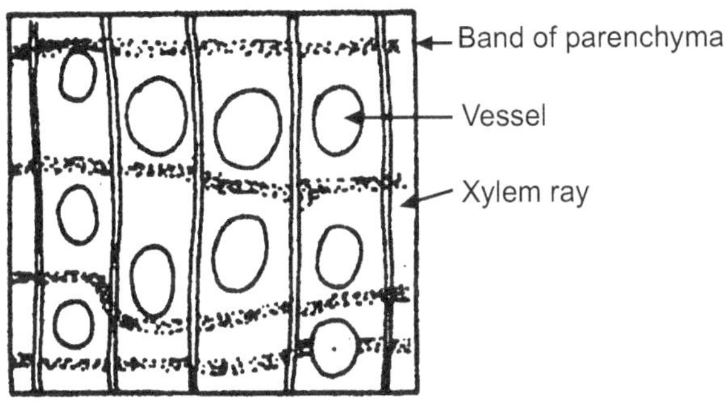

Fig. 5.10: Apotracheal parenchyma

b) Woods with paratracheal parenchyma

In this type of wood, parenchyma exists either in the form of continuous sheath around many vessels or in the form of separate sheath for each vessels or present only on one side of the vessels. When paratracheal parenchyma forms a sheath around the vessels it is called vascicentric paratracheal parenchyma.

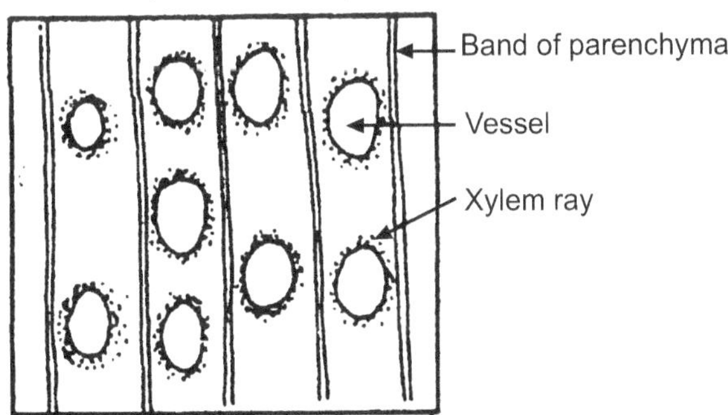

Fig. 5.11: Paratracheal parenchyma

(iv) Spring and Autumn Wood

- **Spring wood:** They are also called early wood as they are formed early in the growing season. It is lighter and has low density. The tracheary elements of xylem are thin walled with wide lumen.
- **Summer wood:** They are also called late wood as they are formed late in the growing season. It is darker and has higher density. The tracheary elements of xylem are thick walled with narrow lumen.

5.4 ANOMALOUS SECONDARY GROWTH IN *BIGNONIA* AND *DRACAENA* STEM

5.4.1 Anomalous Secondary Growth in *Bignonia* Stem

The anomalous secondary growth in the stem of *Bignonia* is an adaptation required by the plant to avoid breaking or cracking of the stem. As *Bignonia* is a climber, its stem is relatively weak and it requires some support for climbing. When the stem grows around the support its inner side get compressed and outer side get stretched. If only hard tissues like secondary xylem remain in the central part of the stem, during compression and stretching, the stem would break or crack. To avoid the breaking or cracking of the stem it requires some soft tissues in the central region. These soft tissues are provided in the form of additional secondary phloem patches intruding secondary xylem cylinder due to abnormal behaviour of cambium and help the plant in climbing. In this way there is a direct relation between abnormal secondary growth and climbing habit of the *Bignonia* plant. Therefore the anomalous secondary growth in *Bignonia* stem is considered as an adaptive feature of the plant.

During abnormal secondary growth following events occur.

- In the beginning, fascicular cambium and interfascicular cambium join to form a cambial ring.
- The cambium behaves normally producing more secondary xylem towards the inner side and less secondary phloem to the outside.
- After some time, cambium produces lesser amount of secondary xylem and more amount of secondary phloem at four diagonal points.

- These phloem masses form four deep wedges supported by transverse bands of sclerotic cells.
- The four wedges of secondary phloem intrude into secondary xylem.
- Thus four wedges of secondary phloem and four ridges of secondary xylem are formed.
- Periderm formation is normal as the activity of cork cambium is normal.

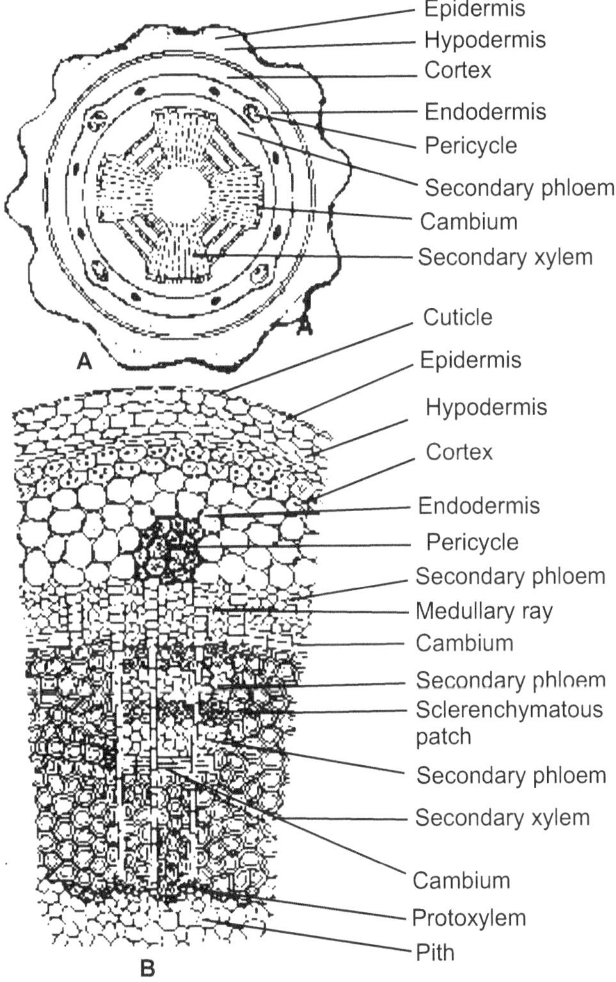

Fig. 5.12: Anomalous secondary growth in *Bignonia* stem

T. S. of *Bignonia* stem shows following anatomical features:

1. **Outline of the stem:** Stem shows wavy outline with prominent ridges and furrows
2. **Epidermis:** Epidermis is single layered with cuticle
3. **Hypodermis:** Hypodermis is collenchymatous
4. **Cortex:** Cortex is parenchymatous
5. **Endodermis:** Endodermis is not prominent
6. **Pericycle:** Pericycle is single layered
7. **Vascular Bundles:** Vascular bundles are conjoint, collateral, open and arranged in a ring around pith with endarch xylem

5.4.2 Anomalous Secondary Growth in *Dracaena* Stem

Dracaena is a typical example of anomalous secondary growth in monocots. Secondary growth is absent in monocots. Therefore, secondary growth itself is an anomaly as *Dracaena* is a monocot.

In *Dracaena* stem secondary growth starts to increase the thickness of the stem. During such secondary growth vascular bundles are produced without forming thick continuous secondary xylem cylinder. Therefore in such monocot plants even after secondary growth there is no formation of wood of commercial importance.

In *Dracaena* the cambium produces three types of secondary tissues i.e. xylem, phloem and conjunctive tissue. The anomalous secondary growth in *Dracaena* which increases the thickness of the stem is of non adaptive type. It neither has any relation with the habit of the plant nor does it have any special physiological function. Therefore the anomalous secondary growth in *Dracaena* is considered as non-adaptive anomalous secondary growth of the plants.

In *Dracaena* stem abnormal secondary growth is due to

a) The formation of extra stellar cambial ring in the cortex and

b) Abnormal activity of cambium

During Secondary growth following events occur

- The secondary meristem or secondary cambium develops in the inner region of parenchymatous cortex.
- The activity of cambium is abnormal.

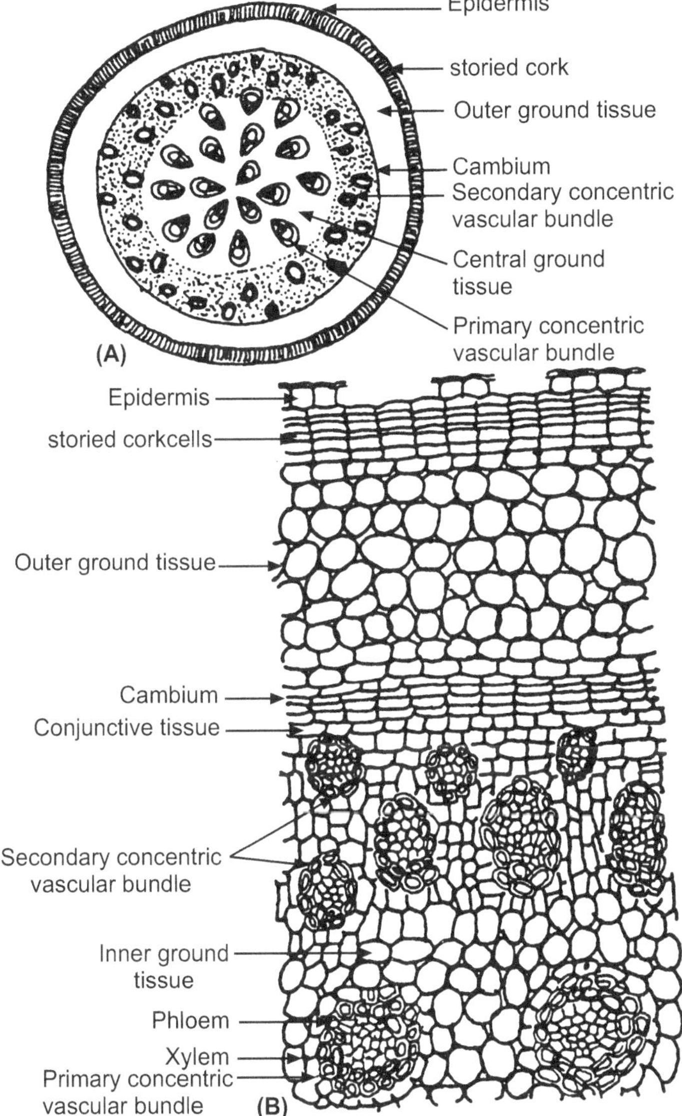

Fig. 5.13: Anomalous secondary growth in *Dracaena* stem

- It produces secondary vascular bundles on its inner side only and parenchymatous cells on the outer side.
- The secondary vascular bundles are amphivasal (Centrophloeic) where phloem is surrounded by xylem.
- The cambium produces more parenchymatous cells to the inside that pushes newly formed vascular bundles to the centre.
- The position of vascular bundles keep on changing and vascular bundles are arranged in concentric rings.
- The second ring of vascular bundles alternates in position with the first ring.
- The vascular bundles in the last inner ring are embedded in a mass of lignified conjunctive tissue.
- The activity of cork cambium is normal and produces cork and secondary cortex at the outer region.

The cross section of young stem of *Dracaena* shows typical monocot stem structure as below:

1. **Epidermis:** Epidermis is single layered
2. **Hypodermis:** Hypodermis is sclerenchymatous
3. **Vascular bundles:** Many closed, collateral vascular bundles with endarch xylem are scattered in the parenchymatous ground tissue

EXERCISE

I. Multiple Choice Questions

1. Secondary growth includes the formation of secondary vascular tissues and -------

   (a) Periderm (b) Plerume

   (c) Epidermis (d) Cortex

2. Suberization occurs in ------

   (a) Cortex (b) Cork

   (c) Xylem (d) Phloem

3. The secondary tissue is formed by the activity of --------
   (a) Apical meristem
   (b) Vascular and cork cambium
   (c) Parenchyma tissue
   (d) Collenchyma tissue
4. During secondary growth in dicot root the entire cambial ring produces -------- on the inner side and secondary phloem on the outer side.
   (a) Secondary xylem
   (b) Primary xylem
   (c) Primary phloem
   (d) Sclerenchyma
5. Annual rings are not well developed in the plants of ------- region
   (a) Tropical
   (b) Temperate
   (c) Alpine
   (d) Arctic
6. Phellogen is a ----- meristem
   (a) Apical
   (b) Intercalary
   (c) Lateral
   (d) None of these
7. The older stems show the presence of outer light coloured region called as -------
   (a) Sapwood
   (b) Heart wood
   (c) Annual ring
   (d) Duramen
8. The abnormal secondary growth in *Bignonia* stem is due to -----
   (a) Abnormal activity of normal cambium
   (b) Normal activity of normal cambium
   (c) Abnormal activity of abnormal cambium
   (d) None of these

ANSWERS

1-a; 2-b; 3-b; 4-a; 5-a; 6-c; 7-a; 8-a;

II. Two Marks Questions

1. What is secondary growth?
2. What is the type of secondary vascular bundles in *Dracaena* stem?
3. What is heartwood?

4. Explain in brief the woods with apotracheal parenchyma
5. What is secondary growth? Mention two lateral meristems required for secondary growth
6. Why does the heartwood become dark coloured?

III. Four Marks Questions

1. Write about the structure and function of lenticel
2. Write abnormal features of interest in *Bignonia* stem
3. Explain how the abnormal secondary growth is useful for *Bignonia* plant.
4. Comment on any two wood types you have studied
5. Write a brief account of annular rings
6. Describe the primary and secondary vascular bundles in *Dracaena* stem

IV. Five Marks Questions

1. Comment on non-porous and porous wood
2. Explain the basic structure of wood? Comment on any two wood types
3. What is periderm? Describe the process of periderm formation
4. Describe the various events that occur during abnormal secondary growth in *Dracaena* stem
5. Comment on the annular rings and lenticel

V. Seven Marks Questions

1. What do you understand by secondary growth? Describe the process in detail in a typical dicot stem.
2. What do you understand by secondary growth? Describe the process in detail in a typical dicot root
3. Describe the process of abnormal secondary growth in *Bignonia* stem
4. Describe the process of abnormal secondary growth in *Dracaena* stem

6

CHAPTER

TAXONOMY OF ANGIOSPERMS

6.1 COMBRETACEAE

Kingdom - Plantae

Division - Phanerogames/ Spermatophyta

Subdivision - Angiosperms

Class - Dicotyledonae

Venation reticulate, flowers pentamerous, cotyledons two.

Subclass - Polypetalae

Flowers with distinct calyx and corolla, petals free.

Series - Calyciflorae

Sepal united, flowers perigynous or epigynous.

Order - Myrtales

Stamens definite, rarely indefinite, flowers perigynous or epigynous.

Family - Combretaceae

General Characters

- **Habitat and Habit:** The members of this family are commonly trees, shrubs and climbers.
- **Roots:** Tap root type.
- **Stem:** The stem is aerial, erect, branched, solid, woody, cylindrical, grey coloured.

- **Leaf:** Leaves are simple, usually opposite, petiolate, entire and exstipulate.
- **Inflorescence:** The inflorescence is racemose; it may be a spike or panicle.
- **Flower:** The flowers are pedicellate, bracteate, usually hermaphrodite but may be unisexual, usually actinomorphic with a tendency to become zygomorphic, epigynous, penta or tetramerous.
- **Calyx:** It consists of 4 or 5 sepals; calyx tube dilated distally. The tube remains adnate to the ovary and is produced above. Aestivation is valvate.
- **Corolla:** It consists of 4 or 5 petals; small, alternating with sepals. The petals may be absent. Aestivation usually contorted.
- **Androecium:** Stamens usually double the number of sepals. In two whorls, the lower one opposite the petals may be 4, 5 or numerous also. They are situated on the calyx. The upper stamens sometimes reduced. They may bend inwards in the bud. Anthers are dithecous and introse.
- **Gynoecium:** Carple 1, ovary inferior, unilocular, usually angular. The angles usually equal to sepals in number, ovules 2-5 anatropous, rarely more, pendulous from the top of the ovary. Style long, filiform with a pointed or rarely capitate stigma. The receptacle tube bears a disc.
- **Fruit:** Usually 2-5 angled, coriaceous (leathery) or drupaceous ones. The angles sometimes forming wings.
- **Floral Formula:** ⊕, ⚥, K_5, C_5, A_{5-10}, $\overline{G_1}$

Distinguishing Features

- Leaves simple and exstipulate.
- Panicle inflorescence.
- Flowers bisexual, actinomorphic, epigynous.
- Stamens double the number of the petals.
- Ovary unilocular, inferior.
- Fruits dry drupe.

Economic Importance

1. ***Quisqualis indica*** (Rangoon creeper)**:** The flowers arising in groups are fragrant and white or pink in colour. It is an important ornamental plant.
2. ***Terminalia catappa*** (Jangli Badam)**:** Ornamental plant, grown in gardens for its large leaves. The bark used in tanning and fruits in dyeing.
3. ***Terminalia cuneata*** (Arjuna)**:** The green bark, leaves and fruits are used in medicine. The bark and ash used in tanning. It is also grown as avenue tree.
4. ***Terminalia bellirica*** (Beheda)**:** The fruits are used in medicine. It is also used in tanning, dyeing and preparation of ink. It can be grown as avenue tree.
5. ***Terminalia chebula*** (Hirda)**:** The fruits from the myrobalan of commerce are used in medicine. It is also used in tanning and dyeing.

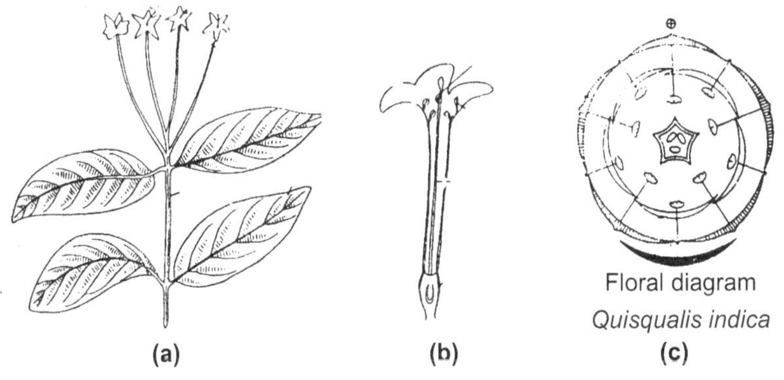

Fig. 6.1: Combretaceae. (a) A flowering twig of *Quisqualis indica* (b) Flower in vertical section

6.2 ASCLEPIADACEAE

Kingdom - Plantae

Division - Phanerogames/ Spermatophyta

Subdivision - Angiosperms

Class - Dicotyledonae

Subclass - Gamopetalae

Flowers with distinct calyx and corolla, petals united.

Series - Bicarpellatae

Ovary superior, carpels two, stamens epipetalous.

Order - Genetianales

Flowers actinomorphic, leaves opposite or whorled, carpels free, pollinium present, anthers fused with stigmatic disc to form gynostegium, fruit etaerio of follicles.

Family - Asclepiadaceae

General Characters

- **Habitat and Habit:** Mostly xerophytic; shows thick succulent stems, and leaves reduced to scales or spines. Twinning herbs, stout climbing shrubs or large erect shrubs.
- **Roots:** Tap root type.
- **Stem:** Aerial, erect, branched, herbaceous, solid, thick, and succulent with milky latex.
- **Leaf:** Leaves are simple, shortly petioled, and exstipulate. In most of the members of this family the leaves are fleshy and covered with wax; opposite and decussate, rarely alternate or whorled.
- **Inflorescence:** The inflorescence is usually a dichasial cyme, arising in the leaf axil or sometimes it is racemose or umbellate.
- **Flower:** The flowers are pedicellate, bracteate, complete, bisexual, actinomorphic and hypogynous, rarely zygomorphic, pentamerous.
- **Calyx:** Sepals 5, united below to form a short calyx tube. The aestivation is quincuncial or rarely valvate.
- **Corolla:** Petals 5, usually coloured, gamopetalous, valvate or twisted. Corolla is rotate, salver-shaped. The corolla tube or throat is often with a corona which is in the form of a ring of hair, scales.

- **Androecium:** Stamens 5, rarely free but mostly epipetalous and alternate with corolla lobes. Filaments flat united forming a fleshy staminal tube. The apex of staminal tube often united to a pentangular stigmatic disc or gynostegium. Anthers are two celled, usually adnate to the stigma, each cell producing a pollinial mass which is waxy. The pollinia are united by the stalk called caudicles to carpusculum.
- **Gynoecium:** Bicarpellary, apocarpous, ovary superior, unilocular. Ovules many, placentation marginal, 2 styles united at the top, stigma is pentangular disc fused with stamens to form gynostegium.
- **Fruit:** The fruit is dehiscent, pair of follicles.
- **Floral Formula:** Br, ⊕, ⚥, K_5, $\overset{\frown}{C_{(5)}, A_{(5)}, \underline{G}_{(2)}}$

Distinguishing Features

- Herbs or shrubs with milky latex.
- Leaves opposite, decussate.
- Inflorescence cymose.
- Corona arising as outgrowths from petals or stamens.
- Gynostegium present
- Pair of follicles.
- Seeds light and comose.

Economic Importance

1. ***Asclepias curassavica*** (Haldi-Kunku): It is cultivated as an ornamental plant. The plant has great medicinal value. The root is used as a purgative and a medicine of piles.
2. ***Calotropis procera / C. gigantea*** (Rui): The floss obtained from the seed, is used for stuffing purpose. The stem yields a fibre. All parts of the plant are used medicinally. The fresh leaves are used as poultice in the swellings.
3. ***Ceropegia oculata*** (Kandilpuspa/ Khantodi): The tubers are edible.

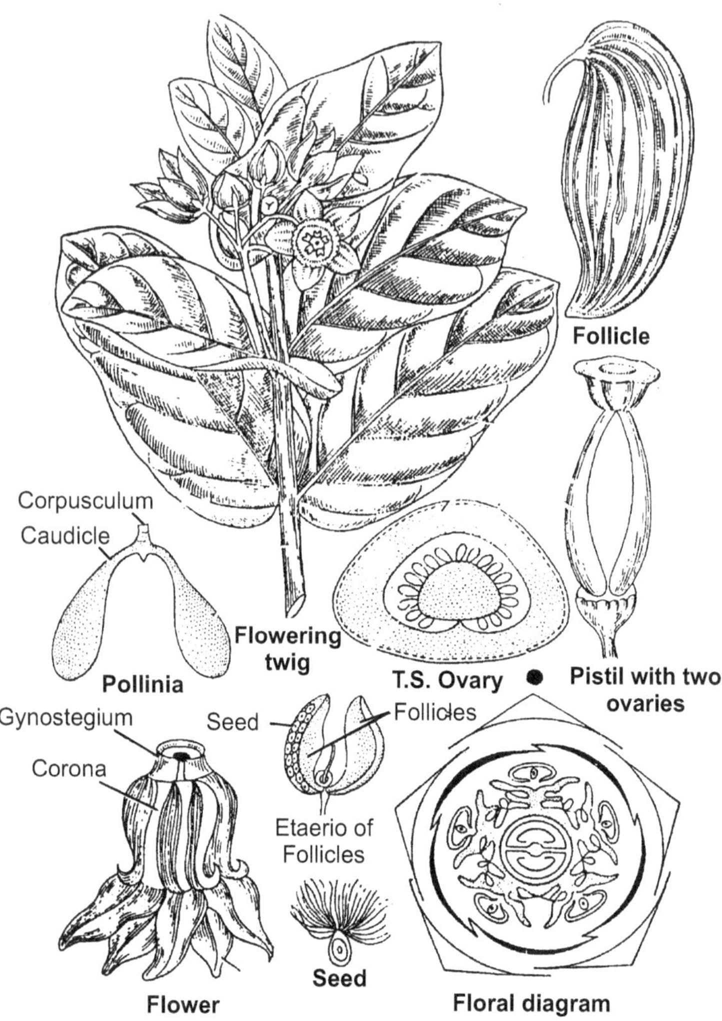

Fig. 6.2: Asclepiadaceae. *Calotropis procera*

4. ***Gymnema sylvestre*** (Gurmar/Bedki cha pala): The roots are used as antidote for snake-bite. The leaves are used as a remedy for diabetes.
5. ***Sarcostemma viminale*** (Somvel/Ransher): It is used to destroy white ants from sugar cane fields.
6. ***Tylophora indica*** (Potmari): It is used as emetic, diaphoretic, and expectorant.

7. ***Cryptostegia grandiflora*** (Chabuk churee): Common weed. Inferior quality rubber is obtained from latex.

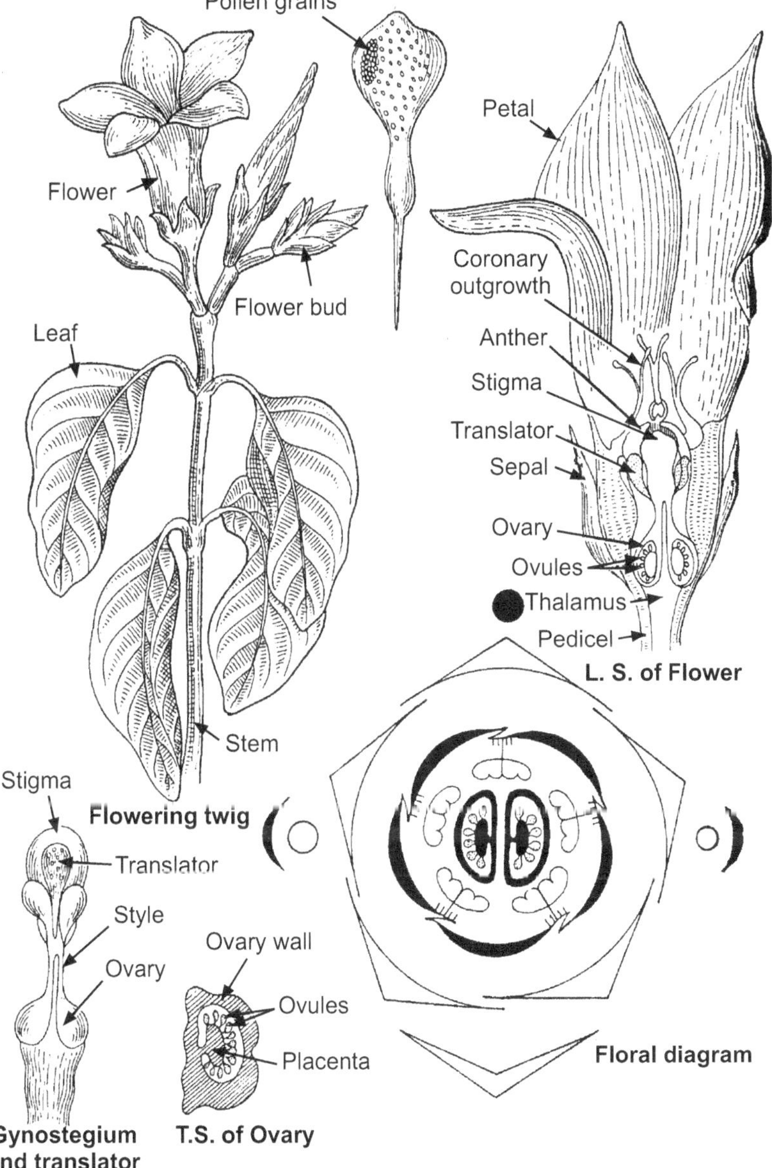

Fig. 6.3: Asclepiadaceae. *Cryptostegia grandiflora*

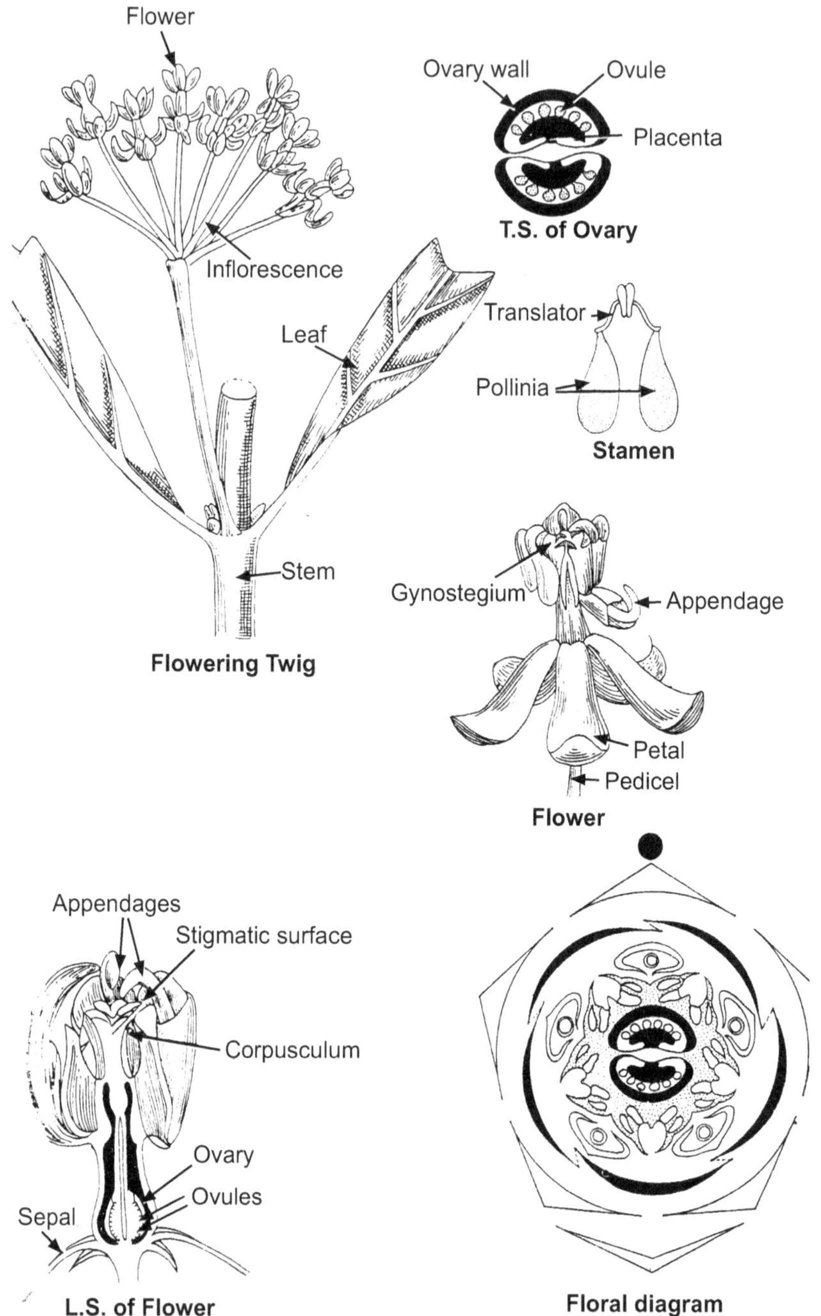

Fig. 6.4: Asclepiadaceae. *Asclepias curassavica*

6.3 AMARANTHACEAE

Kingdom - Plantae

Division - Phanerogames/ Spermatophyta

Subdivision - Angiosperms

Class - Dicotyledonae

Subclass - Monochlamydeae

Perianth single, green, not differentiated into sepals and petals.

Series - Curvembryae

Carpels united, ovule 1, embryo curved.

Family - Amaranthaceae

General Characters

- **Habitat and Habit:** Annual or perennial herbs, rarely under-shrubs.
- **Stem:** Aerial, erect, cylindrical, angular, branched, solid covered with spines, hairy. Herbaceous or woody.
- **Leaf:** Alternate or opposite. The leaves are simple, entire, exstipulate and pinnately nerved.
- **Inflorescence:** The small flowers are arranged in spikes or globose heads or sometimes in axillary clusters.
- **Flower:** The flowers are bracteate and bracteolate, bracts and bracteoles are scarious. The flowers are regular, incomplete, bisexual, monochlamydeous, pentamerous, hypogynous; rarely unisexual and monoecious.
- **Perianth:** The perianths are 3-5; scaly, membranous or chaffy, sometimes coloured. Free or connate at the base. Aestivation is imbricate or quincuncial.
- **Androecium:** The stamens are as many as perianth and opposite to them, and may be free or united at the base. In some cases, there are five fertile stamens alternating with five staminodes. The anthers are sometimes coloured, dithecous.

- **Gynoecium:** The gynoecium is bicarpellary or tricarpellary, syncarpous and superior. Usually unilocular with one basal ovule. Style 1-3, with capitate or hairy stigmas.
- **Fruit:** It may be a circumscissile capsule or may be nut enclosed in perianth.
- **Floral Formula:** Br, brl, ⊕, ⚥ or ♂ or ♀, $P_{(3-5)}$, $A_{(5)}$, $G_{\underline{(2-3)}}$

Distinguishing Features

- Herbs or small shrubs, stipules absent.
- Flowers small, subtended by scarious or paper bracts.
- Perianth persistent.
- Staminodes present.
- Carpels 2-3, superior ovary.
- Capsule or utricle or nutlet fruit.

Economic Importance

1. ***Amaranthus spinosus*:** (Kathe-math): The ash of the leaves is used in dyeing. The roots possess medicinal properties. This is also used as vegetable and fodder.
2. ***Achyranthes aspera*** (Aghada): Ornamental plant, grown in gardens for the large leaves. The bark used in tanning and fruits in dyeing. The plants are used medicinally for several diseases such as piles, colic, boils, etc. This is also used as an antidote for snake bite and scorpion sting.
3. ***Alternanthera tenella:*** Ornamental plant, commonly planted in gardens.
4. ***Celosia argentea*** (Kombada): Cultivated in gardens for showy and attractive feathery inflorescence.
5. ***Gomphrena globosa*** (Old man's button): Cultivated as an ornamental plant in the garden for showy and variously coloured inflorescence.

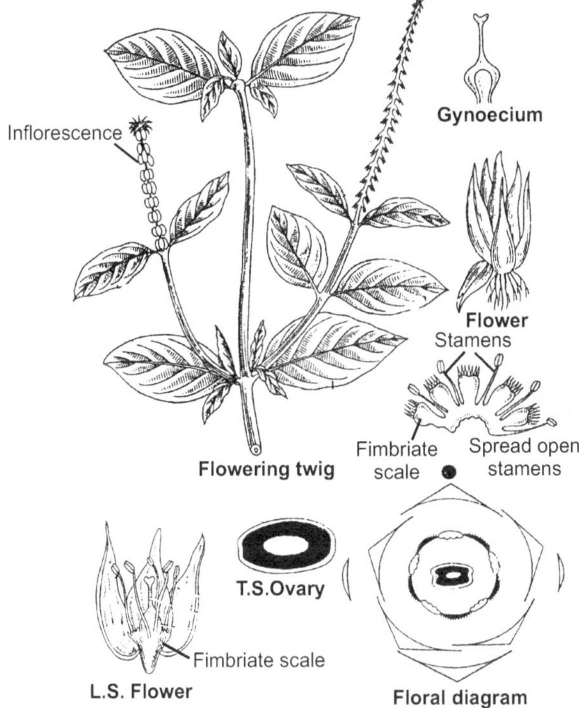

Fig. 6.5: Amaranthaceae. *Achyranthes aspera*

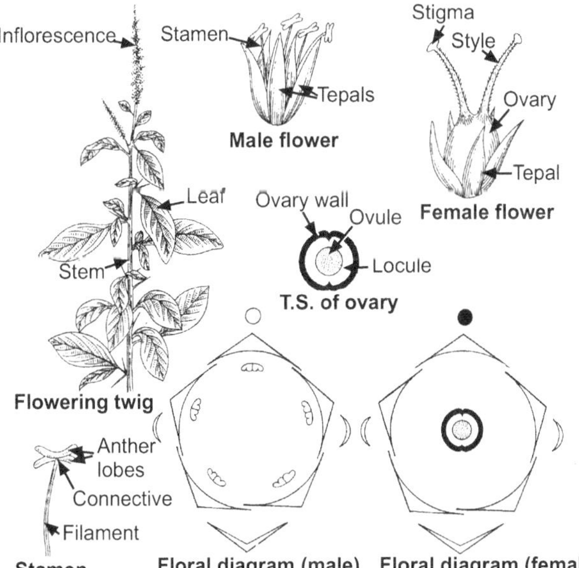

Fig. 6.6: Amaranthaceae. *Amaranthus spinosus*

6.4 LILIACEAE

Kingdom - Plantae

Division - Phanerogames/ Spermatophyta

Subdivision - Angiosperms

Class - Monocotyledons

Tap root system. Leaves isobilateral with parallel venation, Flowers trimerous, Cotyledon one.

Series - Coronarieae

Ovary superior, carpels united, perianth petaloid.

Family - Liliaceae

General Characters

- **Habitat and Habit:** Mesophytes or xerophytes, mostly herbaceous, persisting by underground tuberous stems. Some perennial herbs are weak-stemmed, climbing, scrambling herbs with leaves modified into hard, curved spines.
- **Roots:** Adventitious root type.
- **Leaf:** Leaves radical, simple alternate. The venation is usually parallel. In some cases leaves are fleshy, in some they are reduced to scales or spines. In some cases the leaf apex and stipules are modified into tendrils.
- **Stem:** Stem is underground tuberous, bulb, corm, and rhizome, aerial; branched, may be herbaceous or woody, solid or fistular, in some cases there are cladodes.
- **Inflorescence:** It is terminal or axillary, solitary or simple raceme on a stout scape. It shows variations like raceme, panicle, cymose, umbel, spike.
- **Flower:** Bracteate, usually hermaphrodite rarely unisexual, actinomorphic, trimerous and hypogynous.
- **Perianth:** The perianths are usually petaloid, arranged into two or three whorls. The tepals are free, equal and regular.
- **Androecium:** Stamens six, epiphyllous, and arranged in two or three whorls.

- **Gynoecium:** Tricarpellary, syncarpous, trilocular with one or more ovules in each locule, axile placentation and superior. The stigma is entire or trilobed.
- **Fruit:** The fruit is globose, berry or coriaceous septicidal capsule or loculicidal capsule. The fruits are many seeded.
- **Floral Formula:** Br, ⊕, ⚥, $P_{(3+3) \text{ or } 3+3}$, $\overset{\frown}{A_{3+3}}$, $\underline{G}_{(3)}$

Distinguishing Features

- Herbs with bulb, corm or rhizome.
- Leaves alternate or whorled leaves.
- Flowers bisexual, trimerous
- Perianth with 6 petaloid tepals.
- Stamens 6, filaments free.
- Carpels 3 united, ovary superior, placentation axile.
- Fruit a capsule.

Economic Importance

1. ***Aloe vera*** (Korphad): It is one of the constituents of several laxative preparations. It is also valuable in treatment of piles and fissures. The mucilage is useful for inflammations.
2. ***Asparagus officinalis*** (Shatavari): The shoots are consumed as vegetables. Leaves used for decoration in flower arrangement and in bouquet. The roots are used as powerful tonic.
3. ***Chlorophytum tuberosum*** (Kusali): The leaves are consumed as vegetable.
4. ***Dipcadi montanum*** (Suichi Bhaji): Leaves used as vegetables.
5. ***Gloriosa superba*** (Bachnag/ Kal-lawi): An ornamental climbing herb with beautiful flowers. It has many medicinal properties. It is used as a remedy for stomach ache.
6. ***Asphodelus tenuifolius***: Taken for colds and hemorrhoids (seeds); a febrifuge; used for rheumatic pain.
7. ***Allium cepa*** (Onion)**:** The bulbs are used as vegetable. The green leaves are also edible. The plant posseses medicinal properties and is a stimulant, diuretic and expectorant.

8. ***Allium sativum*** (Garlic)**:** The bulbs are used as a condiment and flavouring substance for vegetables. It also serves as carminative and gastric stimulant in medicinal preparations.
9. ***Asparagus africanus*** (African lily): This is an ornamental herb.
10. ***Pancratium triflorum:*** This is an attractive summer and winter flowering herb, grown as an ornamental plant.

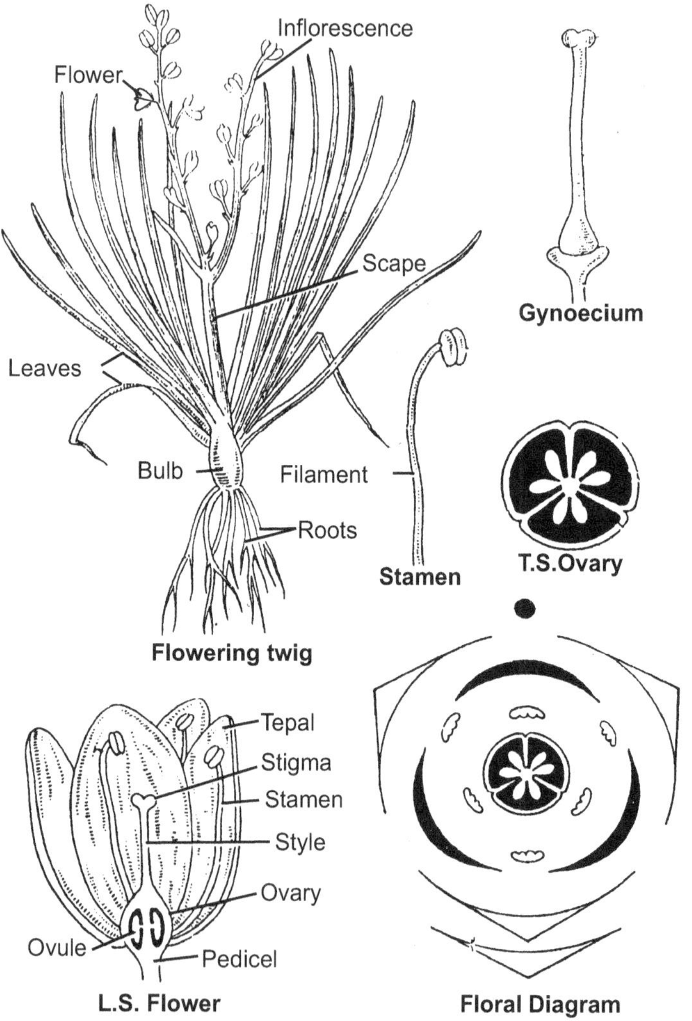

Fig. 6.7: Liliaceae. *Asphodelus tenuifolius*

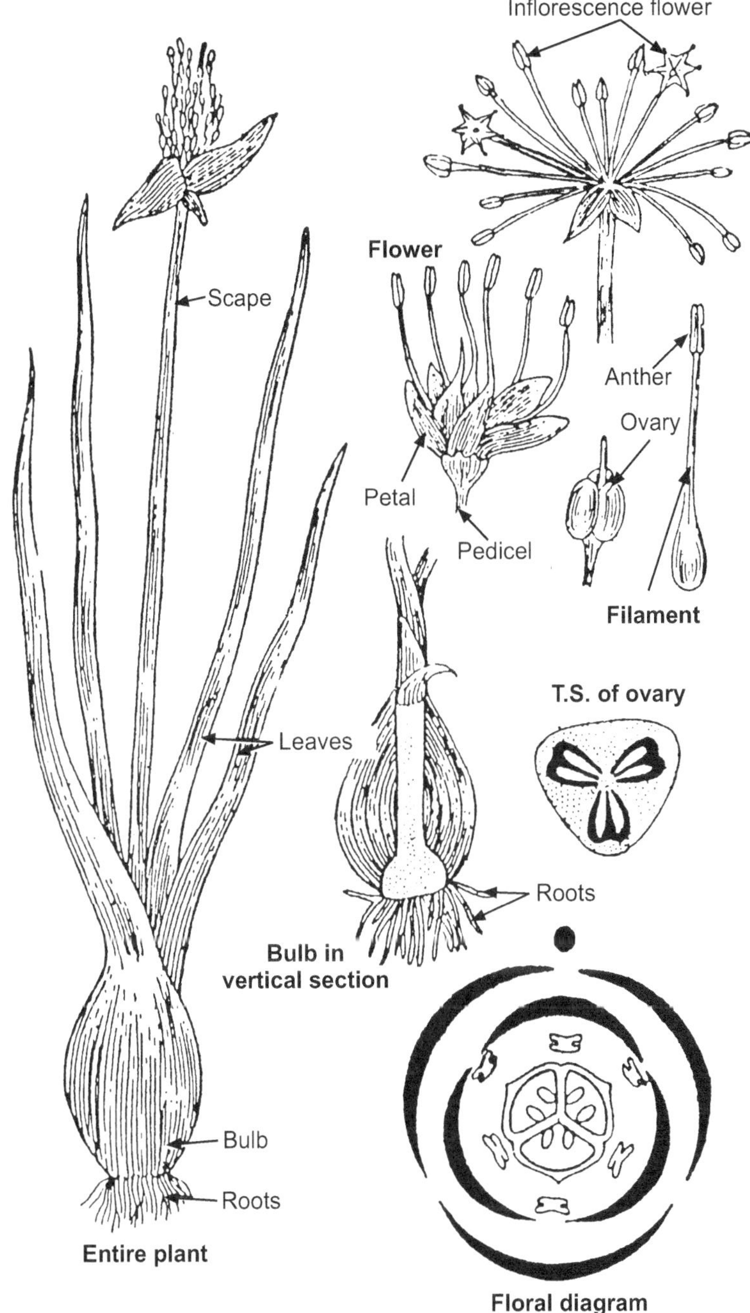

Fig. 6.8: Liliaceae. *Allium cepa*

EXERCISE

I. Multiple Choice Questions

1. *Quisqualis indica* belongs to family ....
   (a) Combretaceae (b) Asclepiadaceae
   (c) Amranthaceae (d) Liliaceae
2. Pollinia are the distinguishing character of .... family.
   (a) Combretaceae (b) Asclepiadaceae
   (c) Amranthaceae (d) Liliaceae
3. Umbel type of inflorescence is found in the .... family.
   (a) Combretaceae (b) Asclepiadaceae
   (c) Amranthaceae (d) Liliaceae
4. Gynostegium is present in the .... family.
   (a) Combretaceae (b) Asclepiadaceae
   (c) Amranthaceae (d) Liliaceae
5. Pair of follicle type of fruit is found in .... family.
   (a) Combretaceae (b) Asclepiadaceae
   (c) Amranthaceae (d) Liliaceae
6. The vernacular 'Korphad' name belongs to .... plant
   (a) *Aloe vera* (b) *Asparagus officinalis*
   (c) *Chlorophytum tuberosum* (d) *Dipcadi montanum*
7. Milky latex in the stem is characteristic feature of .... family.
   (a) Combretaceae (b) Asclepiadaceae
   (c) Amranthaceae (d) Liliaceae
8. Perianth is present in the .... family.
   (a) Combretaceae (b) Asclepiadaceae
   (c) Amranthaceae (d) none of these
9. *Achyranthes aspera* belongs to .... family.
   (a) Combretaceae (b) Asclepiadaceae
   (c) Amranthaceae (d) Liliaceae
10. .... is stem vegetable plant.
    (a) *Aloe vera* (b) *Asparagus officinalis*
    (c) *Chlorophytum tuberosum* (d) None of these

ANSWERS

1-a; 2-b; 3-d; 4-b; 5-b; 6-a; 7-b; 8-c;
9-c; 10-b;

II. Two Marks Questions

1. Give the class of family Combretaceae with reasons.
2. Give the division of family Liliaceae with reasons.
3. Write any two distinguishing characters of family Asclepiadaceae .
4. Mention two economic importance of family Amranthaceae
5. Sketch and label the pollinia of *Asclepias curassavica.*
6. Describe the pair of follicle fruit of family *Asclepiadaceae.*
7. Describe the structure of gynostegium
8. Give the economic importance of *Aloe vera*
9. Describe flower structure of Liliaceae
10. Mention economic importance of *Asparagus officinalis*

III. Four Marks Questions

1. Give the distinguishing characters of any one family you have studied.
2. Give the economic importance of any one family you have studied.

IV. Five Marks Questions

1. Give the distinguishing characters of any one family with economic importance of a plant you have studied.

V. Seven Marks Questions

1. Assign the following plant to their respective family with reasons and add its economic importance.
   (a) *Terminalia catappa* (b) *Calotropis procera*
   (c) *Achyranthes aspera*
2. Give the distinguishing characters of any one family and add an economic important plant with its uses.
   (a) Combretaceae (b) Asclepiadaceae
   (c) Amranthaceae (d) Liliaceae

PAPER - IV

1
CHAPTER

INTRODUCTION

Introduction

Ecology is a branch of biology which deals with the study of relationships between organisms and their environment and to one another.

The name *ecology*, was coined in 1866 by German biologist Ernst Haeckel. According to Haeckel "Ecology is the study of reciprocal relationship between living organisms and their environment." Ecology is derived from two Greek words "*Oikos*" meaning house and "*logos*" meaning the study. Therefore, ecology is the study of organisms at their natural habitat.

Environment refers to everything outside the body of the living organisms which includes light, soil, temperature, water, etc. Environment indicates wide spectrum of physical conditions whereas habitat specifies the 'natural home' of the living organisms.

Plant ecology is broadly classified as Autecology and Synecology. Autecology deals with the study of individual species in relation to their environment. Synecology deals with the study of plant communities in relation to their environment. The study of plant community structure is also called Plant sociology or Phytosociology.

Ecology may be studied according to the nature of community and habitat such as

- **Forest ecology:** It refers to the study of forest community in relation to its environment
- **Grass land ecology:** It deals with the study of grassland community in relation to its environment
- **Fresh water ecology:** It refers to the ecological study of aquatic communities that are present in fresh water bodies such as rivers, lakes, etc in relation to their environment

- **Marine ecology:** It deals with study of organisms residing in saline water bodies such as sea, ocean, etc in relation to their environment.
- **Desert ecology:** It refers to the study of organisms residing in areas with scarcity of water in relation to their environment.
- **Conservation ecology:** It deals with application of ecological principles for the proper management of resources leading to high and sustained yield of useful biological materials for human welfare.
- **Resource ecology:** It deals with the study of plants, animals, water and mineral resource and their judicious management.
- **Pollution ecology:** It deals with the problems of environmental deterioration and ways and means of keeping the environment clean.
- **Ecosystem ecology** is a broad term in which both plant and animal communities along with their total environment are studied.

1.1 CLIMATIC FACTORS

Weather describes the condition of the atmosphere over a short period of time e.g. from day to day or week to week, while climate describes average conditions over a longer period of time.

The climate of an area or country is known through the average weather over a long period of time. If an area has more dry days throughout the year than wet days, it would be described as a dry climate; a place which has more cold days than hot days would be described as a cold climate.

The intensity and duration of light, temperature, humidity, wind velocity, precipitation constitutes the climate of any place. The different climatic factors that affect the life of organisms are described below.

i) Light: Light is one of the most important abiotic factors. Life cannot exist without light. Sunlight is the main source of light.

Sunlight reaches the earth surface in the form of energy rich tiny particles termed as photons. It is required for the activation of photosynthetic process in the green plants and primary production of plant materials upon which all other living organisms depend directly or indirectly. Light is abundantly received on the surface of earth and on an average approximately 2-3 % of this solar energy is used in primary productivity by plants. On the basis of requirement of light intensity for luxuriant growth the plants are classified into two groups such as **heliophytes and sciophytes**.

Heliophytes grow in direct sunlight and sciophytes grow in shade. But most of the plants are not very rigid in their requirement of light intensity. The heliophytes that grow only in sunlight are called obligate heliophytes while the heliophytes that grow in shade though not so well are called facultative sciophytes. In the same way the sciophytes which grow only in shade are called obligate sciophytes and the sciophytes that grow in sun though not so well are called facultative heliophytes.

In the water bodies like lake, pond, ocean, etc. the intensity of light decreases rapidly with depth. Thus the plant distribution in water reservoirs is governed by light factor. The occurrence of reed swamps on marsh, submerged species in shallow regions, rooted species with floating leaves in deeper zones and free floating forms in deep regions show ecological adaptations of life forms mainly in response to variation in light intensity. Phytoplanktons move up and down in water and adjust their position during the 24 hours cycle in relation to diurnal fluctuation in light intensity.

Light regulates the opening and closing of stomata, CO_2 and O_2 exchanges between plants and atmosphere and the rate of transpiration. Plants which are directly exposed to sunlight develop certain common adaptive features in their morphology, anatomy and physiology. For example the stem becomes more compact, hard with short internodes and more branching. The leaves are thick and short with closely arranged small stomata.

Similar to light intensity the duration of light also plays an important role in plant growth. In higher plants the formation of floral buds is the commencement of reproductive growth. Different plant species require different light duration for flowering. This requirement of light duration is called photoperiodism. All plants have a critical photoperiod i.e. the duration of light they require to survive. On the basis of response of plants to photoperiod the plants are classified as Long day plants (LDP), Short day plants (SDP) and Day neutral plants (DNP).

a) **Long Day Plants (LDP):** Long day plants flower only when they receive day length more than critical day length. e.g. Radish, Potato, Spinach, etc.

b) **Short Day Plants (SDP):** Short day plants flower only when they receive day length less than critical day length. e.g. Cereals, Tobacco, Cosmos, *Dahlia*, etc.

c) **Day Neutral Plants (DNP):** In day neutral plants, the flowering behaviour is irrespective of day length. e.g. Cotton, Balsam, Tomato, etc.

ii) Temperature: Temperature plays an important role in the life of living organisms as it affects plant metabolism, seed germination, plant growth and development, plant reproduction etc. Minimum, optimum and maximum are the three cardinal points which differ from plant species to species. At optimum temperature all these processes take place at maximum rate however below and above the optimum temperature the rate of all these processes are declined. Very low temperature may cause chilling injury while high temperature causes heat injury or burning of plant tissues and organs. On the basis of temperature conditions the vegetation of the world has been divided in to the following four classes by Ecologists.

a) **Megatherms:** The vegetation of the region where high temperature prevails throughout the year is called megatherms. The dominant vegetation in this region is tropical rain forest.

b) **Mesotherms:** In this vegetational belt high temperature alternates with low temperature. The vegetation of this region is represented by tropical deciduous forest.

c) **Microtherms:** In this region, the low temperature remains throughout the year. This region is dominated by coniferous forests.

d) **Hekistotherms:** This region is represented by alpine vegetation due to very low temperature.

iii) Humidity: Humidity refers to the atmospheric moisture in the form of invisible vapour. The humidity of air is expressed in terms of relative humidity values. Relative humidity (RH) is the amount of water vapor in the air, expressed as the proportion (in percent) of the maximum amount of water vapor it can hold at certain temperature. For example, an air having a relative humidity of 60% at 27°C temperature means that every kilogram of the air contains 60% of the maximum amount of water that it can hold at that temperature. The humidity affects the life of plants in various ways. The relative humidity affects the opening and closing of the stomata which regulates loss of water from the plant through transpiration as well as photosynthesis. Humid conditions are essential for the germination of spores and growth of different types of fungi. The plants like orchids, lichens and mosses directly use atmospheric moisture for their growth.

iv) Wind: Wind is nothing but air in motion. It is one of the important climatic factors. This climatic factor serves as a vector of pollen from one flower to another thus aiding in the process of pollination. It is therefore essential in the development of fruit and seed from wind-pollinated flowers as in many grasses. Moderate winds favour gas exchanges, but strong winds can cause excessive water loss through transpiration as well as lodging or toppling of plants. When transpiration rate exceeds that of water absorption, partial or complete closure of the stomata may ensue which will restrict the diffusion of carbon dioxide into the leaves. As a result, there will be a decrease in the rate of photosynthesis, growth and yield.

v) Precipitation (Rainfall): Precipitation is the main source of water. Precipitation occurs in different forms such as drizzles, rain, snow, dew, frost, sleet and hail. Drizzles are the minute water droplets floating in air. Rain is the drops of liquid water, snow refers to the solid form of moisture, dew and frost are formed due to condensation of moisture directly on surface of objects, soil, plants and animals. Small pellets or grains of ice are the sleets while hails are the balls or lumps of ice.

On global scale mean annual rainfall is 85.7 cm. Out of the total rainfall 23% is received by land and 77% by oceans. The atmosphere receives 16% of water from land and 84% water from oceans in the form of water vapours. 70% of earth surface is occupied by water. It is present in the form of water reservoirs like ocean, sea, rivers, lakes.

Water is universal solvent and is essential for life because all the metabolic processes of living organisms take place in the medium of water. Being universal solvent nutrients enter in to the plant body in dissolved condition through water. Thus water helps in nutrient absorption. As an essential constituent of photosynthesis water is needed in the manufacture of carbohydrates. Protoplasm which is basis of life is mostly made up of water.

1.2 EDAPHIC FACTORS

The factors which are related to the structure and composition of soil are called edaphic factors. Soil is a very complex medium in which plants grow. A fertile soil contains 40% mineral matter, 10% organic material, 15% water and 25% air.

Soil is defined as the weathered (or broken particles) surface of the earth's crust which is mixed with organic material derived from dead organisms. The development of soil from parent rock by weathering and its modification through interaction between biological, topographic and climatic factors is called pedogenesis and the soil science is called pedology.

Disruption of parental rock material by physical, chemical and biological processes is called weathering.

Action of water, temperature, glaciers, gravity may cause weathering of rocks through processes like wetting-drying, heating-cooling, freezing, glaciation, etc. This type of weathering is called physical weathering.

Chemical weathering includes hydration, hydrolysis, carbonation, chelation and oxidation-reduction. The chemical weathering occurs due to the chemicals produced by living organisms such as bacteria, fungi, lichens, bryophytes, etc and the chemicals that are present in the atmosphere.

Biological weathering refers to the activities of living organisms responsible for disruption of parental rock material. The living organisms like lichens, bacteria and fungi that are growing on rock surface retain water for a long period during which chemical processes can proceed which disintegrate the parental rock material by hydrolysis and carbonation.

The different processes that are involved in soil formation include laterization, melanization, podzolization and gleization

i) **Laterization:** In tropical areas due to high temperature and high rainfall silicate minerals are leached in the form of silicic acid and there is accumulation of sesquioxides of aluminium and iron in the soil. This accumulation of these sesquioxides is called laterization.

ii) **Melanization:** This process is very common in the areas with low humidity. In this process the humus formed in upper horizons get mixed in 'A' horizon along with water. Due to melanization 'A'horizon becomes dark coloured.

iii) **Podsolization:** This process generally occurs in the temperate regions receiving moderate rainfall. These regions show conifers and members of family Ericaceae as chief vegetation. The litter produced by these plants is rich in phenolic (acidic) compounds. The phenolic (acidic) compounds inhibit microbial activities. The water percolating through this acidic litter being acidic dissolves minerals and humus content from 'A' horizon. The leached minerals and humus get accumulated in the 'B' horizon in the form of hard, distinct layer. Due to loss of chemicals the 'A' horizon becomes light ash coloured. This process is called podsolization. The soil developed by this process is termed as 'Podsol'.

iv) **Gleization:** Under water logging conditions the rate of organic matter decomposition is very low as well as these soils become blue- grey or grey coloured due to the accumulation of ferrous compounds in the soil. Due to these reasons there is accumulation of a sticky, compact layer of blue-grey or grey colour at the bottom of 'B' horizon. This process is known as gleization and the soil formed by gleization is termed as 'Gleys'.

1.2.1 Soil Profile

As the process of pedogenesis is influenced by different factors; different types of soils are formed. The different types of soils are described and identified by reference to their profiles. Soil profile is the vertical section of soil showing various superimposed horizons or layers. Each layer has different structure, thickness, consistency, texture, porosity, colour and chemical composition. Soil profile changes from place to place and it is influenced by parent rock, vegetation and climate. Soil profile shows six different horizons which are designated as O-horizon (organic horizon or litter zone), A-horizon (top soil), B-horizon (sub soil) C-horizon (weathering rock), D-horizon (weathering rock), and R-horizon (bed rock).The different layers in soil profile can be described as follows

1. O-horizon (organic horizon or litter zone): This is the topmost layer of earth's crust. It is generally found in forest but absent in desert, grassland and cultivated land. It is composed of fresh or partially decomposed organic matter. This horizon is rich in saprophytic fungi, bacteria and protozoa.

2. A-horizon (top soil): It is a top soil-zone. It is also called as leaching or eluviation zone. This zone is subdivided into two zones such as A1and A2

i) **A1-horizon:** This layer is dark coloured and rich in humus, mineral soil, bacteria and fungi. It is also designated as humic or melanized region.

ii) **A2-horizon:** This layer is light in colour and contains less humus. This is a zone of maximum leaching hence from this zone silicates, clay, iron oxide, aluminium oxides and organic chemicals are lost downward during rainfall making this zone light coloured.

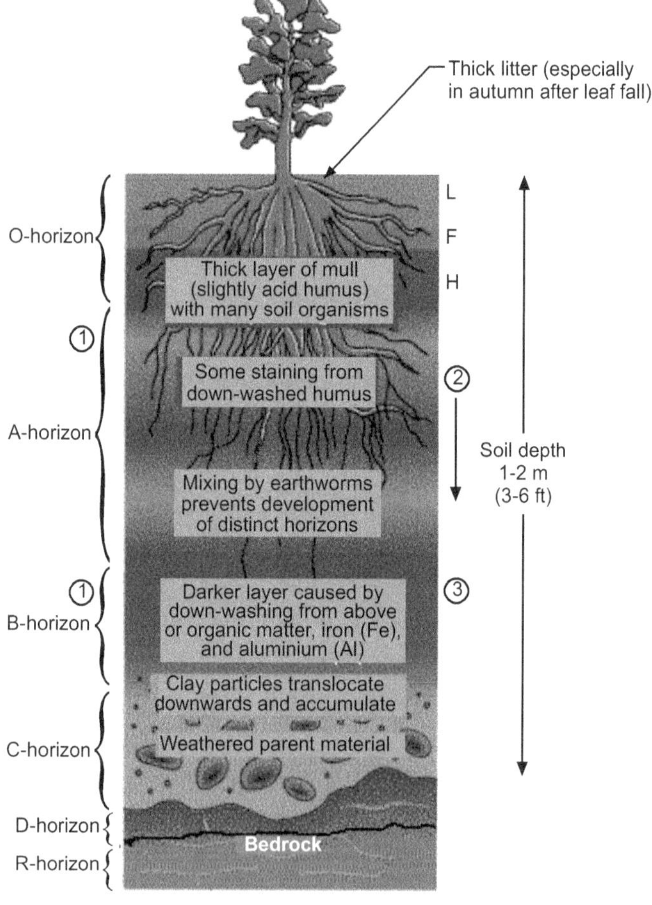

Fig. 1.1: Soil Profile

3. B-horizon (sub soil): This horizon is present below the 'A' horizon. It is divided into B1, B2 and B3 sub zones depending on the stages of soil development in the region. This is also called as zone of illuviation (collection of materials) because the chemical compounds leached from A2 region get collected in this zone. It is dark coloured and coarse-textured due to the presence of silica rich clay, hydrated oxides of aluminium and iron as well as organic colloids. Roots of shrubs and trees reach up to this horizon.

4. C-horizon: This is thick and contains large masses of partially weathered mineral materials.

5. D-Horizon: This layer shows presence of rocks in active weathering state.

6. R-horizon (Bed rock)**:** This is the lowermost layer of unweathered parental rock. It is hard and on this layer percolating gravitational water gets collected.

Soil Classification

There are different systems of soil classification. On the basis of manner of soil formation they are classified in to the following types

i) **Residual soils:** In these soils the complete process of soil formation i.e. weathering and pedogenesis occurs at the same place i.e. parental rock.

ii) **Transported soils:** In these type of soils weathered parental rock material is transported away from their place of weathering by various agencies and then process of pedogenesis occurs. Based on the involvement of agents in transportation the transported soils are sub classified as

   a) **Alluvial:** Soil transported by river or running water.

   b) **Colluvial:** Soil transported by gravity

   c) **Glacial:** Soil transported by ice or glaciers

   d) **Eolian:** Soil transported by wind.

1.2.2 Physical Properties of the Soil

i) Soil Colour

Soil colour gives an indication of the various processes going on in the soil as well as the type of minerals in the soil. For example the red colour in the soil is due to the abundance of iron oxide under oxidised conditions (well-drainage) in the soil; dark colour is generally due to the accumulation of highly decayed organic matter; yellow colour is due to hydrated iron oxides and hydroxide; black nodules are due to manganese oxides; mottling and gleying are associated with poor drainage and/or high water table. Abundant pale yellow mottles coupled with very low pH are indicative of possible acid sulphate soils. Colours of soil matrix and mottles are indicative of the water and drainage conditions in the soil. Soil colour is described by the parameters called hue, value and chroma. Hue represents the dominant wave length or colour of the light; value refers to the lightness of the colour; chroma, relative purity or strength of the colour. The colour of the soil in terms of the above parameters could be quickly determined by comparison of the

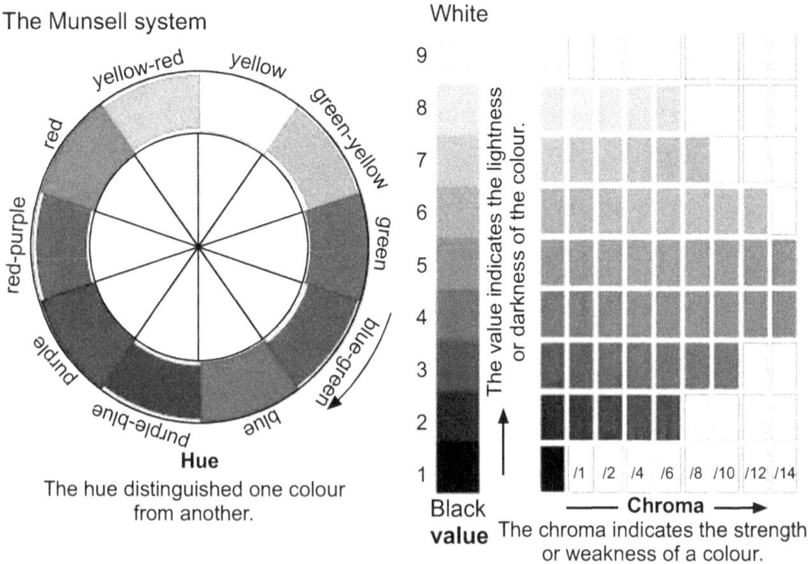

Fig 1.2: Munsell Soil Colour Charts

sample with a standard set of **Munsell Soil Colour Charts** (1973). In these charts, the right hand top corner represents the Hue; the colour chips mounted in a note-book called vertical axis, the value; and the horizontal axis, the chroma.

ii) Soil Texture

Soil is formed by the weathering of parental rock material. It contains minerals such as Ca, Mg, K, P, Mn, Fe, Mo, etc. The mineral composition of soil depends on the mineral content of parental rock material. Soil texture refers to the proportion of the soil "separates" that make up the mineral component of soil. These separates are called sand, silt, and clay. These soil separates have the following size ranges:

Name of Particles	Size (mm)
Clay	<0.002 mm
Silt	0.002-0.02mm
Fine sand	0.02-0.2 mm
Coarse sand	0.2-2.0 mm
Fine gravel	2.0-5 mm
Gravel	> 5 mm

Sand and silt are the "inactive" part of the soil matrix, because they do not contribute to the soil's ability to retain soil water or nutrients. These separates are commonly comprised of quartz or some other inactive mineral. Because of its small size and sheet-like structure, clay has a large amount of surface area per unit mass, and its surface charge attracts ions and water. Because of this, clay is the "active" portion of the soil matrix. On the basis of proportion of the above soil particles the soils are classified into different textural classes such as

a) **Sandy Soil:** This group includes all soils in which the sand separates make up at least 85% and the clay or silt or both clay and silt separates make up 15% by weight. The properties of such soils are therefore characteristically those of sand in contrast to the stickier nature of clays or silts. Two specific textural classes are recognised in this group - sandy and loamy sand (70% sand and 30%clay or silt or both silt and clay)

b) **Silt:** This group includes soils with 90% silt and 10% sand. Naturally the properties of this group are dominated by those of silt. Only one textural class - Silt is included in this group.

c) **Clay:** To be designated clay, a soil must contain at least 35% of the clay separate and in most cases not less than 40%. In such soils the characteristics of the clay separates are distinctly dominant, and the class names are clay, sandy clay and silty clay. Sandy clays may contain more sand than clay. Likewise, the silt content of silty clays usually exceeds clay fraction.

d) **Loam:** This group is a more complicated soil textural class since it contains many subdivisions. An ideal loam may be defined as a mixture of sand, silt and clay particles that exhibits the properties of those separates in about equal proportions. Loam soils do not exhibit dominant physical properties of sand, silt or clay. Loam does not contain equal percentage of sand, silt and clay. However, exhibit approximately equal properties of sand, silt and clay.

Importance of Soil Texture

Soil texture plays a crucial role for nutrient supplies, aeration, root development, moisture content, etc.

a) **Nutrient supplies:** The fine textured soils are high in nutrient status; but sandy soils are low in nutrient content

b) **Aeration:** Coarse-textured soils are better aerated than clayey soils.

c) **Root development:** Percentage of soil particles affect root development.

d) **Moisture:** Coarse-textured soils are easily drained, fine-textured soils are poorly drained and hold much water on the large surface area.

iii) Soil Structure

The soil separates can become aggregated together into discrete structural units called "peds". These peds are organised into a repeating pattern that is referred to as soil structure. Between the peds are cracks called "pores" through which soil air and water are conducted. Soil structure is most commonly described in terms of the shape of the individual peds that occur within a soil horizon. The soil structure is described as follows

a) **Granular:** Roughly spherical, like grape nuts. Usually 1-10 mm in diameter. Most common in A horizons, where plant roots, microorganisms and sticky products of organic matter decomposition bind soil grains into granular aggregates.

b) **Platy:** Flat peds that lie horizontally in the soil. Platy structure can be found in A, B and C horizons. It commonly occurs in A horizon as a result of compaction.

c) **Blocky:** Roughly cube-shaped, with more or less flat surfaces. If edges and corners remain sharp, we call it angular blocky. If they are rounded, we call it subangular blocky. Sizes commonly range from 5-50 mm across. Blocky structures are typical of B horizons, especially those with high clay content. They form by repeated expansion and contraction of clay minerals.

d) **Prismatic:** Larger, vertically elongated blocks, often with five sides. Sizes are commonly 10-100mm across. Prismatic structures commonly occur in fragipans.

e) **Columnar:** The units are similar to prisms and are bounded by flat or slightly rounded vertical faces. The tops of columns, in contrast to those of prisms, are very distinct and normally rounded.

f) **Single grained:** Soil is broken into individual particles that do not stick together; loose consistency; commonly found in sandy soil.

Fig. 1.3: Soil Structures

Importance of Soil Structure

Soil structure has the following importance

i) It affects soil moisture and soil air relations

ii) It is an indication of nutrient status and activity of micro-organisms in the soil

iii) **Soil Consistence:** Soil consistence refers to the ease with which an individual ped can be crushed by the fingers. Soil consistence, and its description, depends on soil moisture content. Terms commonly used to describe consistence are:

Moist soil

- **Loose:** non coherent when dry or moist; does not hold together in a mass
- **Friable:** when moist, crushed easily under gentle pressure between thumb and forefinger and can be pressed together into a lump
- **Firm:** when moist crushed under moderate pressure between thumb and forefinger, but resistance is distinctly noticeable

Wet soil

- **Plastic:** When wet, readily deformed by moderate pressure but can be pressed into a lump; will form a "wire" when rolled between thumb and forefinger.
- **Sticky:** When wet, adheres to other material and tends to stretch somewhat and pull apart rather than to pull free from other material.

Dry Soil

- **Soft:** When dry, breaks into powder or individual grains under very slight pressure
- **Hard:** When dry, moderately resistant to pressure; can be broken with difficulty between thumb and forefinger

iv) **Bulk Density:** Bulk density is the proportion of the weight of a soil relative to its volume. It is expressed as a unit of weight per volume, and is commonly measured in units of grams per cubic centimeters (g/cc). Bulk density is an indicator of the amount of pore space available within individual soil horizons, as it is inversely proportional to pore space:

Pore space = 1 – bulk density/particle density

v) **Soil Porosity:** Soil porosity refers to the space between the soil particles in given volume. The pore spaces are essential for holding the water and for free exchange of gases like carbon dioxide and oxygen between root cells of growing plants and the soil surface. Porosity of soil depends up on the soil texture. The coarse textured soil has more porosity than fine textured soil. The porosity of fine textured soil can be increased by the addition of organic matter to the soil.

vi) **Soil permeability:** Soil permeability is the ability of the soil to transmit water and air. As the soil layers or horizons vary in their characteristics, the permeability also differs from one layer to another. Pore size, texture, structure and the presence of impervious layers such as clay pan determines the permeability of a soil. Clayey soils with platy structures have very low permeability.

vii) **Soil temperature: S**oil temperature is influenced by soil colour, texture and water and also by altitude and slope. It is affected by climate and vegetation type. Black soil absorbs more heat. Sandy soil absorbs more heat and radiates it quickly at night than clay and loamy soil.

viii) **Soil atmosphere:** It refers to the gases present in the soil pores. It contains three main gases such as oxygen, carbon dioxide and nitrogen. It differs from atmospheric air because it contains more carbon dioxide, moisture and less oxygen than atmospheric air. The soil air is influenced by temperature, wind, rainfall and pressure.

ix) **Soil water:** Rainfall is the main source of soil water. In addition to rainfall soil may be irrigated with water from wells, canals, etc. The soil contains water in different forms such as hygroscopic water, capillary water, gravitational water, combined water and water vapors.

a) **Hygroscopic water:** The water that is tightly held by adhesive and cohesive forces on the surface of soil colloid is called hygroscopic water. This is not available to the plants.

b) **Capillary Water:** This water is available for the plants. The water molecules are present in the inter-particular spaces of soil which form the capillary like structure.

c) **Gravitational water:** This water moves downward due to force of gravity and reaches to deep layers of hard rock. It accumulates there. The upper surface of it is called water table.

d) **Combined water:** This water is present as hydrated oxides of aluminium, iron, silicon, etc.

e) **Water vapour:** The soil also contains some amount of water in the form of water vapour in inter-particular spaces of the soil.

Total water content of soil is termed as **Holard.** The easily available water to plants is called **Creshard** and tightly bound, unavailable water is known as **Echard.**

1.2.3 Chemical Properties of the Soil

Chemical properties of soil include soil composition, soil pH, cation exchange capacity (CEC), soil enzymes and soil humus.

i) Soil Composition: Chemical composition consists of both organic and inorganic compounds. Inorganic compounds include mainly Ca, Mg, Fe, Al, Si, Na, K and traces of Mn, Zn, Co, I, and Cu. It influences the pH of soil. Organic compounds found in soil are of different types such as proteins, amino acids, aromatic compounds, purine, pyrimidines, sugar, alcohol, fats, oils, resins, waxes and lignin. These organic compounds are derived from dead remains of plants and animals. Organic matter and humus forms the organic compounds. Chemical nature of soil greatly influences the plant growth and type of vegetation.

ii) Soil Reaction (Soil pH): pH is defined as negative logarithm of hydrogen ion concentration. It is a measure of the active hydrogen ion (H^+) concentration. It is an indication of the acidity or alkalinity of a soil, and also known as "soil reaction". The pH scale ranges from 0 to 14, with values below 7.0 acidic, and values above 7.0 alkaline. A pH value of 7 is considered neutral. A pH range of 6.0 to 6.8 is ideal for most crops because it coincides with optimum solubility of the most important plant nutrients.

Soil pH ranges between 2.00 -10.5. Some soils are acidic and some are alkaline. Soil pH is influenced by mineral content, climate, weathering and rainfall. Soil pH determines the vegetation type of an area for example Sal grows at pH 4.5 to 5.5 while Teak requires a pH of 6.5 to 7.6. Warm and dry climate soils are strongly basic. The acidic soils occur in high rainfall regions like Western ghats, Kerala and Assam. The soil pH affects the availability of nutrients and minerals. Some minor elements (e.g., iron) and most heavy metals are more soluble at lower pH. In acid soils, hydrogen and aluminum are the dominant exchangeable cations. Increase in pH-increases calcium availability. Nitrogen is available at 6 to 8 pH. The soil pH affects the microbial activity in the soil. Below pH 5 fungal and bacterial activities are reduced. Hence lowering the soil pH below 5 may be helpful to control the soil borne diseases like root-rot of cotton, root-rot of tobacco and potato scab while club-root of crucifers and *Rhizoctonia* root-rot can be controlled by increasing the soil pH.

iii) Cation Exchange Capacity (CEC): Ability of the soil particles to adsorb and exchange cations that are loosely bound to its surface is called cation exchange capacity (CEC).

Some plant nutrients and metals exist as positively charged ions, or "cations", in the soil environment. Among the more common cations found in soils are hydrogen (H^+), aluminum (Al^{+3}), calcium (Ca^{+2}), magnesium (Mg^{+2}), and potassium (K^+). Most heavy metals also exist as cations in the soil environment. Cation exchange capacity is highly dependent on soil texture and organic matter content. Clay and organic matter particles are predominantly negatively charged (anions), and have the ability to hold cations from being "leached" or washed away. The adsorbed cations are subjected to replacement by other cations in a rapid, reversible process called "cation exchange". Organic matter has both (+) and (–) sites.

Cations leaving the exchange sites enter the soil solution, where they can be taken up by plants, react with other soil constituents, or be carried away with drainage water. The soil having more percentage of clay and organic matter shows higher CEC.

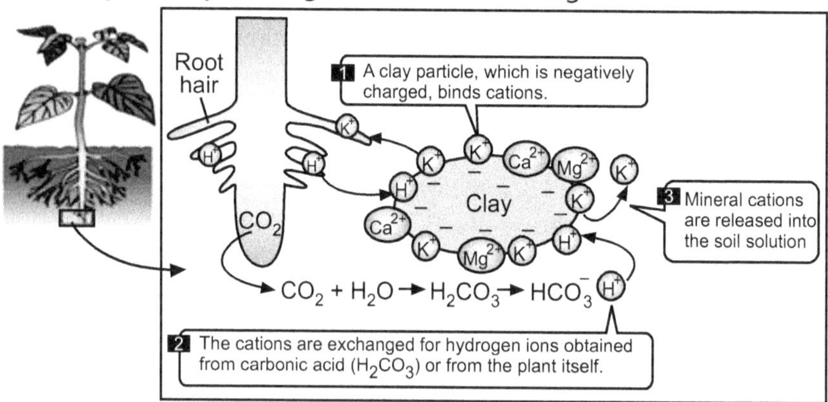

Fig. 1.4: Cation Exchange Capacity (CEC) Of Soil

iv) Soil Enzymes: There are 50 enzymes in various types of soil. The main source of soil enzymes are microorganisms, soil animals/ insects and plant roots. These enzymes catalyse biological reactions in the soil, maintain soil fertility and support plant life. Common enzymes that are found in soil are amylases (wheat roots) catalases, invertases, dehydrogenases, phenol oxidases, glycerophosphatases and urease (earthworm) etc. Saline soils have high activity of ureases while the activity of dehydrogenase is highest in forest soil and absent in alkali soils.

v) Soil Humus: Humus is a dark coloured complex organic substance resulting from the disintegration of dead remains of plants and animals. The process of humus formation is called humification. It is formed either naturally or from composting. Depending on the level of decomposition, humus can be classified into Mor, moder, mull.

a) **Mor:** It is the least decomposed humus. It shows low biological activity in soil. (Coniferous forest soils) Litter of large thickness. C/N ratio is more than 20, and pH is acidic.

b) **Moder:** It is a transitional stage of decomposition. It is found in grassland soils where litter of low thickness (2-3 cm) is present. It is medium humified humus having C/N ratio ranging between 15-25. In this type of humus mineral-organic complexes are weakly bound

c) **Mull:** This is a fully decomposed organic matter showing high biological activity. It is dark coloured having C/N ratio – 10 and neutral pH. It creates a stable mineral-organic complexes.

Soil Organisms

Soil is the site of residence of different types of microorganisms like bacteria, fungi and actinomycetes as well as useful insects/rodents like earthworms and harmful insects/rodents like nematodes. Microorganisms disintegrate dead remains of plants and animals in to humus. The bacteria like *Rhizobium* and *Clostridium* fix atmospheric nitrogen and add it to the soil and help in increasing fertility of soil. The earthworms makes the soil porous and improves soil aeration, its excretory products are rich in content of plant growth promoters which are beneficial for the luxuriant growth of plants. Soil also contains harmful animals like nematodes which enter in to the phloem of root and block the phloem transport therefore their eradication from soil is essential to achieve luxuriant plant growth.

EXERCISE

I. Multiple Choice Questions

1. The term ecology was first used by ---------
   (a) Reiter (b) Odum
   (c) Sharma (d) Haeckel
2. ------- deals with the ecology of plant communities
   (a) Autecology (b) Synecology
   (c) Phytosociology (d) Marine ecology
3. -----------grow in direct sun light.
   (a) Heliophytes (b) Sciophytes
   (c) Obligate sciophytes (d) None of these
4. At ----- temperature all the metabolic processes in the plants are at maximum.
   (a) Optimum (b) Minimum
   (c) Maximum (d) All of these
5. ----- are the balls or lumps of ice.
   (a) Hails (b) Dew
   (c) Drizzles (d) Rain
6. Accumulation of sesquioxides of iron and aluminium in the soil is called ------
   (a) Laterization (b) Melanization
   (c) Podsolization (d) Gleization
7. The soil particles less than 0.002mm in diameter are called -------
   (a) Silt (b) Clay
   (c) Fine sand (d) Gravel
8. Total water content of soil is called ------
   (a) Echard (b) Creshard
   (c) Holard (d) None of these
9. ----- is the least decomposed humus.
   (a) Mor (b) Moder
   (c) Mull (d) None of these
10. ----- refers to the space between the soil particles.
    (a) Soil porosity (b) Soil Structure
    (c) Soil permeability (d) Bulk density

ANSWERS

1-a; 2-b; 3-a; 4-a; 5-a; 6-a; 7-b; 8-c;
9-a; 10-a.

II. Two Marks Questions

1. Define autecology and synecology
2. What are heliophytes?
3. What are sciophytes?
4. Enlist different soil separates
5. Comment up on any to structural types of soil you have studied
6. What is humus? Enlist different types of humus
7. Comment on soil enzymes

III. Four Marks Questions

1. Discuss the effect of temperature on plants
2. Comment on water as climatic factor
3. What is soil humus? Discuss different types of humus based on their stage of decomposition
4. Comment on soil organisms
5. What is photoperiodism? Classify the plants according to their requirement of light duration for flowering.
6. Comment on the cation exchange capacity of the soil

IV. Five Marks Questions

1. Discuss 'Light' as a climatic factor
2. Comment up on the soil profile
3. Discuss about soil humus and soil organisms
4. Explain soil reaction and cation exchange capacity of soil
5. What is soil texture? Comment up on the 'Textural classes' of soil
6. Discuss 'Temperature' as a climatic factor

V. Seven Marks Questions

1. Discuss in detail any three physical and any two chemical properties of soil
2. Comment up on the soil texture and soil structure
3. What is the difference between weather and climate? Discuss any two climatic factors you have studied
4. Discuss the impact of light and wind on plant life.

2

CHAPTER

COMMUNITY ECOLOGY

Introduction

In last chapter we have studied various climatic and edaphic factors that affect the life of organisms. In this chapter, we are going to study the relationship of different kinds of populations at particular habitat in relation to the environment. The assemblage of different types of populations at particular habitat is considered as community. Ecologists consider community as basic unit of vegetation. Each community represents many groups of organisms persisting year after year. Henry J. Oosting has defined community as an "aggregation of living organisms having mutual adjustment among themselves and to their environment". The populations of animals and plants living together at particular habitat constitute a biotic community. Only assemblage of animals in the habitat is considered as **animal community** while that of plants is called plant community. In the recent literature on plant ecology the **plant community** is defined as "Uniform floristic composition". The species living together in groups at a habitat exhibit various degrees of adjustments among themselves and with their surrounding (physical environment). The relationship of individuals in community among themselves and their physical environment is called community ecology.

2.1 FORM AND STRUCTURE OF COMMUNITIES

2.1.1 Form of the Community

The "Form" of a community is described in number of ways by different ecologists by considering different aspects. The individuals in the community have different growth habits such as herbs, shrubs, trees, etc. This external appearance of the individuals in the plant community is generally termed as Form or Life form or Growth Form.

A. Life Forms

Danish botanist Raunkiaer (1934) referred growth habit of plants as life form. He categorised the individual plants in the community into different life form classes based on the relation of the ground surface to the plant's regenerating (meristematic) tissue which is generally referred to as bud. The bud remains inactive during unfavourable conditions and sprout under favourable conditions. Raunkaier classified plants into five different life form classes based on the position of perennating buds on plants and the degree of their protection during adverse conditions such as phanerophytes, chamaephytes, hemicryptophytes, cryptophytes and therophytes (**Fig. 2.1**).

Fig. 2.1: Raunkiaer's Life Forms: (a) Phanerophytes (b) Chamaephytes (c) Hemicryptophytes (d) Cryptophytes and (e) Therophytes

1. **Phanerophytes:** The term phanerophyte is derived from two Greek words *"phenoros"* meaning open or visible and *"phyton"* meaning plant. The term visible or open refers to the perennating organs or buds. Thus, the plants having perennating buds directly

exposed (open) to the environment are called phanerophytes. In these plants, the buds are naked or covered with scales and are situated high up on the twigs and branches of plant. They are directly exposed to the atmosphere. The plants belonging to this life form class include trees, shrubs, lianas, some large perennial herbs and epiphytes. On the basis of height phanerophytes are again divided into different sub-classes such as megaphanerophytes, mesophanerophytes, microphanerophytes and nanophanerophytes.

i) **Megaphanerophytes:** In these plants perennating buds are situated at a distance of 30 metres or more than 30 meters from the ground surface.

ii) **Mesophanerophytes:** In these plants perennating buds are situated at a distance of 8 to 30 metres from the ground surface.

iii) **Microphanerophytes:** In these plants perennating buds are situated at a distance of 2 to 8 metres from the ground surface.

iv) **Nanophanerophytes:** In these plants perennating buds are situated at a distance of 25 cm to 2 metres from the ground surface.

2) **Chamaephytes:** The term chamaephytes is derived from two Greek words *"chamai"* meaning near or close to the soil and *"phyton"* meaning plant. Thus, the chamaephytes are the plants in which perennating buds are near the soil surface. The plants of this class are less than 25 cm in height however their perennating buds are above the soil surface. During the unfavourable season the buds are protected by the dead fallen leaves on lower altitudes and by snow on higher altitudes. Many perennial herbaceous plants belong to this life form class.

3) **Hemicryptophytes:** The term Hemicryptophyte is derived from three Greek words *"Hemi"* meaning half or partial, *"Cryptos"* meaning hidden and *"phyton"* meaning plant. The term hemicryptophyte refers to the plants in which perennating buds are partially hidden under soil surface or fallen leaves during

unfavourable season. These are herbaceous plants found on the soil surface as runners and their buds and shoots are protected by soil and dead leaves. Many biennial and perennial plants are included in this life form class.

4) **Cryptophytes:** The term Cryptophyte is derived from two Greek words "*Cryptos*" meaning hidden and "*Phyton*" meaning plant. The cryptophytes are the plants whose perennating organs (buds) are hidden or buried under soil surface or water surface. The cryptophytes are again subdivided as geophytes, helophytes and hydrophytes.

   i) **Geophytes:** The term Geophyte is derived from two Greek words "*Geos*" meaning earth or soil and "*Phyton*" meaning plant. The geophytes are the terrestrial plants with underground perennating buds. They are of different types such as Rhizome geophytes (e.g. Ginger, *Canna*), Stem tuber geophytes (e.g. Potato), Bulb geophytes (e.g. Onion, Garlic).

   ii) **Helophytes:** The term Helophyte is derived from two Greek words "*Helos*" meaning marsh (water saturated soil) and "*Phyton*" meaning plant. The term helophyte refers to the plant of marshy places. These plants grow in marshy places; their rhizomes are underground while the leaves and flower are aerial e.g. *Typha*.

   iii) **Hydrophytes:** The term hydrophyte is derived from two Greek words "*Hydros*" meaning water and '*phyton*" meaning plant. The plants growing in water medium are referred to as hydrophytes. *Eichhornia*, *Hydrilla*, Lotus are the examples of hydrophytes.

5) **Therophytes:** The term therophyte is derived from two Greek words "*Theros*" meaning summer or hot season and "*Phyton*" meaning plant. This life form of plants includes annual summer plants which survive in the form of seeds under unfavourable period. These plants are seasonal plants and complete their life cycle under favourable conditions and die at the onset of summer or unfavourable conditions. The perennating bud is an embryo of the seed. The seeds germinate under favourable

conditions and produce new seedlings. This group includes many seasonal plants and grasses.

B. Phytoclimatic Spectrum

The life forms are not evenly distributed over the earth surface. Their distribution varies with the climatic zone. Each climatic zone has its own spectrum of life forms. In the tropical zone huge trees or phanerophytes are abundant, in desert higher number of annuls or therophytes are observed and temperate zone shows dominance of cryptophytes and hemicryptophytes. The array of percentages of different life forms in any plant community at a habitat is called phytoclimatic spectrum.

Raunkiaer prepared a normal phytoclimatic spectrum. This normal spectrum provides a base line. Deviation in percentage in any life form from the normal spectrum reflects the change in climate of that region. The higher percentage of phanerophytes is indicative of phanerophytic climate or humid tropical climate. Maximum percentage of therophytes (More than 40%) indicates dry subtropical (arid) climate. In the cold arctic climate phanerophytes are absent while the percentage of chamaephytes, hemicryptophytes and geophytes is large. Though the phytoclimatic spectrum is indicative of climate there are some limitations to usefulness of phytoclimatic spectrum as an indicator of climate because at certain habitats it does not indicate the existing climatic conditions, for example, the actual climate of Indogangetic plain is favourable for luxuriant growth of phanerophytes however in Indogangetic plain therophytes are maximum in number which is an indicator of dry, subtropical climate.

Raunkiaer's Phytoclimatic Spectrum in Various Climates

Type of Climate	*Large Phanero phytes%*	*Small Phanero phyte%*	*Chamae phyte%*	*Hemi Crypto phyte%*	*Crypto phytes*	*Helo and Hydro phyte%*	*Thero phyte%*	*Total %*
Humid, Tropical	*10*	*50*	*06*	*12*	*03*	*02*	*17*	*100*
Cold, Arctic	*-*	*01*	*22*	*60*	*13*	*02*	*02*	*100*

Dry, Subtropical	-	06	13	19	09	02	51	100
Normal	06	39	09	28	03	01	14	100

C. Growth Forms

The method of recognising different growth forms was proposed by ecologist Pierre Dansereau in 1951. According to him the individuals in the plant community can be categorised in to

- Six growth forms such as trees, shrubs, herbs, bryoids, epiphytes and lianas
- Three sizes such as tall, medium and low
- Four leaf habits such as deciduous, semi- deciduous, evergreen and evergreen succulent
- Six leaf shapes such as needle or spine, graminoid, medium or small, broad, thalloid and compound
- Four leaf textures such as filmy, membranous, sclerophyll, succulent or fungoid and
- Four aspects of coverage such as barren, discontinuous, in tufts or groups and continuous.

2.1.2 Structure of the Community

The pattern of the spatial and trophic arrangement of members of the community is called structure of the community. The structure of the community with respect to the spatial arrangement is studied under two heads such as Zonation and Stratification while the food relationship of different organisms in the community is considered as trophic structure.

1. Zonation: When the community is divided horizontally into sub-communities it is called zonation. Each sub-community represents different life forms depending on the climate of that region. Change in both altitude (height above mean sea level) and latitude (distance from the equator) are related with change in vegetation. Therefore, altitudinal and latitudinal zonations are observed in the vegetation. According to G.S. Puri the vegetation at different altitudes is determined by temperature, rainfall and soil conditions.

On mountains up to the height of 1800 feet from mean sea level the vegetation represented is tropical rain forest. The altitudinal zone from 1800 feet to 4000 feet shows presence of grassland or desert. The deciduous forest occurs at a zone present between 4000 feet to 7500 feet. The coniferous forests are present above 7500 feet and spread up to a height of 12000 feet. Tundra biome is the vegetation of zone extending from 12000 feet to 14500 feet and above 14500 the snow line is present.

The variation in temperature along latitude (distance from the equator) is responsible for the formation of vegetational zones such as tropical rain forest, grassland or desert, deciduous forest, coniferous forest, tundra and ice or snow. **(Fig. 2.2)**

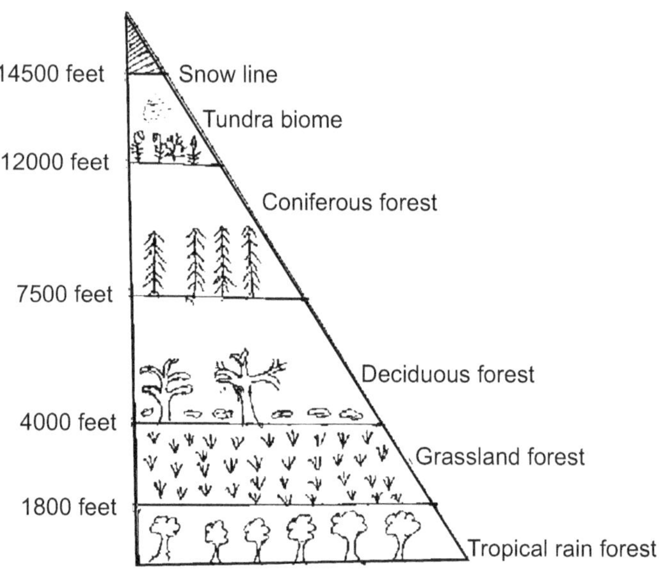

Fig. 2.2: Zonation

2. Stratification: Stratification of community means formation of vertical layers by different life forms existing in the community. The plant community is an aggregation of different types of growth forms such as trees, shrubs, herbs, mosses, thallophytes, lichens, etc. These growth forms have different heights and each growth form occupies a definite vertical position forming different layers. The different plant communities have different patterns of their stratification. For example, grassland community has three different strata while forest community shows five different strata. **(Fig. 2.3)**

(a) Stratification in Grassland Community

The grassland community has three strata which can be described as follows:

i) **Root and Rhizome Layer:** This is underground layer and is occupied by roots and under ground modified stems such as rhizomes, tubers, bulbs, corms, etc.

ii) **The ground layer:** The ground layer is occupied by thalloid bryophytes such as *Riccia*, *Anthoceros* and fungi.

iii) **Herbaceous layer:** The herbaceous layer consists of aerial parts of the grasses and herbs.

(b) Stratification in Forest Community

The forest vegetation shows presence of five strata such as:

i) **Subterranean or underground stratum:** In this stratum, under ground modified stems such as bulbs, rhizomes, tubers, corms and roots of aerial vegetation are present.

ii) **Forest floor:** Forest floor represents the vegetation of thalloid bryophytes, mosses, fungi, etc.

iii) **Ground layer:** The individuals in this vegetation may extend up to the height of one meter. This layer is occupied by herbs.

iv) **Under storey trees and Shrub layer:** This layer extends from 1 to 5 metres. This layer is occupied by shade loving small trees and shrubs.

v) **Top storey or Canopy layer:** This layer extends from 5 to 15 meters in most of the forests but sometimes it may extend up to 25-30 metres in coniferous forests and in rain forest it may extend up to 40 to 50 metres. The *Sequoia* forest shows a canopy layer of trees having height more than 100 metres.

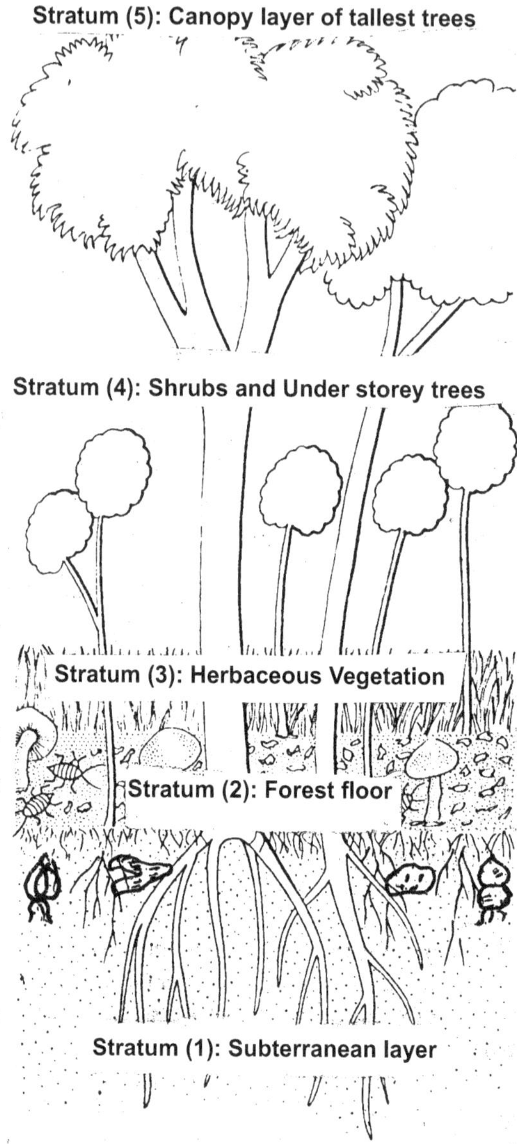

Fig. 2.3: Stratification in Forest community

3. Trophic Structure: In any biological community, there exists a food relationship amongst the different individuals present in the community. Some members especially green plants have autotrophic mode of nutrition while some members are heterotrophs. On the basis of food relationship the different members of community are categorised as producers, consumers and decomposers and transformers.

i) **Producers:** Producers are the autotrophic members mainly green plants. They use radiant energy of sun for the process of photosynthesis in which radiant energy of sun is converted or transformed in to chemical form of energy. As the producers transduce or convert the radiant energy of sun into chemical form they are called transducers or convertors by E.J. Kormondy. In the process of photosynthesis carbohydrates are synthesised. In addition to carbohydrates the producers can synthesise various macromolecules like proteins and lipids. As the plants produce the food material in the form of macromolecules such as carbohydrates, proteins and lipids they are called producers. Algae, green purple bacteria, cyanobacteria, different types of herbs, shrubs, trees, bryophytes, pteridophyes are all included under the category producers.

ii) **Consumers:** The living members of the community which utilise or consume the food material synthesised by producers are called consumers. This category includes different types of animals and insects which feed on plants. The consumers are again classified as Primary consumers, Secondary consumers and Tertiary consumers.

   a) **Primary Consumers:** Primary consumers are herbivorous animals which are dependent for their food on plants or producers. Insects, rabbits, rodents, deer, elephants, camels, goats are the examples of primary consumers in terrestrial community while small crustaceans and molluscs are the examples of aquatic community. The carnivores use herbivores as main source of food hence the herbivores are named as "Key industry animals" by Elton (1939).

   b) **Secondary Consumers:** Secondary consumers are the carnivores and omnivores. Carnivores are flesh eating animals and they consume herbivores while omnivores can eat both flesh and vegetables hence they are adapted to utilise herbivores as well as plants as their food. The secondary consumers include fox, wolves, dogs, cats, snakes, sparrow, crow, etc.

c) **Tertiary Consumers:** These are the top order carnivores which eat herbivores, omnivores and other carnivores. Tigers, lions, hawk, vultures are the examples of tertiary consumers.

d) **Decomposers and Transformers:** Decomposers and transformers are the bacteria and fungi. A group of bacteria and fungi that disintegrate dead remains of plants and animals and degrade the complex organic substances into simpler components are called decomposers. The simple organic matters are then attacked by another group of bacteria called transformers which convert simple organic matter into inorganic forms that are suitable for reuse by the producers.

2.2 CLASSIFICATION AND PHYSIOGNOMY

On the basis of habitat, species composition, dominance and physiognomy the plant communities are categorised in to different classes.

i) **Classification based on habitat:** The plant communities prefer to grow in different places or habitats containing different water content. On the basis of habitat plant communities are classified into five groups such as Wetland community, Wet-Mesic community, Mesophytic community, Dry-Mesic community and Dry land community.

ii) **Floristic classification:** The floristic classification is developed by an ecologist Frederic Clements. While classifying communities he has given emphasis on various aspects of community development such as succession, dominance, constancy and diagnostic species. According to Clements vegetation can be classified into different units such as formation, association, faciation, consociation, location, societies and clans.

a) **Formation:** In Clements's view formation is the major unit of vegetation. The plant formation is the largest vegetational unit showing different dominant growth forms such as trees, shrubs, herbs, etc. For example: forest is characterised by the presence of huge trees. When the community becomes stable and shows no further change then it is called climax community while a changing community is known as seral community. Forests, woodlands, savanna, scrub, prairie, meadow, steppe, desert, tundra and crusts are examples of formation types.

b) **Association:** Each formation is divided into a few associations which are considered as units of climax communities in which a few species are dominant. An association is named after two or three dominant species.

c) **Consociation:** Consociation is a unit with a single dominant species. The developmental or communities of a climax consociation are known as conscious.

d) **Faciation:** Faciation is an association developed under different microclimatic conditions within the same general climate. It contains two or more dominant species and is characterised by specific precipitation, evaporation and temperature. The seral communities are accordingly known as facies.

e) **Location:** This is a localised variant of an association, differing from it in the composition of some main subdominant and chief secondary species. Seral communities are accordingly called locies.

f) **Society:** Society is a community with one or more sub-dominants. The seral communities are called Society.

g) **Clans:** Each society is composed of two or smaller climax units. These small climax units are called clans.

iii) **Physiognomy and Classification based on physiognomy:** The term Physiognomy refers to the external appearance of the plant community. The plant community is recognised by the name of dominant life form that is present in the plant community. For example, if a community shows dominance of huge trees intermingled with shrubs and herbs then it is recognised as forest while a community showing more number of grasses than other life forms then it is termed as grassland community. The forest community is identified by the name of dominant plant species for example, if the forest is dominated by teak plants then it is recognised as Teak forest; if a forest is dominated of oak and hickory plants then it is identified as Oak-Hickory forest.

Dansereau (1958) classified plant communities by observing their external appearance as follows.

(a) Forest: The plant community showing the dominance of huge trees intermingled with under storey trees, shrubs and herbs is designated as forest.

(b) Woodland: The plant community having scattered distribution of tallest trees is called woodland.

(c) Savanna: The plant community containing flat topped, less branched, small trees (less than 10 meters in height) and other woody plants scattered regularly or clumped in small groups is known as savanna.

(d) Scrub: This plant community shows continuous stand of medium sized bushy plants (shrubs) separated by patches of herbaceous vegetation or bare land.

(e) Prairie: The plant community showing continuous stand of tall dense grasses is recognised as prairie.

(f) Meadow: This plant community contains herbaceous vegetation mainly belonging to family Poaceae. It does not contain woody plants.

(g) Steppe: It is a plant community containing bunch grasses and scattered shrubs.

(h) Desert: This plant community is represented by succulent, woody, evergreen perennial plants (Xerophytes) scattered in habitat.

(i) Tundra: This plant community consists of very low woody vegetation, trailing shrubs, cushion plants and mosses.

(j) Crusts: This plant community is represented by lichens, algae and fungi growing on soil or rock surface.

2.3 COMMUNITY CHARACTERISTICS

Like population, a community too has its own characteristics, which are not shown by its individual component species. These characteristics have meaning only with reference to community level of organisation. Each community is characterised by its species diversity, growth forms and structure, dominance, succession trends, etc. A number of characters are taken into consideration for studying the details of these aspects of a community. These characters are then used to express the characteristics of a community. These various characters are broadly classified into two major categories such as Analytical characters and Synthetic characters

Analytical characters are those which can be either described or measured, while the synthetic characters are generalisations based on analytical characters.

A) Analytical Characters

These are of two types, namely

1) Qualitative Characters: These can only be described and not measured.

i) **Species diversity:** Each biotic community is an aggregation of different kinds of organisms such as plants, animals, microbes. The individuals of the community differ from each other with respect to morphology, anatomy, physiology and taxonomy. The biosphere shows two levels of species diversity such as a) Regional diversity of whole nations or part of continents in which different communities are present and b) Local diversity in a given nation where different communities are found at different latitudes. If two distant habitats have same climate and similar type of vegetation then they are called **biotopes**. The vegetation in a plant community is a reflection of climate. Each species of community has definite range of tolerance towards environmental conditions of the habitat. The range of environment that species of community can tolerate is called its **ecological amplitude**.

ii) **Species dominance:** A plant community is an assemblage of different kinds of species at particular habitat. In plant community, only few species are found in abundance. The species which are more abundant in number and contain more biomass than other species of community are recognised as dominant species. Different plant communities are named after their dominant species. For example, if a forest community is represented by more number of teak plants as compared to other plant species then it is named as Teak forest.

iii) **Growth forms and Structure:** Each plant community contains different growth forms such as trees, shrubs, herbs, etc. The plant community is described in terms of major growth forms that exist in plant community. The plant community containing trees as major growth form is described as forest. The structure of community refers to the spatial arrangement of plant species in a community. Communities exhibit horizontal layering or zonation and vertical layering or stratification.

iv) **Coexistence:** It is a natural tendency of living organisms including plants to live in association and not as isolated individuals. This tendency of organisms to live in association is called coexistence. The coexisting populations have some sort of interaction amongst organisms of the same population as well as with other populations. The interactions between coexisting species may be obligatory in one direction or both. The nature of interaction between two coexisting species is categorised as exploitation, mutualism, competition and neutralism.

- **Exploitation:** In this type of coexistence, one species lives at the expense of other. For example, parasite *Cuscuta* lives at the expense of host plant.
- **Mutualism:** In this type of coexistence, both coexisting organisms and populations benefit from each other but none suffer. For example, symbiotic *Rhizobium* bacteria in the root nodules of legume plants. *Rhizobium* bacteria provide nitrogen for plant growth and root nodule cells provide food material for the life of bacteria.

- **Competition:** The individual plant species or populations in the community compete for the available resources such as soil water, soil minerals, sunlight, etc.
- **Neutralism:** In this type of coexistence the populations in the community are not dependent on each other and neither population affects the other.

v) **Succession:** The community develops on bare area. The evolution of community on bare area is prolonged process which involves a number of stages. Each stage is characterised by assemblage of particular plant species. This assemblage of plant species at each stage takes place according to existing environment. Change in environment results in the change of community. The change in community continues to take place until the establishment of balance between developed community and environment. The replacement of one community by the other till the development of climax community is called succession.

vi) **Trophic structure:** Trophic structure represents the nutritional relationship amongst the individuals of the community. They are recognised as producers, consumers and decomposers.

vii) **Periodicity:** Periodicity refers to the regular seasonal occurrence of various processes such as photosynthesis, growth, pollination, flowering, and ripening of fruits and seeds; and the manifestations of these processes, such as formation of leaves, elongation of shoots, appearance of flowers, and dissemination of seeds. Periodicity results from inherent genetic characteristics of each species under the influence of a particular combination of environmental conditions.

viii) **Phenology:** Phenology is the scientific study of seasonal changes in the life cycle of organism. In case of plants different species have different periods of seed germination, vegetative growth, flowering, fruiting, seed and fruit dispersal, etc. All these events are recorded day and date wise hence phenology is considered as the calendar of events in the life history of plant. These events are shown by a hexagon called phenogram. The angles of the hexagon are numbered as 1, 2, 3, 4, 5 and 6. These numbers are used to indicate the specific stage in the life history of plant species such as 1 for germination, 2 for vegetative growth, 3 for flowering, 4 for fruit formation, 5 for seed maturation and 6 for death. The vertical line drawn at angle indicates commencement of that phase in life cycle of plant species. **(Fig. 2.4)**

Plants	March	July	August	September	October	December
Heteropogon contortus						
Digitaria marginata						
D. royleana						
Aristida sp.						

1, 2, 3, 4, 5, 6

1 Germination
2 Vegetative growth
3 Flowering
4 Fruit formation
5 Seed maturation
6 Death

Phytophases

Fig. 2.4: Phenology of some Grasses

viii) Vitality (Vigour): Vitality is related to the condition of a plant and its capacity to complete the life cycle, while vigour refers more specifically to the state of health or development within a certain stage; a seedling or mature plant may be vigorous, or it may be feeble and poorly developed. In order to appraise the degree of vigour one needs to know the appearance of normal plants, preferably under optimum conditions, in the various stages of growth.

A number of criteria may be used in determining the vigour of plants such as the rate and total amount of growth, especially in height; rapidity of growth, renewal in the spring or following mowing or grazing; quantity or area of foliage; colour and turgidity of leaves and stems; degree of damage by disease or insects; time of appearance and number and height of flower stalks; rate of growth and extent of the root system; appearance and development of new stems and leaves; and the extent of dead portions, especially in bunch or mat-formers.

The following classification of vitality has been widely used:

Class 1 : Well-developed plants which regularly complete their life cycles.

Class 2 : Vigorous plants which usually do not complete their life cycle or are poorly developed. Sparsely distributed plants spread vegetatively.

Class 3 : Feeble plants that never complete their life cycles but do spread vegetatively.

Class 4 : Plants occasionally appearing from seed but which do not increase in number, such as ephemeral plants.

ix) Sociability (Gregariousness)

Sociability refers to the proximity of plants or shoots to one another. It is dependent upon the life-form and vigour of the plants, habitat conditions, and competitive and other relations between individuals. The Braun-Blanquet scale, given below, for rating sociability of species, has been widely used in analysing communities.

Class 1 : Shoots growing singly.

Class 2 : Small groups of plants such as *Chenopodium* spp., or scattered tufts, such as *Aristida* spp.

Class 3 : Small, scattered patches or cushions, e.g., patches of grama grass or buffalo grass, or large clumps of prickly pear cactus.

Class 4 : Large patches or broken mats.

Class 5 : Very large mats or stands of nearly pure populations that almost completely cover a large area, such as Andropogon scoparius grassland.

Association of Species

Association of species, or interspecific association, is the growing together of two or more species in close proximity to one another as; for example, Kentucky bluegrass and white clover in many pastures, *Stipa comata* and *Bouteloua gracilis* in some grasslands in the Great Plains, and *Agropyron spicatum* and *Poa secunda* in the lower grassland zone in British Columbia. Association of species may be brought about by the similarity in ecological amplitudes of two or more species.

b) Quantitative Characters

These are expressed in quantitative terms and they include frequency, density, abundance, cover and basal area and dominance.

(i) Frequency

Frequency is an important parameter of vegetation analysis, which reflects the spread, distribution or dispersion of a species in a given area. For example, a species which is distributed uniformly in an area has greater probability of its occurrence in all quadrants (sampling units) and it would have high frequency. If a species is clustered or present only in a part of the area, it will occur only in few quadrants and hence it would have lesser frequency. The frequency of a species in a given area is studied either by quadrant method or transects and is calculated by the following formula:

$$\text{Frequency (\%)} = \frac{\text{No. of sampling units in which the species occurred}}{\text{No. of sampling units studied}} \times 100$$

Thus, if a species occurs in 2 out of total 4 quadrats studied, its frequency would be 50%. If a species occurs in all the quadrats studied, its frequency would be 100%. Frequency is a very important quantitative parameter. Raunkiaer (1934) studied 8000 quadrats and made an elaborative study on the frequency of species. Based on his data, he divided plant species into five frequency classes such as A, B, C, D and E. The distribution of frequency in five classes is given in **Table 2.1.**

Table 2.1: Raunkiaer's frequency classes

Sr. No.	Frequency Class	Frequency Range
1.	A	1 - 20%
2.	B	21 - 40%
3.	C	41 - 60%
4.	D	61 - 80%
5.	E	81 - 100%

According to Raunkiaer (1934) the number of species in frequency class A is greater than B; B is greater than C, class C is greater than or less than or equal to the class D and class D is less than class E. This can be shown as A > B > C = D < E. This assumption is also known as Raunkiaer's frequency law.

Relative frequency of a species

The spreading pattern of a species in relation to the dispersion of all the species is termed as relative frequency of a species. It is calculated by using the following formula.

$$\text{Relative frequency of a species} = \frac{\text{Frequency of a species in a study area}}{\text{Sum of frequencies of all species in the study area}} \times 100$$

(ii) Density

Density, broadly considered, denotes the number of individual plants or stalks in an area, but in a strict sense it refers to the number of individuals or stalks in a unit space or unit area. Density represents the numerical strength of an individual plant species in the community. Density gives an idea of competition that may exist in the members of plant community. When the measured unit area is divided by the number of individuals, the average area occupied by each individual is obtained. It is calculated by using the following formula

$$\text{Density} = \frac{\text{Total number of individuals of the species in all the sampling units}}{\text{Total number of sampling units studied}}$$

Relative Density

It is defined as the proportion of a density of an individual species to that of density of all species in study area. It is calculated by using the following formula

$$\text{Relative Density} = \frac{\text{Total number of individuals of the species in all the sampling units}}{\text{Total number of individuals of all species in sampling units studied}} \times 100$$

(iii) Cover and Basal area

Cover, or specifically herbage cover, signifies primarily the area of ground occupied by the leaves, stems, and inflorescences, i.e., the above-ground parts of plants, as viewed from above. Basal area, however, refers to the ground actually penetrated by the stems, and readily seen when the leaves and stems are clipped at the ground surface. "Basal area" has also been used to denote the area occupied by the vegetation at one or at some other level, above the ground. In forest the basal area is the cross sectional area of a tree measured at a height of 4 to 5 feet from ground surface. In grasslands the basal area refers to the coverage of ground by stems and leaves of plant one inch above the ground surface. Basal area of tree is calculated by using following formula

$$\text{Basal area per tree} = \frac{\text{Total basal area}}{\text{Number of trees}}$$

(iv) Abundance

Abundance refers to the number of individuals of any species per sampling unit of occurrence. It is calculated by using following formula

$$\text{Abundance} = \frac{\text{Total number of individuals of the species in all the sampling units}}{\text{Number of sampling units in which the species occurred}}$$

By calculating the abundance, the plant species are assigned to respective abundance classes.

The abundance classes are mentioned below.

Sr. No.	Abundance Class	Plant species per Sq. metre quadrat
1.	Rare	1 to 4
2.	Occasional	5 to 14
3.	Frequent	15 to 29
4.	Abundant	30 to 99
5.	Very abundant	100 or more

Association index and Index of Similarity

Existence of two or more plant species at a habitat is generally referred to as an association. Association index and Index of similarity are used to evaluate inter-specific association. The following example gives an idea of Association index and Index of Similarity. Suppose 100 sampling units or quadrats are studied for the determination of association index and index of similarity of hypothetical plant species A and B. Out of 100 quadrates A is found in 50 quadrates. Species A is found in association with B in 20 quadrates. Then association index of species A is calculated by dividing the total number of quadrats in which A occurred in association with B by the total number of quadrats in which A is found.

$$\text{Association index of A} = \frac{20}{50} = 0.4$$

Index of similarity is calculated as follows:

Suppose there are two groups of coexisting species. In one group number of plant species is 30 and in the other group the number is 20. 15 species are common to both groups. Then index of similarity is calculated as

$$\text{Index of Similarity} = \frac{2 \times \text{No. of common species}}{\text{Total number of species in both associations}} \times 100$$

$$\text{Index of Similarity} = \frac{2 \times 15}{30 + 20} \times 100 = 60$$

B) Synthetic Characters

To describe the community structure Nicholas (1930), Cain (1932) and Braun-Blanquet (1932) used three synthetic characters such as fidelity, presence and constance.

1. Fidelity

The faithfulness of a species to its community is referred to as fidelity. It is the degree with which a species is restricted in its distribution to one kind of community. That means each and every plant species requires a specific set of the environmental factors, if such environment occurs in the habitat then that species grow there. Therefore, some species are confined to one particular community such species are called indicator species. If a species has high fidelity value then such species occurs in the restricted habitat having favourable environmental conditions and is unable to grow elsewhere. According to Pandeya (1960) the species having high fidelity value have low ecological amplitude.

2. Presence

This synthetic character indicates the existence of species in a study area. The presence of a species is described by observing their frequency as Rare (1 to 20%), Seldom present (21 to 40%), Often present (41 to 60%), Mostly present (60 to 80%), Constantly present (81 to 100%).

3. Constance

Constance is the degree of existence of a species in an unit area instead of whole study area. It is determined by observing the frequency of plant species and assigned to five different classes such as Constance Class-I (1 to 20% frequency), Constance Class-II (21 to 40% frequency), Constance Class-III (41 to 60% frequency), Constance Class-IV (61 to 80% frequency), Constant Class-V (81 to 100% frequency).

EXERCISE

I. Multiple Choice Questions

1. Assemblage of plants in a habitat is called ------
   a) Plant community b) Animal community
   c) Biological community d) All of these
2. In ----- perennating buds are situated at a distance of 30 metres or more than 30 metres from the ground surface
   a) Megaphanerophytes b) Mesophanerophytes
   c) Microphanerophytes d) Nanophanerophytes
3. Horizontal division of community into different sub communities is called ------
   a) Zonation b) Stratification
   c) Growth forms d) Phytoclimatic spectrum
4. -------- means formation of vertical layers by different life forms existing in the plant community.
   a) Zonation b) Stratification
   c) Growth forms d) Phytoclimatic spectrum
5. Green plants are the -------
   a) Producers b) Primary consumers
   c) Secondary consumers d) Tertiary consumers
6. The plant community showing dominance of huge trees is designated as -----
   a) Savana b) Forest
   c) Woodland d) Prairie
7. In ----- association one species lives at the expense of other.
   a) Exploitation b) Mutualism
   c) Neutralism d) None of these
8. The species having high --------- value have low ecological amplitude
   a) Fidelity b) Presence
   c) Constance d) None of these

ANSWERS

1-a; 2-a; 3-a; 4-b; 5-a; 6-b; 7-a; 8-a;

II. Two Marks Questions

1. What is plant density? Give the formula for calculating density.
2. What is phenology? Draw phenogram of any one plant species you have studied.
3. Comment on the association between Rhizobium and root nodule cells.
4. Define cryptophytes. Give two examples of geophytes.
5. Explain the role of decomposers in an ecosystem.
6. What is physiognomy? Give any two physiognomic classes of the community.

III. Four Marks Questions

1. What is life form? Enlist various life form classes suggested by Raunkiaer (1934) and discuss any one of them.
2. What is life form? Comment on the phanerophytes as one of the life form class.
3. What is stratification? Discuss stratification in forest community.
4. Comment on the classification of plant community based on the habitat.
5. What are qualitative characters of the plant community? Discuss any two qualitative characters you have studied.
6. What is phenology? Explain phenogram using any suitable example.

IV. Five Marks Questions

1. Explain with suitable example Association Index and Index of Similarity.
2. Enlist various life form classes and comment on any two life form classes.

3. What is physiognomy? Enlist various physiognomic classes of the community and comment on one of them.
4. What are quantitative characters of the community? Explain any two quantitative characters you have studied.
5. What are synthetic characters of the community? Explain any two synthetic characters you have studied.

V. Seven Marks Questions

1. What are analytical characters of the plant community? Explain any two qualitative and any two quantitative characters of the plant community.
2. Discuss in detail the floristic classification of plant community as suggested by Clements.
3. Discuss the trophic structure of the plant community.
4. What is life form? Comment on the life form classes suggested by Raunkiaer.

3

CHAPTER

ECOSYSTEM

3.1 CONCEPT AND TYPES

3.1.1 Concept of Ecosystem

An organism is always in the state of perfect balance with the environment. The environment refers to the things and conditions around the organism which directly or indirectly influence the life and development of the organisms and their population. The organisms and environment are non-separable factors. The organisms interact with each other and also with physical conditions that are present in their habitat. Keeping this view in mind the term 'ecosystem' was coined by British ecologist A. G. Tansley in 1935. He defined it as "The system resulting from the integration of all living and non-living factors of the environment." Ecosystem is a major ecological unit. It has both structural and functional groups of individuals having similar properties and living in the same area which are called populations. When various populations interact with one another they form a community. The interaction of such community and its physical environment constitute an ecosystem and ecosystem then refers to the organisms and physical environment that supports their life. The ecosystem can be defined as an ecological complex formed by the interactions of the organisms and the physical features of the habitat.

3.1.2 Types of Ecosystem

There are mainly two types of ecosystem

1. Natural Ecosystems and
2. Artificial Ecosystems

1. Natural Ecosystems

Natural ecosystems operate by themselves under natural conditions without any major interference by man. Based on the habitat natural ecosystems are again divided into two subtypes such as

A) Terrestrial Ecosystem: The ecosystem existing on land is termed as terrestrial ecosystem. e.g. Forest, Grass land.

B) Aquatic Ecosystem: The ecosystem existing in a water body is termed as aquatic ecosystem. Aquatic ecosystems are of two types such as:

i) **Fresh water ecosystems:** These ecosystems develop in non-saline or fresh water e.g. River, Ponds, Lake, Dam, etc. This is further divided into

   a) **Lotic ecosystem:** The ecosystem of running water is termed as lotic ecosystem. e.g. River, Spring, Stream, etc.

   b) **Lentic ecosystems:** The ecosystem of standing water is termed as lentic ecosystem.

   e.g. Lake, Pond, Dams, etc.

ii) **Marine ecosystems**: These are the ecosystems of saline water. e.g. Sea, Ocean, Estuaries, etc.

2. Artificial Ecosystems

These are maintained artificially by man. In these ecosystems the natural balance is regularly disturbed due to interference by man. In these ecosystems man tries to control the biotic community as well as physicochemical environment. e.g. Crop lands like Maize, Wheat, Jowar, Rice, etc. and different types of orchards.

3.2 COMPONENTS AND ORGANISATION OF ECOSYSTEM

Components and organisation of ecosystem refers to the structure of the ecosystem.

Structure and functions are two main aspects of any ecosystem. The structure refers to the composition of biological community, the amount and distribution of non-living material such as nutrients, water, etc. and the range or gradient of conditions of existence such as temperature, light, etc. while the function of ecosystems means:

i) The rate of biological energy flow i.e. photosynthetic and respiration rate of the biological community.

ii) The rate of cyclic flow of various minerals and water.

iii) Regulation of organism by environment and regulation of environment by the organism.

Hence in the study of ecosystem both structure and function are studied together.

3.2.1 Structure of Ecosystem

All ecosystems contain both living or biotic components such as plants, animals and microbes and non-living or abiotic components such as water, soil, energy, air, etc.

1. Biotic or Living Components

The living component of an ecosystem can be divided into three categories depending on their role in maintaining the stable ecosystem as producers, consumers and decomposers.

i) Producers: Producers are autotrophic organisms chiefly green plants. They lock up the radiant energy of the sun in the bonds of carbon compounds (carbohydrates) during the process of photosynthesis. Photosynthetic organisms such as green purple bacteria, microscopic algae and large plants function as producers of organic compounds from inorganic material. Since, the producers convert or transduce the radiant energy into chemical form of energy; E. J. Cormandy suggested an alternative term transducers or converters for producers.

ii) Consumers: The living members of ecosystem which consume the food synthesised by producers are called consumers. Different types of animals that are found in ecosystem are included under the category consumer. Consumers are classified as:

a) Primary consumers: Primary consumers are purely herbivorous. They are dependent upon green plants for their food. e.g. Insects, Rabbit, Buffalo, Goat, Deer, Cow, etc. Herbivores serve as a chief source of the food for carnivores.

b) **Secondary consumers:** These are carnivores and omnivores which eat primary consumers. e.g. – Dog, snake, Wolf, etc.

c) **Tertiary consumers:** Tertiary consumers are the top order consumers which eat other carnivores, omnivores and herbivores. E.g. – Lion, Tiger, Vultures, etc.

d) **Parasites:** Besides different classes of consumers the parasites, scavengers and saprophytes are also included in the category of consumers. The parasitic plant and animal utilise the living tissues of different organisms. The scavengers and saprophytes utilise dead remains of animals and plants as a food.

e) **Scavengers and Saprophytes:** Scavengers and Saprophytes utilise dead remains of plants and animals as their food.

iii) **Decomposers and Transformers:** These are living components of an ecosystem, they are fungi and bacteria. Decomposers attack dead remains of producers and consumers and degrade complex organic substances into simple compounds. The simple organic substances are attacked by other kind of bacteria which finally change organic components into inorganic components that are suitable for reuse to producers. The decomposers and transformers play a very important role in maintaining the dynamic nature of ecosystem.

2. **Non-living or Abiotic components:** The abiotic components of any ecosystem are categorised as physical factors, organic substances and inorganic substances.

A) Physical Factors

The physical factors are of two types such as climatic factors and edaphic factors. Climatic factor include light, temperature, water, etc.

while edaphic factors are the factors related with soil which include soil minerals, soil organisms, soil organic matter, soil water, etc. The edaphic factors are discussed in Unit 1.

B) Organic Substances

These substances include carbohydrates, proteins, lipids found in living organisms and humus formed after the decomposition of dead remains of plant or animal body.

C) Inorganic Substances

Water, minerals and gases are the inorganic substances. They are required for the synthesis of organic substances. They are known as biogenic substances. The quantity of biogenic minerals present in the environment is called standing state or standing quantity.

3.2.2 Examples of Ecosystems

1) Terrestrial Ecosystem: e.g. Forest **(Fig. 3.1)**

Forest is the best example of terrestrial ecosystem. Forest is composed of two types of components such as abiotic and biotic components.

i) **Abiotic components:** The climatic and edaphic factors mentioned above are the abiotic components of forest ecosystem.

ii) **Biotic components:** Biotic components of forest ecosystem are classified as producers, consumers and decomposers.

   a) **Producers:** All green plants including tallest trees, under storey trees, shrubs, herbs, mosses, thalloid bryophytes, photosynthetic bacteria, algal members and lichens are the producers which photosynthesise and prepare their own food material.

   b) **Primary consumers:** Primary consumers are herbivores like grasshoppers, rabbits, deer, monkeys, birds, elephants, camels, wild goats, etc. They feed on the producers.

   c) **Secondary consumers:** Secondary consumers eat primary consumers. Wolves, jackals, pythons, etc. are the secondary consumers in forest ecosystem.

d) **Tertiary consumers:** Tertiary consumers or top order consumers in forest ecosystem are represented by lions, tigers, panthers, hawks, etc. They eat secondary consumers as well as primary consumers.

e) **Decomposers:** Microorganisms like bacteria, fungi and actinomycetes constitute the category of decomposers. They decompose dead remains of producers and consumers and convert them in to simpler inorganic compounds and elements which are added to the soil and reutilised by producers in their nutrition.

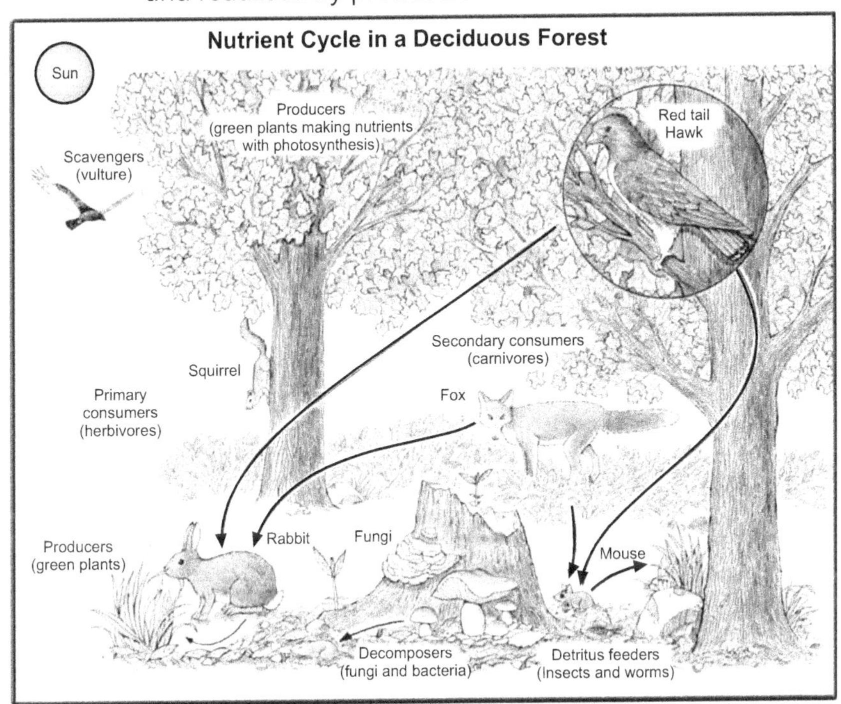

Fig. 3.1: Forest Ecosystem

2) Aquatic Ecosystem

Pond is the best example of aquatic ecosystem **(Fig. 3.2)**. It shows presence of abiotic and biotic components. They are summarised as follows:

i) **Abiotic components:** The abiotic components of aquatic ecosystem include temperature of water, light intensity received at different depths, pH of water and minerals, oxygen, carbon dioxide, nitrogen, calcium, phosphates, humic acid that are dissolved in water.

Pond Ecosystem

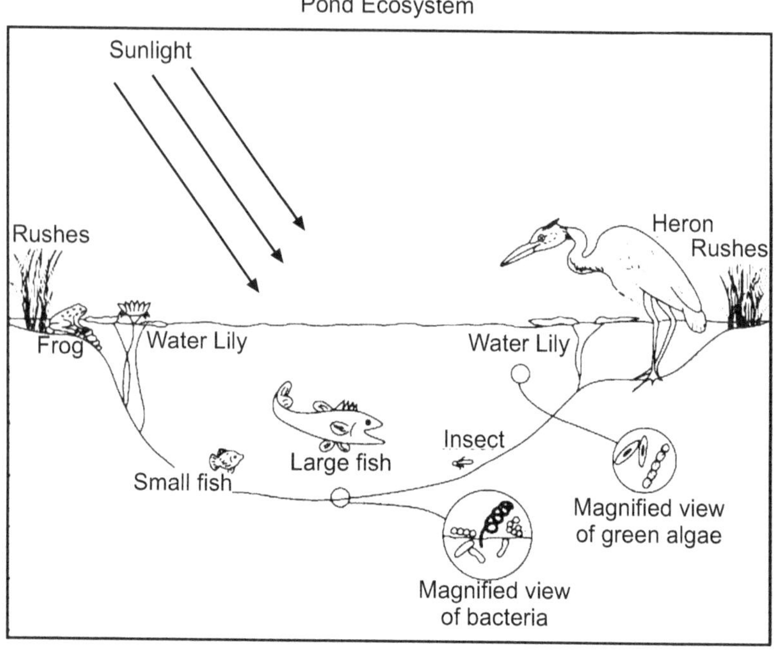

Fig. 3.2 : Aquatic Ecosystem

ii) **Biotic components:** Similar to the terrestrial ecosystem the aquatic ecosystems have different biotic components as producers, primary consumers, secondary consumers, tertiary consumers and decomposers.

a) **Producers:** The producers are autotrophic hydrophytes. They are of two types such as macrophytes and microphytes. Macrophytes include aquatic plants like *Hydrilla, Chara, Vallisneria, Ceratophyllum, Eichhornia Nymphaea* etc. and microphytes include phytoplanktons which are minute floating or suspended algal plants like *Zygnema, Ulothrix, Spirogyra, Oedogonium, Closterium, Cosmarium, Pandorina,* etc.

b) **Primary consumers:** They directly feed on producers. They include insect larvae, fishes, crustaceans, molluscs, beetles, mites as well as zooplanktons like *Brachionus, Asplanchna, Lecane, Euglena, Dileptus*, etc.

c) **Secondary consumers:** They are mainly insects and fish which are carnivorous. They eat primary consumers. The water beetles eat zooplanktons.

d) **Tertiary consumers:** The big fishes feeding on secondary consumers are termed as tertiary consumers.

iii) **Decomposers:** Decomposers are the bacteria and fungi that disintegrate dead remains of producers and consumers in to simpler components and return minerals to the water.

3.3 ECOLOGICAL PYRAMIDS, FOOD CHAINS AND FOOD WEB

3.3.1 Ecological Pyramids

According to Charles Elton (1927) ecological pyramid is nothing but graphical representation of trophic structure. The trophic structure of an ecosystem is a kind of producer-consumer arrangement where each food level is known as trophic level. The structure and function of successive trophic levels may be shown graphically by means of ecological pyramids where the first trophic level or producer level constitutes the base of the pyramid and the successive trophic levels make successive tiers making triangular structure having apex. Ecological pyramids are of three types:

(i) Pyramids of Number

(ii) Pyramids of Biomass

(iii) Pyramid of Energy

(i) **Pyramid of Number:** Pyramid of number shows the number of individual organisms at each trophic level and reveals the relationship between organisms at various trophic levels in terms of their numerical strength.

a) **Pyramid of number in grassland ecosystem:** In grassland ecosystem the pyramid of number is always upright. The producers are mainly grasses which are maximum in number. This number shows decrease towards apex. The number of primary consumers like Rabbits, Grasshoppers, etc. is lesser than the number of grasses. Secondary consumers like Lizards, Snakes are lesser in their number than primary consumers and the tertiary consumers like Hawk and Vulture are the least in number. Therefore, in this pyramid base is occupied by producers and successive tiers are occupied by primary consumers, secondary consumers and tertiary consumers respectively making the pyramid upright. **(Fig. 3.3)**

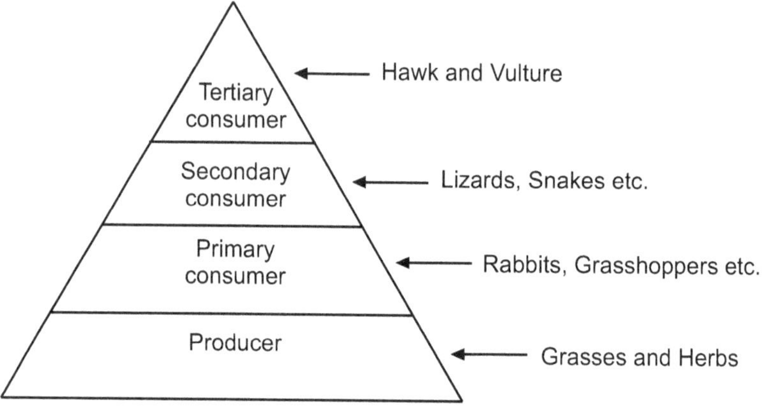

Fig. 3.3: Pyramid of Number in Grassland ecosystem

b) Pyramid of number in pond ecosystem: In pond ecosystem, the pyramid of number is upright. Here the producers which are mainly phytoplanktons (microscopic algae, bacteria) are maximum in number. The herbivores or primary consumers like small fishes, tadpole larvae of frogs, water beetles are lesser in number than producers. The secondary consumers like big fishes are lesser in number than primary consumers and the top order consumers like Turtles, bigger fishes are least in number. In this case, the base is occupied by producers and successive tiers are occupied by primary, secondary and tertiary consumers giving upright appearance of the pyramid. **(Fig. 3.4)**

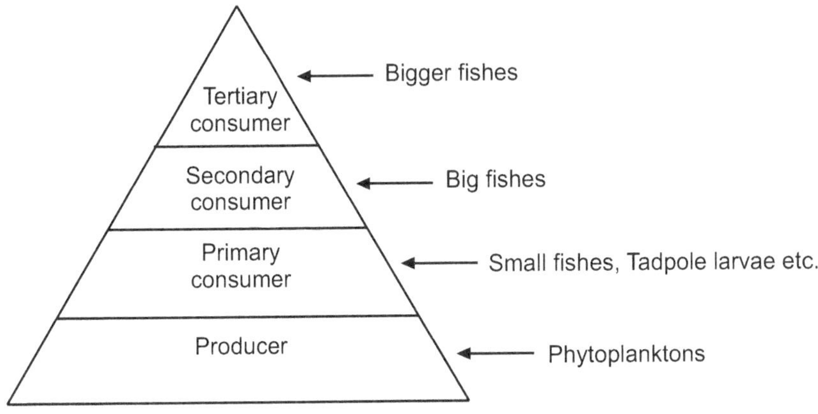

Fig. 3.4: Pyramid of Number in Pond Ecosystem

c) **Pyramid of number in forest ecosystem:** In forest ecosystem the pyramid of number is like arrowhead. Producers which are mainly large sized trees are lesser in number than primary consumers or herbivores like fruit eating birds, elephant, deer etc. and form the narrow base of the pyramid. Then there is gradual decrease in number of secondary consumers like wolf, fox and tertiary consumers like lion, tiger, etc. making the pyramid again upright. Thus making the pyramid arrow headed **(Fig. 3.5)**.

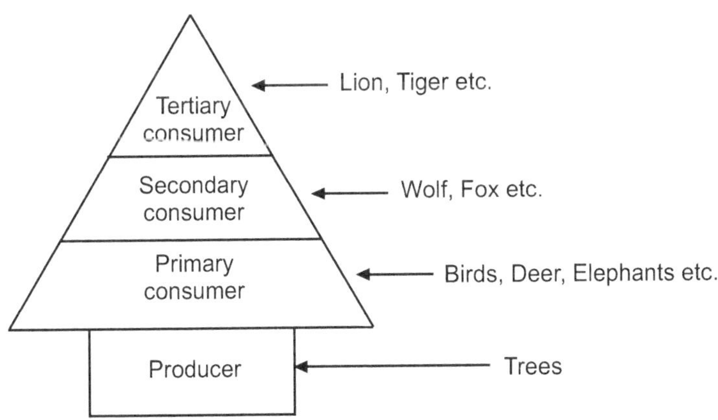

Fig. 3.5: Pyramid of Number in Forest Ecosystem

d) **Pyramid of number in parasitic food chain:** In parasitic food chain, the pyramid of number is always inverted. This is due to the fact that a single plant may support the life of many herbivores (fruit eating birds). Each herbivore (bird) may provide nutrition to several parasites (lice and bugs). Parasites support many hyperparasites (fungi, bacteria, actinomycetes members). Thus from producers towards consumers there is a reverse position i. e. number of organisms show gradual increase making the pyramid inverted in shape. **(Fig. 3.6)**

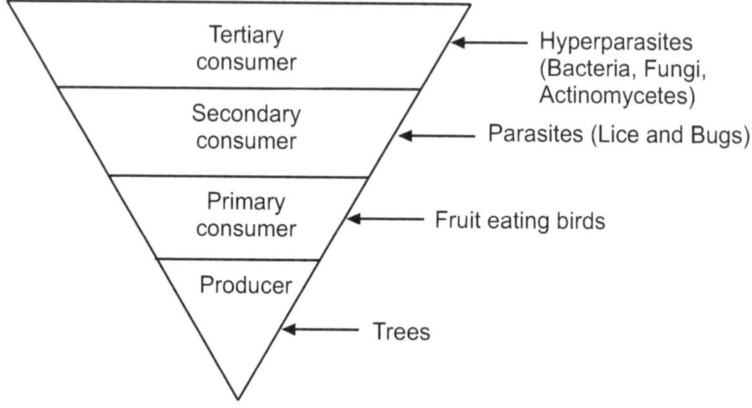

Fig. 3.6: Pyramid of Number in Parasitic Food Chain

(ii) **Pyramid of Biomass:** Pyramid of biomass shows a quantitative relationship of standing crop.

a) **Pyramid of biomass in grassland ecosystem:** In grassland ecosystem, the biomass of producers like grasses, shrubs is always more than primary consumers which are herbivores like insects, grasshoppers, rabbits etc. The biomass of secondary consumers is lesser than the biomass of primary consumers and the biomass of the tertiary consumer is always lesser than the biomass of secondary consumer. As there is a gradual decrease in biomass of successive trophic level, the pyramid becomes upright. (Fig. 3.7)

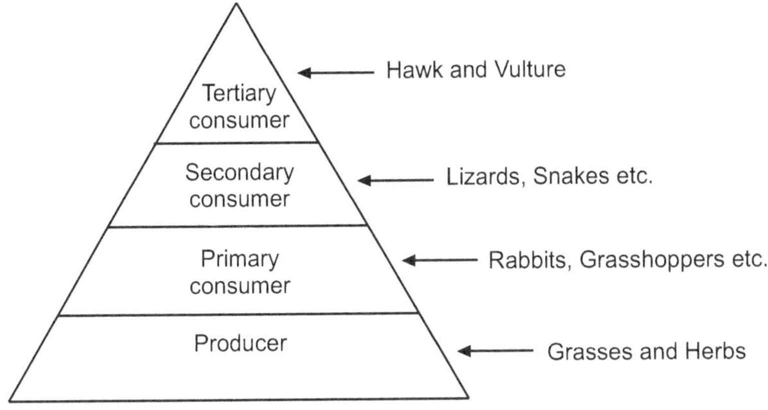

Fig. 3.7: Pyramid of Biomass in Grassland Ecosystem

b) **Pyramid of biomass in forest ecosystem:** In forest ecosystem, the base of the pyramid is occupied by producers especially large sized trees as their biomass is more than the biomass of primary consumers. The primary consumers are herbivorous animals like Rabbit, Elephant, Goat, Sheep, Deer etc. The biomass of secondary consumers like Snake, Lizards, Wolf, Fox is lesser than the biomass of primary consumers. The biomass of tertiary consumers like Lion and Tiger is lesser than the biomass of secondary consumers. In this way, there is gradual decline in biomass of organism in successive tiers (trophic levels) making the pyramid upright. **(Fig. 3.8)**

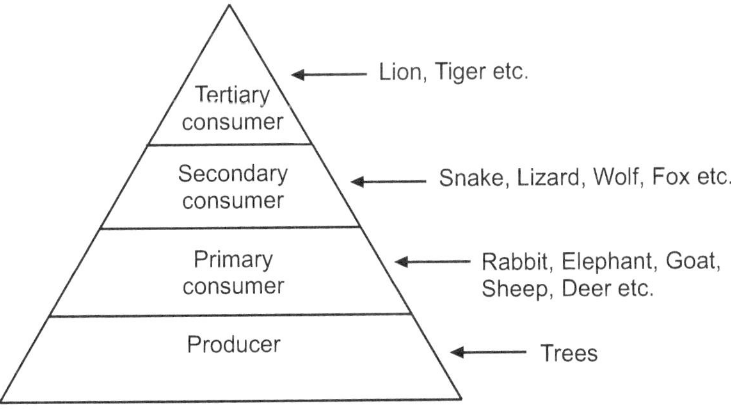

Fig. 3.8: Pyramid of Biomass in Forest Ecosystem

c) **Pyramid of biomass in aquatic ecosystem:** In aquatic ecosystem, producers are microscopic algal members and the top consumers are bigger fishes. In this ecosystem, the biomass of producer is least and the biomass of tertiary consumers is maximum. As there is gradual increase in biomass of organisms at the successive trophic level pyramid of biomass becomes inverted. **(Fig. 3.9)**

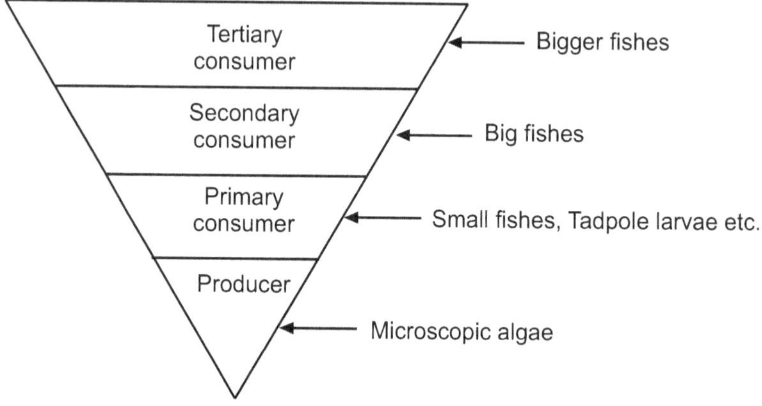

Fig. 3.9: Pyramid of Biomass in Aquatic Ecosystem

(iii) Pyramid of Energy: The food chain illustrates the direction of energy flow but not amount and rate of energy flow from one trophic level to other trophic level. This is represented by energy pyramid. The energy pyramid is a graphic representation of the trophic structure and the amount of flow of energy at successive trophic levels during the particular period in the ecosystem. In energy pyramid, the producers form the base and each successive tier is occupied by different consumers. Each step in the pyramid represents the trophic level and width of each step represents the amount of energy available at that trophic level. Generally, the amount of energy that is available to successive trophic level from its preceding one is 10% because the consumers at each step utilise some amount of energy and some energy is lost in the form of heat. There is always gradual decrease in the energy content of successive trophic level from producers to top order consumers. Therefore, the energy pyramid is always upright. **(Fig. 3.10)**

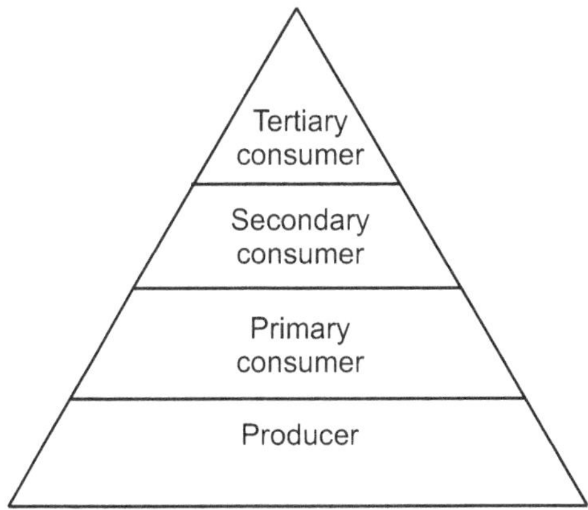

Fig. 3.10: Pyramid of Energy

Energy pyramid reveals the following facts:

- Energy pyramid is always upright.
- The base of the pyramid is always represented by producers.
- Greater amount of energy is available at producer level than at other trophic levels.
- At each trophic level from base to the apex energy goes on reducing.
- Lesser the number of trophic levels more is the energy available to top order carnivores.

3.3.2 Food Chains

In ecosystem, one organism feeds on the other. The food energy passes from one organism to the other. Energy passes from producers to top level consumers through various trophic levels. The sequential arrangement of various organisms through which energy passes is known as food chain. For example, insects feed on plants, insects are eaten by frogs, frogs are eaten by snakes and snakes are eaten by hawks. This eating and being eaten sequence can be represented in the form of chain, called as food chain which is represented as follows:

Grass → Insects → Frogs → Snakes → Hawks

Ecosystem contains number of such food chains. Each food chain starts with producers and ends in the top order consumers. Basically, there are two types of food chains such as:

1. Consumers food chain (Grazing food chain) and
2. Detritus food chain (Decomposers food chain).

1. Grazing or Consumers food chain: It starts from green autotrophs and ends in top level carnivores. The ecosystems having grazing food chains are directly dependent upon influx of solar energy in the form of solar radiations. Thus, this type of food chain depends on the harvesting of solar energy by autotrophs and movement of this acquired energy to herbivores and carnivores. Most of the ecosystems in nature have this type of food chain. The food chain of grassland ecosystem can be represented as follows:

Grass → Insects → Frogs → Snakes → Hawks

The marine food chain can be represented as follows:

Phytoplanktons → Zooplanktons → Crustaceans → Small fishes → Large fishes → Killer fishes

2. Detritus or Decomposers food chain: This type of food chain starts with dead organic matter and goes into microorganisms and then to organisms feeding on detritus (detritivores) and their predators. These ecosystems are practically independent of solar energy and are depend chiefly on the influx of organic matter produced in other ecosystems. 'Odum' (1970) has described detritus food chain based on mangrove leaves in the brackish zone of Southern Korea. Leaves of red mangrove (*Rhizophora mangle)* fall into the warm shallow water. The fallen leaves are acted upon by microbes like fungi, bacteria, protozoa etc. and colonised by phytoplanktonic algae. The leaf fragments are eaten and re-eaten by small animals like crabs, insect larvae, nematodes etc. All these animals are detritus consumers. These small animals are eaten by small fishes. The small fishes serve as the main food of large fishes which are top order consumers.

Detritus (Dead organic matter of plant and animal origin) → Microorganisms (Fungi, bacteria, protozoa) → Detritivores (Crab, Earthworms), Small fishes → Large fishes

All the food chains end with decomposers like bacteria, fungi, protozoa etc. They play an important role in ecosystem because they carry on the following function:

1. They decompose and dispose dead bodies of plants and animals and thus act as scavengers of nature.
2. They help in the formation of humus resulting from decomposition of plant and animal tissue.
3. They help in releasing and recycling of metabolites i.e. they help to maintain biogeochemical cycle.

3.3.3 Food Web (Interlinking pattern of organisms)

In any ecosystem food chains never operate as isolated sequences but are interlinked with each other forming some interlocking pattern which is referred to as food web (Fig. 3.11). Under natural conditions linear arrangement of food chain hardly occur and these remain interconnected with each other at a different tropical level. For example, in grazing food chain of grass land in absence of rabbit grass may be eaten by insects which are then eaten by frogs, frogs by snakes and snakes by hawk. Thus in nature, there are alternatives which all together constitute some sort of interlocking pattern termed as food web. In such a food web of grass land, there may be seen as many as five linear food chains which in sequence are as follow:

i) Grass → Grasshopper → Hawk

ii) Grass → Grasshopper → Lizard → Hawk

iii) Grass → Rabbits → Hawk

iv) Grass → Mouse → Hawk

v) Grass → Mouse → Snake → Hawk

The inter-inking pattern of these five food chains forms a food web which is shown as follows:

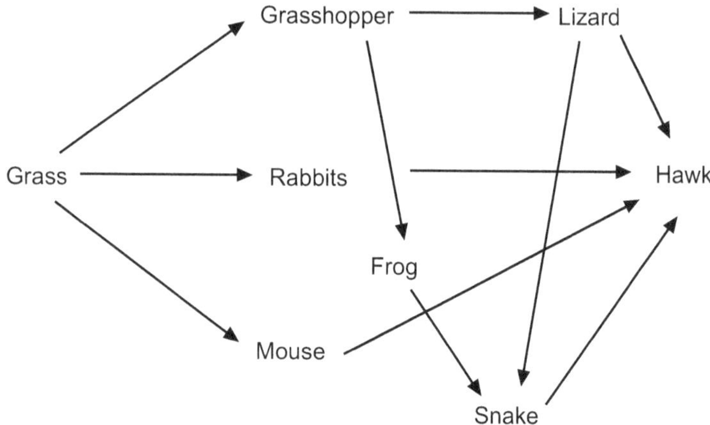

Fig. 3.11: Food Web

Significance of food web

In food web the number of alternative food pathways is open to the organisms at each trophic level. For example, Hawk may feed on snake/mouse/rabbit/grass hopper/lizard, etc depending on whatever is available. The food web thus ensures the food of one or other kinds to all organisms in the ecosystem. The food web maintains stability and balance of an ecosystem.

3.4 ENERGY FLOW IN ECOSYSTEM

An ecosystem is a closely integrated unit of organisms and their biotic and abiotic environment. The existence of all the living organisms in ecosystem depends on two things:

(i) Energy and (ii) Metabolites

Flow of energy is unidirectional, therefore not available for recycling while metabolites run in cyclic manner, hence are non-exhaustible.

Ecosystem starts operating with the influx of radiant energy of sun. Only 14% of the total output of sun's energy reaches the surface of the earth about 1-5% of solar energy is trapped by the green plants during photosynthesis where it is converted into chemical form of energy. It is radiant energy of sun that keeps the wheels of the life turning. Energy flow is the transfer of energy from organism to organism. It starts from green plants which traps solar energy during photosynthesis. Therefore, green plants are called energy fixers or producers. They provide energy directly or indirectly to all life forms, therefore it is said that "All flesh is grass".

The plants are eaten by herbivores (Primary consumers) and thus the food energy is transferred from producers to primary consumers. The primary consumers are eaten by secondary consumers. Thus, along with food the energy is transferred from primary consumers to secondary consumers. Then the secondary consumers are eaten by tertiary consumers. In this way, the food energy ultimately reaches to the top order consumers.

The successive stages of organisms like producers, primary consumers, secondary consumers and tertiary consumers through which food energy passes in an ecosystem, constitutes different trophic levels. At each trophic level energy goes on decreasing because some energy is utilised by organisms at least tropic level and considerable amount of energy is lost in the form of heat. Since, there is a leakage in flow of energy at each trophic level the energy goes on reducing and ultimately is lost to the surroundings, hence is not available for recycling. **(Fig. 3.12)**

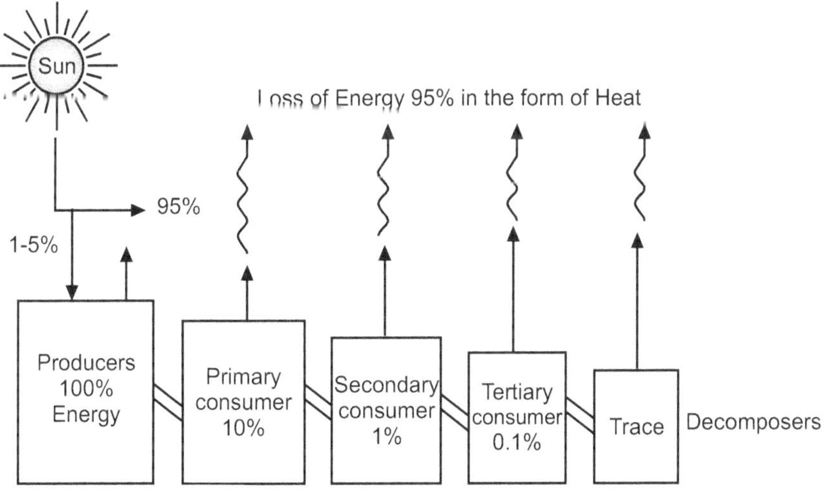

Fig. 3.12: Energy Flow in Ecosystem

Salient features of energy flow in ecosystem

- There is a transfer of food energy from organism to organism.
- It starts with producers which acquire solar energy and ends with the top order consumers. At each trophic level energy goes on decreasing.
- The energy flow is unidirectional.
- Energy flow is constantly replenished from outside in the form of solar radiation.

Productivity of an Ecosystem

Green plants absorb solar radiations and convert solar energy to chemical form of energy. This energy is mainly stored in photosynthates especially in carbohydrates. The amount of dry matter accumulated within a specific time period is called production while the total amount of dry matter present in ecosystem at any given time per unit area is known as standing crop or biomass. Productivity of an ecosystem refers to the rate of production of organic matter by plant tissues. Productivity of an ecosystem is studied under different heads such as Primary productivity, Secondary productivity and Net productivity.

1) Primary productivity: Autotrophs or producers including green plants, chemosynthetic and photosynthetic bacteria accumulate solar energy in the form of chemical bonds of organic compounds. This accumulation of energy by producers is known as Primary production and the rate at which the radiant energy of sun is stored by producers in the form of organic matter is called Primary productivity. Primary productivity is differentiated as Gross Primary Productivity (GPP) and Net Primary Productivity (NPP).

Gross Primary Productivity (GPP): It refers to the total rate of photosynthesis including the organic molecules consumed during respiration at the time of measurement period. The Gross primary productivity depends on the chlorophyll content of photosynthetic tissues. The rate of Gross primary productivity is expressed in terms of chlorophyll content as Chl/g dry weight/unit area or in terms of photosynthetic number (amount of CO_2 fixed/g Chl/hour).

Net Primary Productivity (NPP): The plants require energy for various cellular processes which is obtained by oxidation of organic matter accumulated during photosynthesis in respiration. Hence the plants synthesise excess amount of organic matter. The rate of accumulation of organic matter in plant tissues in excess of respiratory consumption by the producers is known as Net Primary Productivity. NPP is the rate of increase of biomass. It is expressed as the amount of carbon fixed per unit area per unit time excluding the losses due to respiration and deaths of individual plants. Therefore, NPP is expressed as follows:

NPP = GPP – (Losses due to respiration + Losses due to death)

NPP = Mass of Carbon fixed/Unit area/Unit time

2) Secondary Productivity: It refers to the productivity of consumers or heterotrophs. It is the rate at which energy is stored at consumer level.

3) Net Productivity: It is the rate of storage of organic matter not used by consumers. Net productivity is generally expressed as production of $Cg/m^2/day$.

3.5 BIOGEOCHEMICAL CYCLES

The term biogeochemical cycle refers to the cycling of the chemical compounds like nitrogen, oxygen, carbon, phosphorus, etc. through biotic (Producers, Consumers, Decomposers) and abiotic (Lithosphere, Atmosphere, Hydrosphere) components of the ecosystem. In nature, there are three types of biogeochemical cycles such as hydrologic cycle (water cycle), gaseous cycles and sedimentary cycles. Nitrogen, Oxygen and Carbon cycles are gaseous cycles.

3.5.1 Nitrogen Cycle

Of all the elements which plants absorb from the soil, nitrogen is the most important for plant growth because it is required for the synthesis of amino acids, proteins, nucleic acids (RNA and DNA), energy rich molecules ATP and $NADPH_2$ and chlorophyll molecules. This is required in greatest quantity. Atmosphere contains 78% nitrogen. However, plants or animals can not use this inert molecular nitrogen. Green plants obtain nitrogen from the soil in the form of ammonium or nitrates or nitrite ions. The most important source of nitrogen for green plants is nitrogen that is fixed by nitrogen fixing bacteria. Some of the nitrogen fixing bacteria (*Rhizobium*) inhabit the root nodules of leguminous and some other plants (Actinomycetes in Alder plant) and some others are found free in the soil (*Clostridium, Azotobacter*).

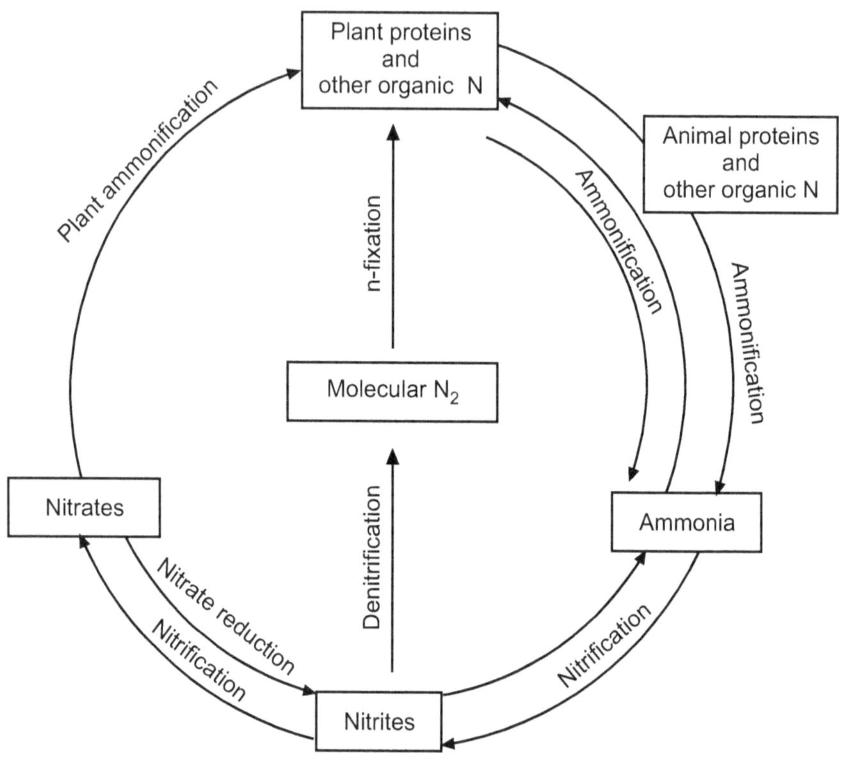

Fig. 3.13: Nitrogen Cycle

Nitrogen is directly taken from the air by nitrogen fixing root nodule bacteria (Rhizobia) or by free living aerobic bacteria (*Azotobacter*) or by anaerobic soil bacteria (*Clostridium*). These bacteria make nitrogen available to the plants for their growth. Some blue green algal members like *Nostoc, Oscillatoria, Anabaena* etc. also fix atmospheric nitrogen. After absorption of nitrogen in the form of nitrate by the plants, it has to be reduced to ammonia before being used in amino acids and protein synthesis. The breakdown of dead tissues by decaying bacteria releases the ammonia from proteins and other nitrogenous compounds. *Nitrosomonas* bacteria oxidise ammonia into nitrites and *Nitrobacter* oxidises nitrite to nitrate. This conversion of ammonia to nitrate is called nitrification. Denitrifying bacteria convert ammonia in to free nitrogen and release nitrogen to atmosphere by the process of denitrification. In this way, the nitrogen is cycled in the ecosystem. **(Fig. 3.13)**

3.5.2 Oxygen Cycle

Oxygen cycle is a gaseous cycle which describes the translocation of oxygen within three main reservoirs such as atmosphere (air), the total biological matter existing on earth surface and the lithosphere. Oxygen is found in free state in atmosphere and in dissolved state in water. The atmosphere contains 21% oxygen. It is liberated as by-product of photosynthesis hence photosynthesis is considered as chief driving factor of oxygen cycle. Oxygen is also added to the atmosphere after photolysis of atmospheric water molecules and nitrous oxide by the high energy ultraviolet rays. The UV radiations split water (H_2O) molecules in to H and O_2 and nitrous oxide (N_2O) molecules in to N and O_2.

i) $2H_2O \xrightarrow{\text{UV-Radiations}} 4H + O_2$

ii) $2N_2O \xrightarrow{\text{UV-Radiations}} 4N + O_2$

Thus, atmospheric oxygen is replenished by light reactions of photosynthesis occurring in green plants and photolytic breakdown of atmospheric water and nitrous oxide molecules by UV-radiations.

The plants, animals and microbes consume atmospheric oxygen for respiration. In respiration, oxidative break down of carbohydrates takes place which results in the liberation of energy and molecules of carbon dioxide (CO_2) and water (H_2O).

$$C_6H_{12}O_6 \xrightarrow{\text{Respiration}} 6CO_2 + 6H_2O + \text{Energy}$$

The lithosphere also utilises atmospheric oxygen for chemical weathering and surface reactions. Formation of iron oxides is an example of chemical weathering.

$$4FeO + O_2 \xrightarrow{\text{Chemical weathering}} 2Fe_2O_3$$

Oxygen is also cycled between lithosphere and biosphere. Marine organisms form shells of calcium carbonates ($CaCO_3$). After the death of marine organisms these shells get deposited on shallow sea floor and are converted to the lime stone sedimentary rocks of lithosphere. Weathering process initiated by organisms makes the oxygen free from lithosphere and adds it to the oxygen pool of atmosphere. In this way a simple yet vital O_2 cycle is maintained in the ecosystem. **(Fig. 3.14)**

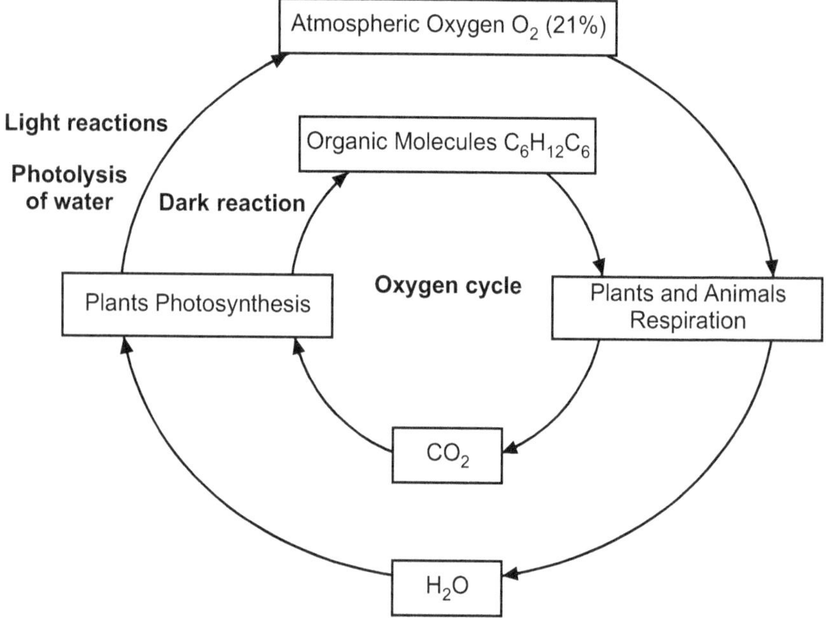

Fig. 3.14: Oxygen Cycle

3.5.3 Carbon Cycle

Carbon is the basic building block of all organic compounds found in living organisms. Atmosphere contains carbon in the form of carbon dioxide (CO_2). About 0.03% part of atmosphere is constituted by CO_2. Water also contains carbon in the form of dissolved carbon dioxide. Autotrophs or producers use carbon dioxide to perform photosynthesis and convert carbon dioxide into carbohydrates, carbohydrates provide carbon skeleton for the synthesis of other macromolecules like proteins and lipids. Primary consumers or herbivores eat plants and primary consumers are eaten by secondary and tertiary consumers and thus carbon from plant body enters in to the animal body. Both plants and animals respire. In respiration, oxygen enters in to the plant and animal body and carbon dioxide is released to the atmosphere. Decomposers (Bacteria and fungi) disintegrate dead remains of plants, animals and animal waste. During decomposition carbon dioxide is liberated which is added to the carbon dioxide pool of atmosphere. Undecomposed organic matter of plant and animal origin gets incorporated into the

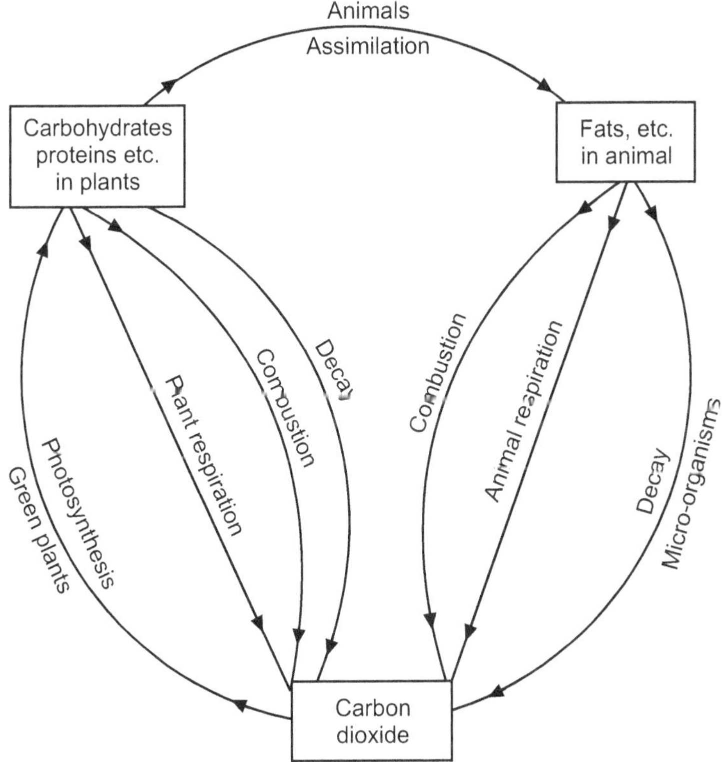

Fig. 3.15: Carbon Cycle

earth's crust as coal, gas, petroleum, limestone and coral reef. Carbon from such deposits may be liberated after a long period of time. The fossil fuels like oil, petroleum are used to run auto-vehicles, after burning of such fossil fuels carbon in the form of carbon dioxide is released to the atmosphere. In this way carbon cycle is maintained in the nature. **(Fig. 3.15)**

EXERCISE

I. Multiple Choice Questions

1. The term 'ecosystem' was coined by British ecologist-------
   a) A. G. Tansley b) O.P. Odum
   c) P.D.Sharma d) T.N.Khoshoo
2. Primary consumers are ---------
   a) Herbivores b) Carnivores
   c) Omnivores d) None of these
3. In forest ecosystem the pyramid of number is---------
   a) Inverted b) Arrow headed
   c) Upright d) All of these
4. In ecosystem energy flow is ------
   a) Scattered b) Unidirectional
   c) Bidirectional d) Cyclic
5. Atmosphere contains ----- carbon dioxide
   a) 0.03% b) 0.3%
   c) 3% d) 30%
6. ------- is the rate of storage of organic matter by producers not used by consumers.
   a) Net productivity b) Primary productivity
   c) Gross productivity d) Secondary productivity
7. The atmosphere contains ------ oxygen.
   a) 21% b) 20%
   c) 23% d) 26%

ANSWERS

1-a; 2-a; 3-b; 4-b; 5-a; 6-a; 7-a

II. Two Marks Questions

1. Enlist biotic components of an ecosystem.
2. What is food chain? Write an outline of any grazing food chain you have studied
3. What is ecological pyramid? Draw sketch of pyramid of number in forest ecosystem
4. Write an outline of Oxygen or Carbon or Nitrogen cycle
5. Write in brief about primary productivity or secondary productivity
6. Write any three salient features of energy flow in ecosystem

III. Four Marks Questions

1. Write the salient features of energy flow in ecosystem
2. What is food chain? Comment on the detritus food chain
3. What is food chain? Comment on the grazing food chain
4. What is food web? Explain the food web in any ecosystem you have studied
5. Define ecosystem and comment on the classification of aquatic ecosystems
6. Discuss the pyramid of energy in any ecosystem
7. Discuss the pyramid of number in forest ecosystem

IV. Five Marks Questions

1. Give a brief account of biotic components of any ecosystem you have studied
2. What is ecological pyramid? Discuss in brief pyramid of biomass in aquatic ecosystem.
3. What is ecological pyramid? Discuss in brief pyramid of number in parasitic food chain
4. Give a brief account of Carbon or Nitrogen or Oxygen cycle

V. Seven marks Questions

1. What is ecosystem? Enlist biotic and abiotic components of an ecosystem and comment on any two biotic and any one abiotic components of ecosystem
2. Comment on the productivity of an ecosystem
3. Discuss in detail about the energy flow in ecosystem

4

CHAPTER

ECOLOGICAL SUCCESSION

4.1 CONCEPT AND PROCESS

4.1.1 Concept

Plant communities are not stable but dynamic. They keep changing more or less regularly over time and space. One community is constantly replaced by other community. Gradual replacement of one type of plant community by other is known as "**Plant succession**". The sequence and direction of change is generally from simple to complex. This process continues till a stable community gets established. The succession is defined as "the occurrence of relatively definite sequence of communities over a period of time in the same area". It is also described as "the gradual replacement of one type of plant community by the other". Halt (1885) used for the first time, the term succession for the orderly changes in communities. Clements (1916) defined succession as "the natural process by which the same locality becomes successively colonised by different groups of communities".

4.1.2 Process

Succession is a series of processes. It is completed through a number of sequential steps *viz.*: (I) Nudation, (II) Invasion, (III) Competition and coaction (IV) Reaction and (V) Stabilisation.

I. **Nudation:** It is the formation of bare area. The causes of nudation may be

   (i) Topographic factors: These include erosion, deposition of sand, land slides, volcano, etc.

   (ii) Climatic: Glaciers, storm, frost, fire, etc. may destroy vegetation.

(iii) Biotic: Disease and pest attack, destruction of forests, grass lands for industry, housing, and roads.

II. Invasion (Entry): This refers to entry of new organisms and formation of community. It is completed by:

(i) Migration: Seeds, spores, propagules enter the new area by winds, water, animals, etc.

(ii) Ecesis (establishment): The new migrants adjust with new climate and establishment occurs. This is known as ecesis.

(iii) Aggregation: The increase in number of individuals by colonisation and reproduction is known as aggregation.

III. Competition and Co-action: Due to aggregation, competition starts between the species or within the species (Inter or Intra) for space, light, food, etc. In competition those which can adjust will survive and increase in population. The weaker ones will gradually disappear. Individual species affect each other's life in various ways. This is called co-action.

IV. Reaction: It is the mechanism of modification of the environment through the effect of living organism on it. As a result of reactions, changes take place in soil, water, light conditions, temperature of the environment. These changes become unfit for the existing community which sooner or later is replaced by another community.

V. Stabilisation: Due to 'reaction' the climate changes, it becomes less favourable for the existing and more favourable for new invaders. The old ones are replaced by new. As plant succession progresses the animals in the community also change. In this way gradual evolution takes place and finally a stable or permanent community is formed. Such a condition is called stabilisation. The stabilised community is called climax community of ecological succession. Community and climate are in complete harmony.

4.2 PRIMARY AND SECONDARY SUCCESSION

Succession is the concept that communities proceed through a predictable, step-by-step process of change over time. Through the process of succession, the original species colonising a site may be replaced completely or they simply become less numerous as different species emerge. For the development of succession bare area is necessary. Depending upon the nature of bare area the succession is divided into two types.

(i) Primary succession: The succession which starts on a bare area and one that was not occupied previously by any vegetation is called primary succession, e.g. rock, sand dune or lake. In primary succession the growth of an ecosystem takes place gradually over a long period of time. The example of primary succession may be a new land formed after volcanic eruption and cooling of lava. This new land will be barren without any living organism. But after some time, simple plants will begin to colonise the new land. The plants that are first to grow and aggregate are called 'Pioneers', primary community or primary colonisers. Typical pioneer species may be lichens, algae, and fungi. These plant species carry out their life processes, they produce waste and some die. This leads to the formation of the organic material that will become soil. After the formation of soil on the top of cooled lava, these simple organisms interact with the environment and make it suitable for the later introduction of more complex species, like vascular plants including herbs, shrubs and trees.

(ii) Secondary succession: Secondary succession begins on an area, which was previously occupied by well developed communities. The communities might have been lost due to fire, cyclone, land slide, drought, flood, etc. The area is usually rich in nutrients hence secondary succession is faster and takes place in shorter period. For example, revival of a forest after a fire, the forest fire destroys different plant species that are growing in the forest. However their seeds, underground organs like bulbs, tubers etc, some aerial shoots and roots remain in and on the soil. After receiving rain showers gradually the plants and trees begin to grow again and eventually return to the state of the original ecosystem.

4.3 HYDROSERE AND XEROSERE

4.3.1 Hydrosere

Succession beginning in aquatic environments like ponds, lakes etc. is called hydrarch succession. The different stages of hydrarch succession are called hydroseres. The various stages of hydroseres are as follows:

1. Phytoplankton Stage

In the hydrarch succession phytoplanktons and zooplanktons are the pioneer colonisers. Blue green algae, green algae, diatoms and bacteria are the first organisms to colonise. All these organisms add large amount of organic matter after their death. This matter settles at the bottom of pond and forms organic manure. These phytoplanktons occur at a depth of 20 to 10 feet water.

2. Submerged Stage

The phytoplankton stage is followed by submerged stage. Due to sedimentation, the soil settles at the bottom of the pond and organic matter is added to this soil. As a result the soil level increases and water depth decreases. This condition, replaces phytoplanktons by submerged hydrophytes like *Chara, Vallisneria, Elodia, Hydrilla, Potamogeton,* etc. The submerged hydrophytes form a tangled mass and have marked effects upon the habitat. When these plants die their remains add at the bottom of the ponds and form fertile soil. This process makes the pond shallow and becomes unfit for the survival of submerged plants.

3. Floating Stage

Decreased water level and the accumulation of sediments, dead organic matter leads to the appearance of fixed floating hydrophytes like Lotus, *Nelumbo*, *Trapa,* etc. as well as some free floating hydrophytes like *Azolla*, *Eichhornia*, *Pistia,* etc.

The sedimentation of soil particles and deposition of organic matter further continues and pond becomes shallow. This habitat is unfit for floating plants and they disappear. This area is now fit for the growth of reed swamp plants.

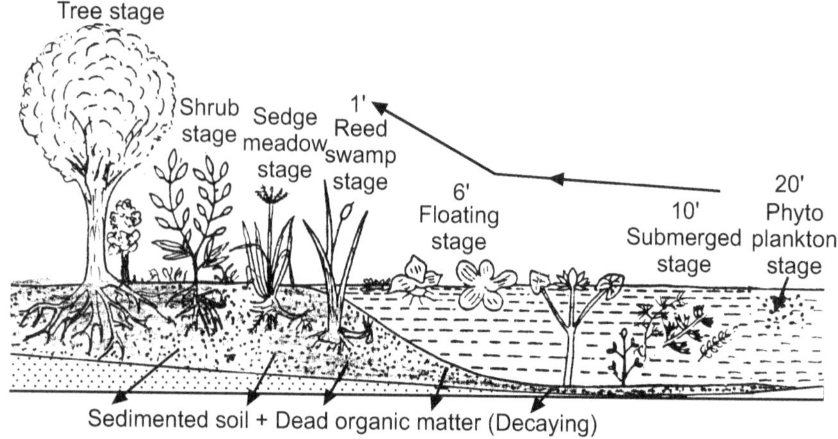

Fig. 4.1: Hydrarch succession showing hydroseres

4. Reed Swamp Stage

The amphibious plants like *Typha, Sagittaria* occupy and become dominant by replacing floating plants. These plants have well developed rhizomes and form dense vegetation. This vegetation makes the area still shallower due to high transpiration, evaporation, sedimentation and deposition of organic matter. The habitat is consequently made unfit for the reed swamp plants and becomes more suitable for marshy plants. The animals like water scorpion, beetles, ducks, kingfishers, etc. now start appearing.

5. Sedge Meadow Stage or Marsh Meadow Stage

Due to the action of reed-swamp plants, deposition of organic matter and sedimentation of soil leads to the loss of reed swamp plants and invasion of sedges like *Juncus, Carex, Polygonum, Cyperus,* Grasses, etc. They aggregate and establish. These plants again react upon the habitat. They transpire enormously as a result the water in the soil becomes less. Marsh-meadow plants can not survive in such dry soil. These are gradually replaced by shrubs and later by trees.

6. Wood-land Stage

Due to the disappearance of marshy vegetation the area is invaded by terrestrial shrubs and trees and wood-land stage is developed. Some medium sized trees like *Cassia, Populus, Terminalia* appear and form wood lands. These plants produce more shade, thus shade loving herb and shrub plants invade. The humus content in the soil increases with rich flora of micro organisms. In this fertile soil, herbs, shrubs, trees, climbers, etc. will start invading and establishing.

7. Forest Stage

This is the climax community. It is represented by all types of plants. The area is completely covered by herbs, shrubs, trees and climbers. Innumerable animals, like herbivorous, carnivorous, will invade and form climatic climax.

In tropical climates with heavy rainfall tropical evergreen forest develops, whereas in temperate regions temperate forests develop. In tropical moderate rainfall area tropical deciduous forests are formed.

4.3.2 Xerosere

Succession beginning in dry conditions is called xerarch succession. The different stages of xerarch succession are known as xeroseres. Here, crustose lichens are the pioneers. The series of successive changes finally form climax forests.

1. Crustose Lichen Stage

Crustose-lichens are the pioneers of xerarch succession. These grow on bare-rocks. They tolerate extreme deficiency of water, nutrients, high light intensity and high temperature. The spores, soredia or fragments of these lichens migrate to rocks through air. These lichens obtain minerals from rock by secretion of carbonic acid. It dissolves rock surface and loosens the rock particles. These particles with decaying lichen thalli form the first thin layer of soil on rock surface.

The crustose lichens like *Rhizocarpon*, *Rinodina*, *Laconora*, etc. grow on rocks. These crustose lichens are gradually replaced by foliose lichens, when some amount of soil forms on the rock surface.

2. Foliose lichen Stage

Foliose lichens develop on the rock partially covered by soil particles and crustose lichen. Foliose lichens like *Parmelia*, *Dermatocorpon* completely cover crustose lichens. As a result light is out off to crustose lichens which leads to the death and decay of crustose lichens. Thus organic matter is added to the soil. The foliose lichens secrete acid which causes disintegration of rock and formation of fertile soil. The water holding capacity of soil also increases due to the addition of humus (organic matter). Such area is unfit for foliose lichen and conducive for mosses.

3. Moss Stage

Mosses like *Polytrichum, Funaria, Bryum,* etc. invade humus-rich soil where foliose lichens are growing. The mosses compete with foliose lichen and they are completely replaced by moss. The mosses form a thick mat, their rhizoids secrete acid and help in the rapid degradation of rock. The addition of dead matter increases humus in the soil. This leads to the formation of fertile soil with more water holding capacity. This habitat later becomes unfit for the mosses and fit for herbaceous plants.

4. Herb Stage

The seeds of xerophytic plants like grasses brought by wind or birds germinate and grow with mosses. Later the mosses die due to the shade resulting from the growth of herbs. Thus, herbs dominate. The disintegration of rock and formation of soil further increases. As a result rich soil with many micro-organisms favours the entry of shrub plants.

5. Shrub Stage

The changed habitat and climatic conditions lead to the invasion and establishment of shrubs. This further enhances the soil formation due to disintegration of rock. Humus also increases due to the addition of dead herbs and parts of shrubs. The climate becomes cooler and soil becomes more fertile. Such climate is fit for xerophytic trees.

6. Forest Stage

In this stage some xerophytic trees invade. The increasing soil formation, humus content, cool climate favour the invasion and establishment more trees. The mesophytic plants completely occupy and develop the forest. Below the big trees, shade loving small trees and shrubs grow and replace the previous xeric plants. The forest floor is covered by some bryophytes, ferns, shade loving herbs, shrubs, climbers, epiphytes, etc. Thus finally climax community establishes.

7. Climatic Climax

In the succession, the competition starts among different group of plants. Only those species which adjust to the environment will survive and multiply. The plants interact with the habitat and modify the environment. Once illuminated areas become shaded and dry area becomes moist. Thus changed climate becomes less favourable for the existing species and fit for the invaders. Old vegetation is replaced by the new one. Gradual changes occur and finally a stable community establishes and reaches climax. Here, no further changes occur. This stable community is called climax community and the existing climate is said to be attended climatic climax.

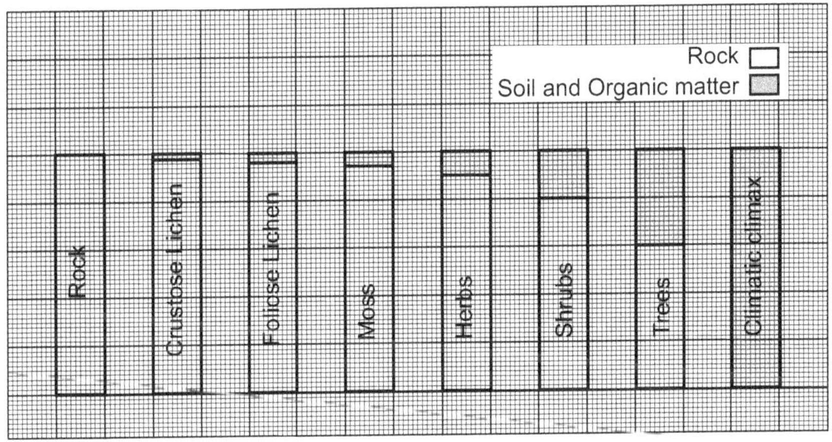

Fig. 4.2: The different stages of xerarch succession

EXERCISE

I. Multiple Choice Questions

1. Gradual replacement of one type of community by other is called -------
   a) Succession
   b) Nudation
   c) Formation
   d) Stabilisation

2. ------ is the formation of bare area.
   a) Nudation b) Reaction
   c) Invasion d) Stabilisation
3. Hydrarch succession begins ---------
   a) On rocks b) In water
   c) On Soil d) On sand
4. ------ is the pioneer stage of xerarch succession
   a) Crustose lichen b) Foliose lichen
   c) Shrub stage d) Moss stage
5. ------ is the pioneer stage of hydrarch succession
   a) Phytoplanktons b) Reed swamp
   c) Woodland d) Moss stage

ANSWERS

1-a; 2-a; 3-b; 4-a; 5-a

II. Two Marks Questions

1. What is plant succession? Give an outline of possible trend of succession in aquatic environment/xeric environment
2. What is plant succession? Comment on Primary succession or Secondary succession
3. What is plant succession? Enlist sequential steps that occur in the process of succession.

III. Four Marks Questions

1. Comment on primary and secondary succession
2. What are the causes of nudation?
3. Discuss the first two stages of xerosere
4. Comment on phytoplankton and submerged stage of hydrosere

IV. Five Marks Questions

1. What is succession? Discuss nudation and invasion in brief
2. What is xerosere? Comment on crustose lichen and foliose lichen stage of xerosere

3. What is hydrosere? Discuss the phytoplankton and submerged stage of hydrosere

V. Seven Marks Questions

1. What is plant succession? Describe various stages of hydrosere ?
2. What is plant succession? Describe various stages of xerosere ?
3. Write an account of process of plant succession.

5

CHAPTER

ECOLOGICAL ADAPTATIONS

Introduction

The survival of an organism depends on the characteristics of the organism. Each organism has both behavioural and physical characteristics, which qualify it to survive in its own habitat. Many environmental factors influence the existence and success of an organism in an ecosystem. In order to withstand adverse conditions of the environment, the organisms develop certain morphological, anatomical, physiological and reproductive adaptations. These ecological adaptations increase the ability of an organism under changing environment and favour the success of an organism in a given environmental condition.

On the basis of their water requirement, plants can be classified as

- **Hydrophytes**: Plants that grows wholly or partly submerged in water.
- **Xerophytes**: Plants which are adapted to survive under very poor supply of water.
- **Mesophytes**: Plants that grow in surroundings receiving an average supply of water.

5.1 XERIC, HYDRIC AND MESIC ADAPTATIONS

5.1.1 Ecological Adaptation of Xerophytes

Xerophytes are the plants that grow in habitats where there is very less water or no water supply. The plants that live in physiologically dry areas are called Xerophytes. The plants that grow in dry or arid zones are known as ephemerals or, drought evaders or drought escapers. There ephemerals are annual plants and they complete their life cycles in 6-8 weeks. The xerophytic plants absorb more water during the rainy season; the absorbed water is stored in different body parts like stem and leaves. These plants are called succulents or drought avoiding plants. These plants store water in the form of mucilage. Some perennial plants withstand prolonged periods of drought and are called non-succulents or true xerophytes.

Examples of succulent plants:

Stem succulents - *Opuntia*

Leaf succulents - *Bryophyllum, Aloe*

Root succulents - *Asparagus*

All these groups of xerophytic plants have some common means of adaptation to survive in dry environment. Some of the ecological adaptations of xerophytes are as follows:

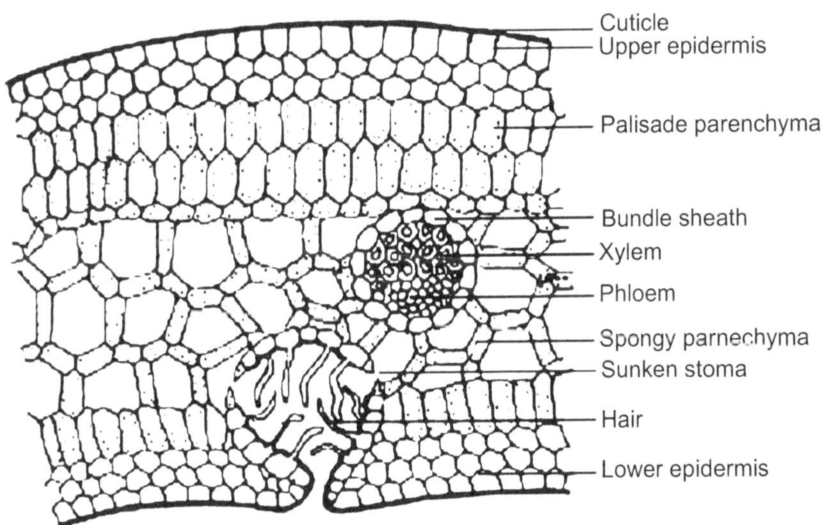

Fig. 5.1 : T.S. of *Nerium* Leaf

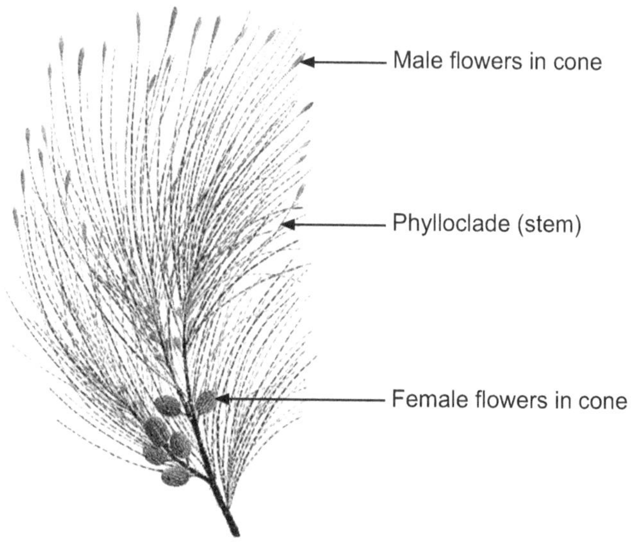

Fig. 5.2: A Branch of *Casuarina equisetifolia*

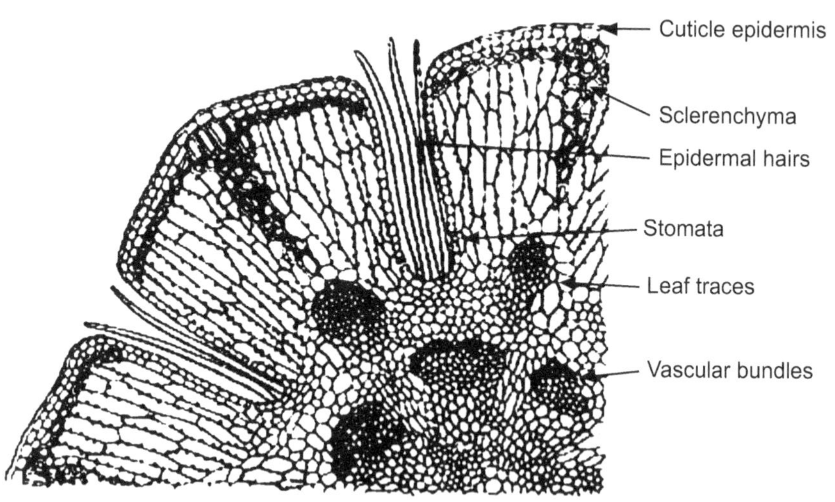

Fig. 5.3: T.S of *Casuarina* stem

A. Morphological adaptations

1. Roots of the xerophytes are very well developed with extensive branching and are usually longer that the shoots system. Root hairs and root caps are very well developed.

These roots enable them to absorb from water tables beneath the soil.

2. Stems of these plants are usually stunted; they are covered with thick bark and are woody. In some species of xerophytes the stem is underground. In some plants like *Optunia* the stem becomes green, fleshy, and shows presence of leaf-like phylloclades which are covered with spines. Stems of these plants are usually covered by hair or waxy coatings.

3. Leaves of these plants are reduced, small, scale-like and sometimes these leaves are modified into spines which help to reduce the rate of transpiration. In plants like *Acacia*, the lamina is narrow, long, needle-like or they may be divided into many leaflets. Foliage leaves like that of the *Aloe*, become thick and fleshy and succulent or tough and leathery in texture. Leaf surfaces of some plants like that of the *Calotropis* have a shiny glaze which reflect light and heat.

B. Anatomical adaptations

1. Epidermis of the leaf is covered by thick cuticle to reduce the rate of transpiration. Cells of the epidermis have silica crystals. In plants like *Nerium*, the epidermis is multilayered. In *Calotropis*, there is a waxy coating present on the leaves and stem.
2. Epidermal cells are thick- walled
3. The stomata in these leaves are less in number, hypostomatus i.e., they are generally confined to the lower epidermis of leaves and sunken
4. Palisade is present on both sides of leaves
5. The cells and vacuoles are small
6. Mechanical tissues and vascular tissues of these plants are well developed.

C. Physiological adaptations

1. Succulent xerophytes contain polysaccharide pentosans and a number of acids by virtue of which they are able to resist

drought. The structural modifications in these succulent xerophytes are directly governed by their physiology. Metabolic reaction which induces development of succulence is the conversion of polysaccharides into pentosans. Pentosans are hygroscopic in nature and absorb water molecules. The accumulation of excess amount of water results in the development of succulence in plant organs like leaf, stem and root.

2. The stomata of succulent plants are open during night and remain closed during the day. This unusual feature is associated with metabolic activity of these plants. During night time, these plants respire and produce acids. The accumulation of acids in the guard cells increases their osmotic concentration which causes inward flow of water in the guard cells. When guard cells become turgid the stomata open. In sunlight, acids dissociate to produce carbon dioxide which is used up in the photosynthesis and as a result of this osmotic concentration of cell sap decreases which ultimately causes closure of stomata.

3. The chemical substances in the cell sap of xerophytes are actively converted into cell wall forming compounds like anhydrous cellulose, suberin, etc that are finally incorporated into the cell walls.

4. In xerophytes the enzymes like catalases, peroxidases, are more active than in mesophytes. The starch hydrolysing activity of an enzyme is also highest in xerophytes.

5. The protoplasm of xerophytic cell shows maximum resistance to heat and desiccation.

6. Regulation of transpiration. Presence of the cuticle, polished surface, compact cells and sunken stomata protected by stomatal hairs regulate the transpiration.

7. The cells of xerophytes have very high osmotic pressure which results in the increase of turgidity. The turgidity of cell sap exerts tension on the cell walls which prevents wilting of cell.

5.1.2 Ecological Adaptation of Hydrophytes

Adaptations in hydrophytes can be discussed under three headings: morphological, anatomical and physiological.

A. Morphological adaptations

Hydrophytes show various kinds of morphological adaptations in their roots, stems and leaves

1. Roots

Roots of hydrophytes are not of much importance, because most hydrophytes are partly or wholly immersed in water.

(i) Roots are totally absent in plants like *Utriculari, Ceratophyllum, Myriophyllum, and Salvinia.*

(ii) Poorly developed roots are found in submerged plants like *Hydrilla, Vallisneria.*

(iii) Root pockets in place of root caps are found in floating hydrophytes like *Pistia* and *Eichhornia* that project the root tip

(iv) Root hairs are poorly developed in most hydrophytes.

(v) Some plants like *Jussiea repens* have two types of roots; one being normal while the other spongy type and negatively geotropic.

2. Stem

(i) In submerged hydrophytes the stem is slender, flexible and long as in *Hydrilla, Potamogeton.*

(ii) In some floating hydrophytes like *Azolla, Pistia* or *Eichhornia*, it is horizontal, spongy and floating.

(iii) In rooted hydrophytes like *Sagittaria, Cyperus, Scirpus, Potamogeton*, the stem is a rhizome or stolon.

3. Petioles

Some hydrophytes show special features in the petioles.

(i) Petioles in submerged plants, with free floating leaves like *Nymphaea* and *Nelumbium*, are long, slender and spongy.

(ii) In the free floating hydrophyte *Eichhornia*, the petiole is swollen and helps in floating

4. Leaves

Hydrophytes show a number of variations in the structure of their leaf lamina.

(i) In submerged hydrophytes like *Utricularia, Myriophyllum* and *Ceratophyllum*, the leaves are finely dissected and in plants like *Vallisneria*, they are long and narrow. In both types of adaptations the intention is to offer little resistance to water currents.

(ii) In free floating hydrophytes, the leaves are smooth, shiny and coated with wax. Presence of wax not only prevents water clogging, but also protects from physical and chemical injuries.

(iii) In floating but rooted hydrophytes like *Nelumbium* and *Nymphaea* the petioles are long and the lamina are peltate with their lower surfaces in direct contact with water and the upper surfaces exposed to air.

(iv) One important feature that is usually shown by hydrophytes is heterophylly (leaf dimorphism), i.e., the presence of two types of leaves. In plants like *Sagittaria, Ranunculus* and *Limnophila heterophylla*, the submerged leaves are ribbon shaped or dissected and the leaves above the surface of water are broad.

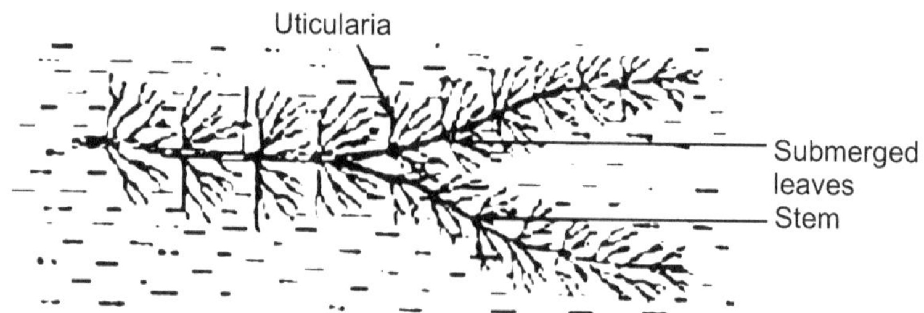

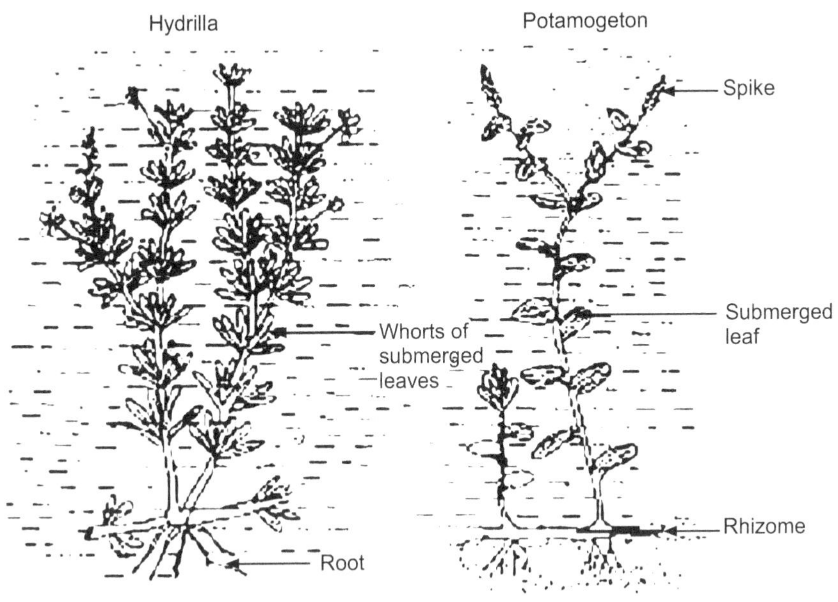

Fig. 5.4: Submerged Hydrophytes

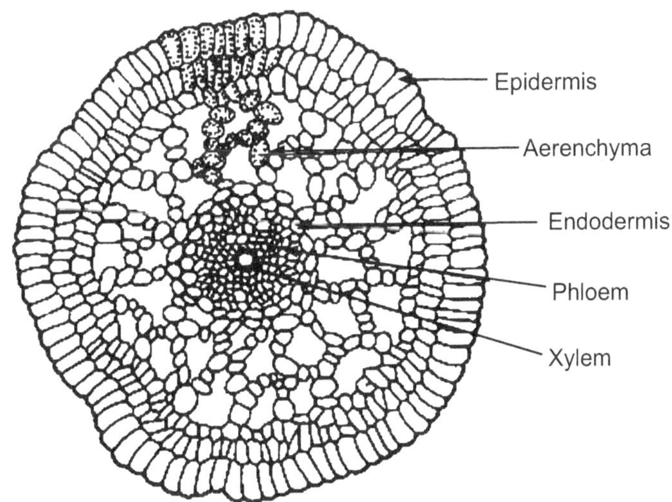

Fig. 5.5: T.S. of *Hydrilla* Stem

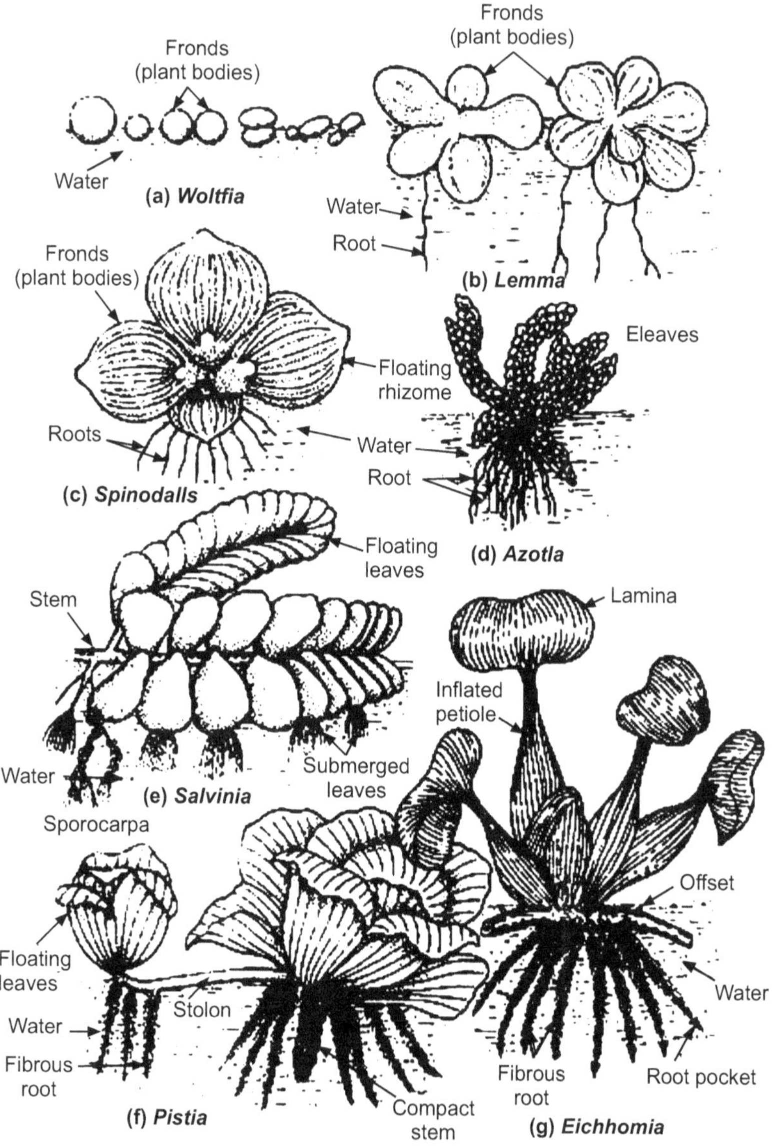

Fig. 5.6: Free floating hydrophytes

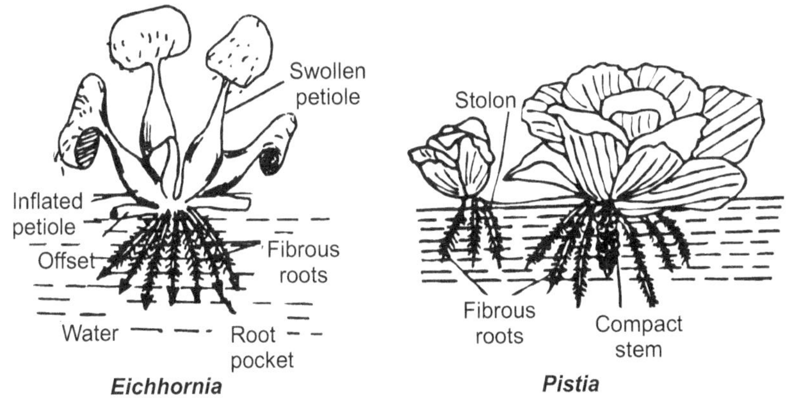

Fig. 5.7: Free Floating Hydrophytes

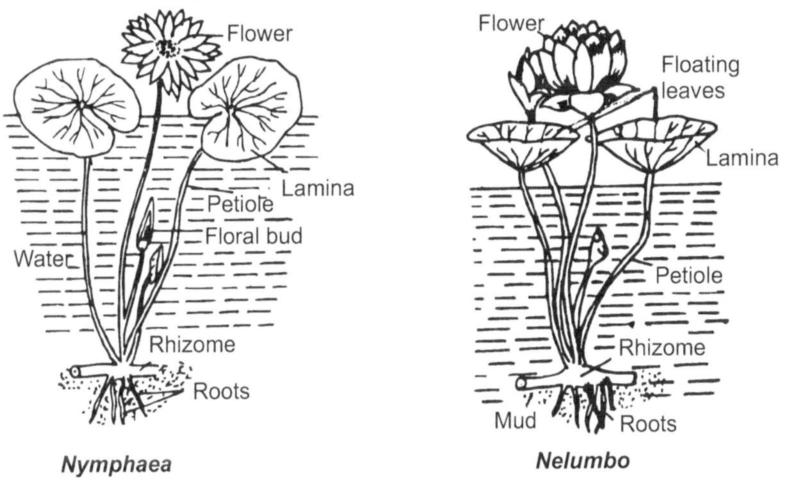

Fig. 5.8: Floating but Rooted Hydrophytes

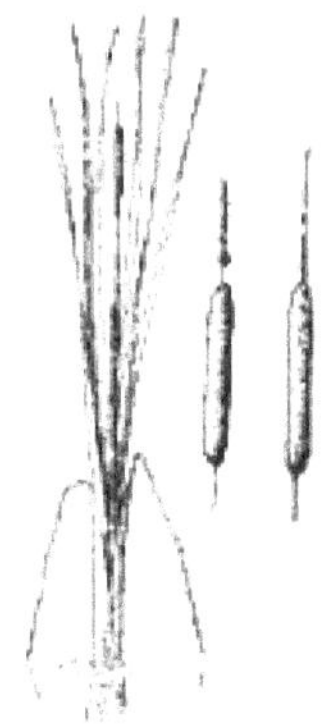

Fig. 5.9: Amphibious Hydrophyte *Typha spp*

B. Anatomical adaptations

In general, hydrophytes show the following trends in anatomical features:

(i) Reduction in protecting structures.

(ii) Reduction in mechanical tissue.

(iii) Reduction in conducting tissue.

(iv) Increase in aeration.

As the above features are seen in most organs of a plant, the anatomical adaptations are better discussed on the basis of such features rather than on the basis of organs.

1. Reduction in protecting structures

(i) Absence of cuticle in the submerged portions.

(ii) Use of epidermis as an absorbing or photosynthesising (when epidermis has chloroplasts) organ rather than a protecting organ.

(iii) Poorly developed hypodermis

2. Reduction of mechanical tissue

(i) Total absence or poor development of sclerenchyma in the submerged portions.

(ii) Presence of special type of sclereids called asterosclereids in some hydrophytes provide mechanical support in the absence of sclerenchyma.

(iii) Presence of sclerenchyma in little or moderate quantities in the aerial portions

3. Reduction of conducting (Vascular) tissue

(i) Vascular bundles are reduced to few or even one and located at the centre.

(ii) Xylem cells are very few as there is hardly any need of conduction.

(iii) Phloem is usually poorly developed but in some cases it is well developed.

(iv) Secondary vascular tissue is never developed. Increase in aeration

(i) Stomata are totally absent or vestigial in submerged parts.

(ii) Stomata are confined to upper leaf surface of rooted but floating hydrophytes.

(iii) In amphibious plants, stomata are scattered on the aerial portions.

(iv) Roots, stems and leaves of most hydrophytes have air chambers. These chambers store gases like $C0_2$ and 0_2 and help in respiration and photosynthesis. Besides, this the air chambers help in buoyancy and provide mechanical support.

C. Physiological adaptations

Besides their adaptations in the morphological and anatomical characters, hydrophytes also show some physiological adaptations. These are

(i) Osmotic concentrations of cell sap are low.

(ii) No transpiration from submerged plants.

(iii) Photosynthetic and respiratory gases are retained in air chambers for later use.

5.1.3 Ecological Adaptations of Mesophytes

Mesophytes are the land plants that grow under moderate soil water content and normal environmental conditions. They do not have any special adaptations to survive in either extremely moist or dry conditions.

A. Morphological adaptations

1. Root system is well developed. In dicots taproot and in monocots adentitious fibrous root system with root hairs is present.
2. Stem is rigid and stout
3. Leaves are large, thin and without waxy coating.

B. Anatomical adaptations

1. Arenchyma is absent
2. Cuticle is present
3. Palisade is well developed
4. Epidermal cells are thick
5. Mechanical and vascular tissues are well developed

C. Physiological adaptations

1. The osmotic pressure of the cell is low hence if the plants are not watered regularly they immediately wilt
2. In summer the plants show temporary wilting during midday
3. During dry months the plants shed their leaves and conserve internal water by checking the rate of transpiration
4. They Show C3 (E.g. Sunflower) or C4 (E.g. Maize) photosynthetic mechanism

EXERCISE

I. Multiple Choice Questions

1. *Opuntia* is an example of --------
   a) Ephemeral b) Succulent
   c) Non-succulent d) Mesophyte
2. Presence of sunken stomata is characteristic feature of ------
   a) Xerophyte b) Hydrophyte
   c) Mesophyte d) None of these
3. *Eichhornia* is an example of ------
   a) Free floating hydrophyte b) Amphibious hydrophyte
   c) Submerged hydrophyte d) Xerophyte
4. Presence of arenchyma is characteristic of -----
   a) Hydrophytes b) Mesophytes
   c) Xerophytes d) All of these
5. Root pockets are present in ----
   a) *Hydrilla* b) *Nerium*
   c) *Aloe* d) *Eichhornia*
6. Vascular bundles are poorly developed and less differentiated in---
   a) *Hydrilla* b) *Nerium*
   c) Maize d) Sunflower
7. Sunflower and maize are the examples of -------
   a) Floating hydrophytes b) Stem succulent
   c) Leaf succulent d) Mesophyte

ANSWERS

1-b; 2-a; 3-a; 4-a; 5-d; 6-a; 7-d

II. Two Marks Questions

1. Define hydrophytes and write any two morphological adaptations of hydrophytes
2. Describe physiological adaptations in xerophytes
3. Describe any three important anatomical adaptations of hydrophytes
4. Describe any three important anatomical adaptations of xerophytes
5. Define xerophytes. Enlist different classes of xerophytes with one example of each class
6. What are hydrophytes? Classify them by giving one example of each class.
7. Write general characters of succulent plants.

III. Four Marks Questions

1. Write any four morphological adaptations in hydrophytes
2. What are xerophytes? Write any three anatomical adaptations in xerophytes
3. What are hydrophytes? Write any three anatomical adaptations in hydrophytes
4. Write any two morphological and any two anatomical characters of mesophytes

IV. Five Marks Questions

1. What are xerophytes? Explain any three morphological and two anatomical adaptations in xerophytes
2. What are hydrophytes? Explain any three morphological and two physiological adaptations in hydrophytes

V. Seven Marks Questions

1. What are xerophytes? Explain the morphological and anatomical adaptations in xerophytes.
2. What are hydrophytes? Explain the morphological and anatomical adaptations in hydrophytes.
3. Describe the morphological and anatomical adaptations in mesophytes.

6

CHAPTER

POLLUTION

6.1 INTRODUCTION

One of the greatest problems the world is facing today is that of pollution, which is increasing with every passing year and causing grave and irreparable damage to the earth. Pollution is defined as the addition of any substance or form of energy to the environment at a rate faster than the environment can accommodate it by dispersion, decomposition, recycling, or storage in some harmless form.

Pollution is drastically rising all over the world due to rise in human activity associated with modern technology and population growth. Hence, pollution is often regarded as the result of human actions. It has a detrimental effect on the environment and makes the planet unsafe for future human survival. Animals, fish and other aquatic life, plants and humans all suffer when pollution is not controlled.

Types of Pollution

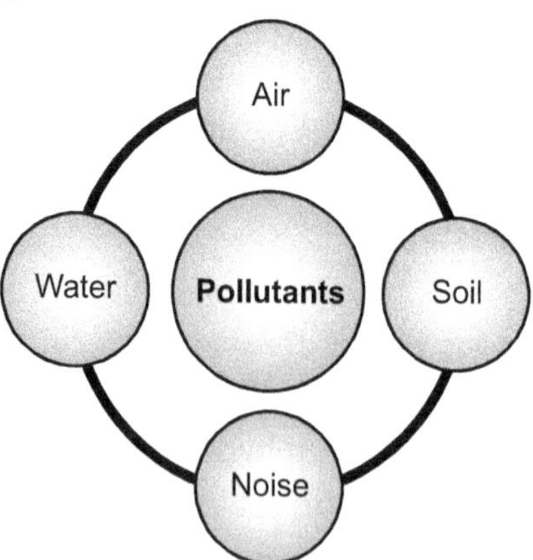

Fig. 6.1: Types of Pollution

Environmental pollution consists of four basic types of pollution, namely, air, water, soil and noise.

1. **Air pollution:** It is considered to be the most harmful form of pollution in our environment. Air has a definite chemical composition comprising of nitrogen, oxygen, water vapour and inert gases. Air pollution occurs when hazardous gases like carbon monoxide, carbon dioxide, sulfur dioxide, methane, methyl isocynate, oxides of nitrogen, chloroflurocarbons (CFCs) and other harmful gases resulting from burning fuels are added to the air.
2. **Water pollution**: It results when large amounts of foreign substances such as organic and inorganic pollutants present in effluents from breweries, tanneries ,dying textiles, paper and pulp mills, steel industries and mining operations chemical and other industries, oils from oil spills, sewage, pesticides and fertilizers from agricultural runoff are introduced to rivers, ponds, lakes, sea and other water bodies. The pollutants include toxins, phenolic compounds, metallic wastes, acids, salts, dyes, cyanides, DDT, heavy metal effluents like Pb, Cd, Hg, Cr, Cu etc. Human activities such as disposal of garbage, flowers, ashes and other household waste as well as bathing and washing clothes in water bodies further adds to water pollution. This makes the water harmful to drink, holds less oxygen and endangers aquatic flora and fauna.
3. **Soil pollution**: It occurs when the concentration of chemicals, nutrients or elements in the soil becomes more than it normally or naturally is, as a result of acid rain, polluted water, fertilizers, chemicals released by spill or underground storage tanks, etc. Polluting the land in this way can lead to entry of pollutants into food chain. The common soil pollutants are hydrocarbons, heavy metals, herbicides, pesticides and chlorinated hydrocarbons. These contaminants can also get infiltrated into ground water and pollute them. Soil pollution can harm living organisms in the soils and humans that come into contact with them by touching, breathing or consuming crops from contaminated soils.

4. **Noise pollution**: It is the disturbance of silent environment by loud noises which include aircraft noise, noise of cars, buses, and trucks, vehicle horns, loudspeakers, and industry noise. When these noises reach harmful levels it leads to noise pollution. Research has shown direct links between noise and health, including stress-related illnesses, high blood pressure, speech interference and hearing loss. This pollution has severe impact especially on old people, small children. Noise also makes wild species communicate louder, which can shorten their lifespan.

6.2 AIR POLLUTION

Air pollution can be defined as the excessive presence or concentration of foreign material in the air, which adversely affects the health and comfort of humans and animals.

6.2.1 Sources of Air Pollution

Based on the basis of mode of generation of pollutants the sources are classified as

A. Natural sources

1. **Forest fires:** In tropical areas or areas of high temperature forest fire is a common feature throughout the year. Very large quantity of smoke and particulate matter is liberated during these fires.
2. **Volcanic Eruption:** During volcanic eruptions large amount of lava along with minute solid particles, gases and radiation is released into the environment.
3. **Dust storms:** They are caused due to movement of hot winds around the surface of land. They dislodge the dust particles from the surface and lift them up into the atmosphere.
4. **Pollen grains:** Pollen grains also contribute to pollution. They are mainly responsible for causing allergy. Plant family like Poaceae, Euphorbiaceae and Asteraceae are some families known to produce allergic pollen grains.
5. **Aerosols:** Aerosols refer to the dispersion of solid or liquid particles of microscopic size in gaseous media such as dust, smoke, mist, fog, fumes.

B. Manmade sources

Domestic Pollution: Carbon monoxide, sulfur dioxide emitted from the incomplete combustion of fossil fuels like coal, petroleum and other factory combustibles is one of the major causes of air pollution. Pollutants emitted from vehicles including trucks, jeeps, cars, trains, airplanes cause immense amount of pollution. We rely on them to fulfill our needs of transportation. However their overuse is killing our environment as dangerous gases are polluting the environment.

Industrial pollution: Most of the air pollutants can be traced back to industries thus the industrial activities are primary cause of air pollution. Waste incinerators, manufacturing industries and power plants emit high levels of carbon monoxide, organic compounds, and chemicals into the air. Every industrial process exhibits its own pattern of air pollution. Petroleum refineries are responsible for extensive hydrocarbon and particulate pollution. Iron and steel mills, metal smelters, pulp and paper mills, chemical plants, cement and asphalt plants all discharge vast amounts of various particulates.

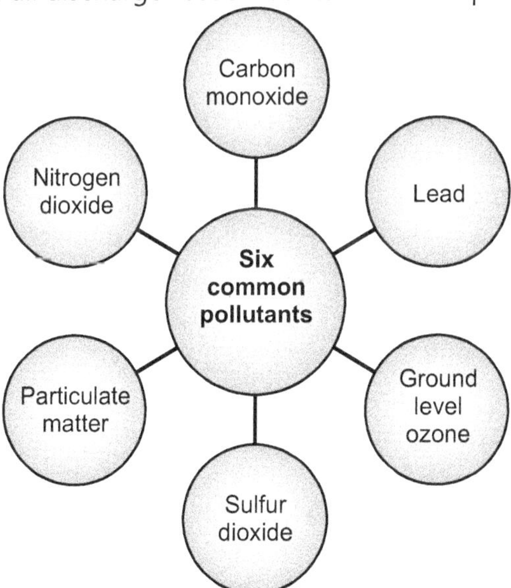

Fig. 6.2: Common Pollutants

6.2.2 Effect of Air Pollution

1. **Health Effects:** The level of effect usually depends on the length of exposure, kind and concentration of the air pollutant that a population or individual is exposed to. People exposed to high levels of toxic pollutants may experience difficulty in breathing, lung and heart problems, wheezing, coughing, irritation of the eyes, nose, and throat. Long term exposure to air pollution can pose serious health concerns such as cancer and damage to the immune, neurological, reproductive and respiratory systems.

2. **Global warming:** The Earth's atmosphere contains naturally occurring gases like CO_2. When CO_2 concentration is normal the temperature of earth surface is maintained due to energy balance of the solar radiations that strike the earth surface and the heat that is radiated back in to space. When CO_2 concentration is increased beyond normal limit it forms a thick layer in the atmosphere. This thick layer of CO_2 allows the sun light to pass in to the space but not the heat to radiate back. Thus the thick layer of CO_2 acts like the glass panels of green house, allowing the sunlight to pass through but preventing the heat being re-radiated in outer space. Thus the temperature of earth surface goes on increasing with increase in addition of air pollutant CO_2. This increase in temperature is called **'Green House Effect'**. The human activities have disturbed this natural balance by producing large amounts of greenhouse gases, including carbon dioxide and methane. As a result, the Earth's atmosphere is trapping more of the sun's heat, causing the Earth's average temperature to rise. This phenomenon is known as global warming. This has a direct effect on the environment as there is, increase in sea levels due to melting of ice from colder regions and icebergs as well as displacement and loss of habitat from many regions.

3. **Acid Rain:** Harmful gases like nitrogen oxides and sulfur oxides are released into the atmosphere when fossil fuels are burnt. When it rains, the water droplets combines with these air pollutants, becomes acidic and falls on the ground in the form of acid rain. Acid rain can cause great damage to human, animals and crops. It acidifies the water bodies, making the water unsuitable for fish and consumption. It also erodes buildings, statues, and sculptures that are a part of our national heritage.

4. **Eutrophication:** Eutrophication is a condition where high amount of nitrogen stimulate blooms of algae. This adversely affects fish and also results in loss of plant and animal diversity. Human activities greatly accelerate eutrophication by increasing the rate at which nutrients enter aquatic ecosystems. Air emissions of nitrogen oxides from power plants, cars, trucks, and other sources contribute to the amount of nitrogen entering aquatic ecosystems.

5. **Effect on Wildlife:** Toxic pollutants in the air, or deposited on soils or surface waters, can impact wildlife in a number of ways. Toxic chemicals present in the air can force wildlife species to move to new place and change their habitat. Like humans, animals can also experience health problems if exposed to sufficient concentrations of air pollutants over time. These pollutants cause birth defects, reproductive failure, and various other diseases in animals. Persistent toxic air pollutants (those that break down slowly in the environment) accumulate in sediments and may biomagnify in tissues of animals at the top of the food chain.

6. **Depletion of Ozone layer:** Ozone present in the Earth's stratosphere is responsible for protecting humans from the harmful ultraviolet (UV) rays of the sun. Earth's ozone layer is depleting due to the presence ozone depleting substances, including chlorofluorocarbons, hydrochlorofluorocarbons, and halons. These substances are used in coolants, foaming

agents, fire extinguishers, solvents, pesticides, and aerosol propellants. Thinning of the protective ozone layer can cause increased amounts of UV radiation to reach the Earth, which can lead to skin cancer, cataracts, and impaired immune systems. UV can also damage sensitive crops and reduce crop yields.

7. **Bhopal Gas Tragedy:** Bhopal Gas Tragedy, 1984 was an event that caused great damage to the life in the world's industrial history. The Union carbide industry in Bhopal was engaged in the synthesis of pesticides like carbaryl. For the synthesis of these pesticides a deadly poisonous gas methyl iso cyanate (MIC) was used. In the early morning hours of December 3, 1984, there was leakage of this gas from the Union carbide plant which resulted in the formation of poisonous gray cloud. The wind spread this cloud through out the Bhopal city and nearby localities. Within hours, the streets of Bhopal were littered with dead bodies of human and animals like buffaloes, cows, dogs and birds. The newspaper reported that 3,800 people died immediately.

This gas not only polluted the air but also polluted drinking water, soils and adversely affected foetus of pregnant women, newly born babies, children and old people. The reports of the hospitals say that near about 200 women delivered dead babies and about 400 babies died within a few hours of their birth. The official reports said that about 10,000 people have been permanently disabled and about 30,000 partially handicapped and bout 1.5 lakh people were the victims of minor disability. This gas affected the liver of new born babies. They developed blue spots on their livers and suffered from cough, asthma and eye trouble.

6.2.3 Control of Air Pollution

Different techniques are used for controlling air pollution. Some of these corrective measures are listed below:

- Industrial estates should be established at a distance away from residential
  areas.

- For controlling gaseous pollutants methods like combustion, absorption and adsorption should be adopted.
- The pollution caused by particulate matter can be controlled by gravity, sudden change flow method, fabric filter, wet scrubbers, electrostatic precipitators.
- Use of tall chimneys shall reduce the air pollution in the surroundings
- Compulsory use of filters and electrostatic precipitators in the chimneys.
- Removal of poisonous gases by passing the fumes through water tower scrubber or spray collectors.
- Use of high temperature incinerators for reduction in particulate ash produced by thermal power stations .
- Use of natural sources of energy like geothermal power, solar power, tidal power, wind power, etc.
- Use of non-lead antiknock agents in gasoline.
- Use of pollution free fuels for automobiles, e.g., alcohol, hydrogen, battery power.
- Automobiles should be fitted with exhaust emission controls.
- Industrial plants and refineries should be fitted with equipment for removal and recycling of wastes.
- Growing plants capable of fixing carbon monoxide, e.g. *Phaseolus vulgaris, Coleus blumei, Daucus carota, Ficus variegata.*
- Growing plants capable of metabolising nitrogen oxides and other gaseous pollutants, e.g., *Vitis, Pinus, Juniperus, Quercus, Pyrus, Robinia pseudoacacia, Viburnum, Crataegus, Ribes, Rhamnus.*
- Better designed equipment and smokeless fuels should be used in homes and industries.
- Automobiles should be properly maintained and adhere to emission control standards.
- More trees should be planted along roadsides and houses.
- Develop awareness in the society for organising various campaigns.

- Legal Control: To control air pollution in India, Indian Government has passed the Prevention and Control of air pollution Act 1981. Section 21(1) of air pollution act says that no person shall, without the previous permission of the State Board, operate any industrial plant specified in the schedule in air pollution area. Section 20 of this act prescribes standards for emission of pollutants from automobiles. Strict implementation of this act may be helpful to control the air pollution up to some extent.

6.3 WATER POLLUTION

Water is considered polluted if some substances or condition is present to such a degree that the water cannot be used for a specific purpose. Olaniran (1995) defined *water pollution to be the presence of excessive amounts of a hazardous substance (pollutant) in water in such a way that it is no longer suitable for drinking, bathing, cooking or other uses.*

6.3.1 Sources of Water Pollution

Water pollution arises from various activities, among which are:

1. **Industrial waste:** Industries produce huge amount of waste which contains toxic chemicals. These include pollutants such as lead, mercury, sulphur, asbestos, nitrates and many other harmful chemicals. Most industries lack a waste management system and dispose the waste in fresh water bodies such as rivers, canals, streams and ponds. When these chemicals are added to the water body, they affect the colour of water, increase the amount of minerals, change the temperature of water and pose serious hazard to water organisms.

2. **Sewage:** The sewage and waste water that is produced by each household carries harmful bacteria and chemicals that can cause serious health problems. The pathogens present in the sewage cause many life threatening diseases. Therefore, it is very important that the sewage be chemically treated and then released into the water body.

3. **Mining activities:** Mining is the process of crushing the rock and extracting coal and other minerals from underground. These elements when extracted in the raw form contain harmful chemicals and can increase the amount of toxic elements when mixed up with water. Mining activities emit several metal waste and sulphides from the rocks and is harmful for the water.

4. **Accidental Oil Spills:** A major water pollutants has been oil spilled in large quantities from tankers of broken oil pipes from oil industries which kills sea weeds, mollusks, marine birds, crustaceans, fishes and other sea organisms that serve as food for humans. This oil does not dissolve with water and drastically affects marine wildlife. Oil spills also reduce oxygen supplies within the water environment.

5. **Chemical fertilizers and pesticides:** Chemical fertilizers and pesticides are used by farmers to increase the productivity and protect crops from attacking pests. However, these chemicals mix with rainwater and flow down into rivers and canals which pose serious damage to aquatic animals.

6. **Radioactive waste:** Radioisotopes and heavy metals from various industries are another source of water pollution. Radioactive substances are used in nuclear power plants, industrial, medical and other scientific processes. Nuclear energy is produced using nuclear fission or fusion. The element that is used in production of nuclear energy is Uranium which is highly toxic chemical. The nuclear waste that is produced by radioactive material needs to be disposed off to prevent any nuclear accident. Nuclear waste can have serious environmental hazards if not disposed off properly.

7. **Urban development:** With the growing population, the demand for housing, food and cloth has also increased exponentially. This has resulted in increased use of fertilizers to produce more food, soil erosion due to deforestation, increase in construction activities, inadequate sewer

collection and treatment facilities, landfills as more garbage is produced, increase in chemicals from industries to produce more materials. All of these contribute to water pollution.

8. **Leakage from the landfills:** Landfills are holes in ground where huge piles of garbage are disposed. When it rains, a substantial amount of waste from the leaking landfills pollute the underground water with large variety of contaminants.
9. **Underground storage leakage:** Transportation of coal and other petroleum products through underground pipes is well known. Accidentals leakage may happen anytime and may cause damage to environment.
10. **Discharge of super heated water:** Another source of water pollution is the discharge of hot water from cooling engines in the industries. This increases water temperature, lowers the metabolic rate of organisms and increases the oxygen demand.

6.3.2 Effects of Water Pollution

1. Human Health

In developed countries, even where there are better purification methods, people still suffer from the health effects of water pollution. Toxins emitted by industries and other urban set ups cause stomach aches and rashes. Lead and cadmium are potent neurotoxic metals present in industrial waste. High toxic nature of certain heavy metals such as silver (Ag), cadmium (Cd), mercury (Hg), lead (Pb), chromium (Cr), arsenic (As) and their deleterious effect on the flora and fauna have forced mankind to find out possible ways of removal of metals from water.

As a result of ageing, the lead which had accumulated in blood starts getting accumulated in secondary organs such as lungs, kidney and at higher levels in bones and soft tissues. Excess nitrogen in drinking water also poses serious risks to infants. Inorganic mercury is a common by product of a number of industrial processes. The level of mercury in fish is mostly dangerous for small children and pregnant women. Mercury interferes with the development of the central nervous system in foetuses and young children, which could potentially lead to a large amount of long-term side effects.

Nitrate contamination can prove fatal for infants as it can restrict the oxygen to the reach the brain causing the 'blue-baby' syndrome. It can also cause digestive tract cancers and eutrophication in water bodies. Arsenic poisoning cause serious liver and nervous system damage, vascular disease and skin cancer.

Minamata Disease

Minamata is a small factory town dominated by the Chisso Corporation. The town is located near the Shiranui Sea. The Minamata Bay is part of this sea. The Chisso Corporation was initially started as Fertilizer Company and gradually advanced to a petrochemical and plastic-maker company.

In a span of about 33 years (1932 to 1968) this company dumped thousands of mercury compounds into Minamata Bay. The dumped mercury compounds found their way in to water which was ingested by fishes and other aquatic animals. These fishes were eaten by people from nearby locality which resulted in methyl mercury poisoning. The disease caused by methylmercury poisoning was named as Minamata disease. It was in May 1956, that Minamata disease was first officially "discovered" in Minamata City, south-west region of Japan's Kyushu Island. The marine products in Minamata Bay showed high levels of Hg contamination (5.61 to 35.7 ppm). The Hg content in hair of patients, their family and inhabitants of the Shiranui Sea coastline were also detected at high levels of Hg (max. 705 ppm).

Typical symptoms of this disease are sensory disturbances, ataxia (Poor coordination and unsteadiness due to the brain's failure to regulate the body's posture and regulate the strength and direction of limb movements), dysarthria (Speech that is characteristically slurred, slow, and difficult to understand), constriction of the visual field, auditory disturbances and tremor (An abnormal, repetitive shaking movement of the body). were also seen.

When the pregnant women ingested the methyl mercury contaminated marine food the foetus was poisoned by MeHg causing serious, and extensive lesions on the brain.

2. Ecological Processes

The entrance of pollutants into waterways can have a wide range of impact. It is possible for the pollutants to raise the temperature of the water thus destroying the ecosystems. The ecosystems in water are affected negatively, as the destruction or introduction of any foreign organism alter the entire food chain. The warm water forces indigenous water species to seek cooler water in other areas, causing an ecological damaging shift of the affected area. This creates an ecological deadzone. Water pollution can also significantly increase the rate of algal blooms. These blooms create massive fish die-offs as the oxygen in the water gets depleted and the fish suffocate. Coral reefs are also affected by the bleaching effect due to warmer temperatures of polluted water. Contamination of groundwater from pesticides causes damage to the reproductive system in the wildlife ecosystem. The non-biodegradable pesticides and chemicals cause mass destruction of aquatic life. Polluted water lead to imbalance in host-parasite relations in the ecosystem, changing the food webs and food chain and thus affects microbial population.

3. Microbial Communities and Animals:

Heavy metals may influence the abundance and diversity of organisms in the environment which may result into changes in the abundance of the major taxonomic groups of microorganisms, as well as particular species of genera. In such situations, microorganisms are able to increase their abundance because of the reduction in competition from organisms which are more metal-sensitive. The overall effect of heavy metals on ecology is a reduction in species diversity; this is a characteristic of stressed environments.

Animals, including water animals die when polluted water is consumed. Immediate impact on the wildlife includes oil-coated birds and sea turtles, mammal ingestion of oil, and dead or dying deep sea coral. Animals are also affected by solid waste thrown into water bodies, as they harm them in many ways. Many animals are stressed and their populations are endangered. Animals that eat dead fish from contaminated streams are affected. The reproduction rate is greatly reduced in aquatic organisms. Bioaccumulative and non-biodegradable pesticides are accumulated in animal bodies and this poses a serious threat if these animals are consumed.

6.3.3 Control of Water pollution

1. Control of pollution should ideally take place at the point of generation, or, in other words, it should be prevented at source i.e. domestic sources to industry sources.
2. Educate farmers to avoid reckless use of fertilizers and pesticides which is the major source of pollution. For example, the amount of fertilizer used and the timing of its application can make a significant difference.
3. Pollution prevention is best achieved by ensuring that each potential point source is properly sited, designed, constructed and managed.
4. Appropriate use of excreta disposal, solid waste disposal and animal waste disposal will help prevent contamination of both surface and groundwater.
5. Springs usually become contaminated when latrines, animal yards, sewers, septic tanks, or other sources of pollution are located on higher land nearby. It is therefore important to have knowledge of the local geology to assess the probability of groundwater contamination.
6. Planting trees would reduce pollution by sediments and will also prevent soil erosion.
7. Avoid run-off of manure. Divert such run-off to basin for settlement. The nutrient rich water can be used as fertilizer in the fields.
8. Avoid overflow of sewage with rain water in rainy season.
9. Separate drainage of sewage and rain water lines should be provided.

10. For controlling water pollution from sewage disposal, treatment of waste waters is essential before being discharged. Parameters like reduction in Total solids, biological oxygen demand (BOD), chemical oxygen demand (COD), nitrates and phosphates, oil and grease, toxic metals etc. should be in permissible levels before discharge.

11. **Legal Control:** Prevention and Control of Water Pollution Act 1974 is appropriate step to praevent water pollution up to some extent.

EXERCISE

I. Multiple Choice Questions

1. ------ is the introduction of particulates, biological molecules, or other harmful gases into Earth's atmosphere.
   a) Air pollution b) Water pollution
   c) Noise pollution d) Soil pollution
2. ------ reduces oxygen carrying capacity of blood
   a) CO b) SO_2
   c) NH_3 d) O_2
3. Typhoid, Cholera and amoebic dysentery are caused due to ---
   a) Air pollution b) Water pollution
   c) Noise pollution d) Soil pollution
4. Peeling of ozone is due to ------
   a) CFC b) CO_2
   c) SO_2 4) None of these
5. Green house effect is caused by ------
   a) CO_2 b) O_2
   c) N_2 d) SO_2
6. Bhopal gas tragedy happened due to the leakage of -----
   a) Methyl isocynate b) Propyl isocynate
   d) Carbon dioxide d) Chlorine

ANSWERS

1-a 2-a 3-b 4-a 5-a 6-a

II. Two Marks Questions

1. Define the term pollutant and pollution
2. Describe in brief the sources of water pollution
3. Define water pollution. Enlist any four diseases caused by polluted water.
4. Enlist any three control measures of water pollution/Air pollution
5. What is air pollution? Enlist any for air pollutants

III. Five Marks Questions

1. Comment on the control measures of Air pollution
2. Discuss in brief the control measures of water pollution
3. What are the causes of Air pollution?
4. What are the causes of Water Pollution?
5. What are the effects of air and water pollution?

IV. Seven Marks Questions

1. What is water pollution? Describe in brief the effects of water pollution on living organisms
2. What is air pollution? Discuss the causes of air pollution
3. What is water pollution? Comment on the causes of water pollution
4. What is air pollution? Discuss in brief the control measures applied to control the air pollution

www.ingramcontent.com/pod-product-compliance
Lightning Source LLC
Chambersburg PA
CBHW050357030726
47503CB00006B/1900
9789351647980